SIMONE VAN DER VLUGT was born in the Netherlands in 1966, and has been internationally acclaimed for her psychological thrillers. She is the author of *The Reunion* which has sold over 200,000 copies in Holland. She lives with her husband and two children in Alkmaar.

Michele Hutchison has worked in the publishing industry for ten years. She was born in the United Kingdom, and now lives in Amsterdam with her Dutch husband and two children.

SIMONE VAN DER VLUGT

Shadow Sister

Translated from the Dutch
by Michele Hutchison

Harper
Press

Harper*Press*
An imprint of HarperCollins*Publishers*
77–85 Fulham Palace Road
Hammersmith
London W6 8JB

www.harpercollins.co.uk
Love this book? www.bookarmy.com

First published in Great Britain by Harper*Press* in 2010
1

Original text © Simone van der Vlugt 2005
English language translation © Michele Hutchison 2009/10
First published in Dutch as *Schaduwzuster* by Anthos, Amsterdam
First published in English by Text Publishing Co Melbourne

Simone van der Vlugt asserts the moral right to be identified as the author of this work

A catalogue record for this book is available from the British Library

ISBN 978-0-00-730138-6

Printed and bound in Great Britain by Clays Ltd, St Ives plc

Mixed Sources
Product group from well-managed
forests and other controlled sources
www.fsc.org Cert no. SW-COC-001806
© 1996 Forest Stewardship Council

FSC is a non-profit international organisation established to promote the
responsible management of the world's forests. Products carrying the FSC
label are independently certified to assure consumers that they come
from forests that are managed to meet the social, economic and
ecological needs of present and future generations.

Find out more about HarperCollins and the environment at
www.harpercollins.co.uk/green

Shadow Sister

Lydia

1.

All of a sudden he's got a knife. The flash as he draws it is so unexpected fear paralyses me. I try to speak, but the sound dies in my throat. I can only stare at the blade glinting in the light streaming through the classroom windows.

Then waves of adrenaline pulse through my body and I can move again. I reverse towards the open door. Bilal steps forwards at the same time so that the knife remains pointed at me, at my chest, my throat.

My thoughts scramble and fall away. I once did a training course on how to handle these kinds of situations. An image of the textbook flashes through my mind. But I can't remember the tips. I can't remember.

Intuition kicks in: Don't make eye contact. Try to escape. But will I make it to the door?

I glance at Bilal. His gaze is strange, fixed, predatory. His eyes register every movement I make, but surely he cannot see the wild heartbeat I can feel in my throat. I try to empty my face of expression, but I've no idea whether I'm succeeding. I probably look more surprised than frightened.

Surprised, because I hadn't seen this coming. But I should have been prepared for it, particularly with Bilal Assrouti.

As he passes the first line of desks, the other students are still quiet, stunned. I stare at the knife and the world contracts into a tunnel through which I can see only the long blade and Bilal's glittering eyes. The nineteen-year-old standing in front of me might be a schoolboy, but he's also a man; he's a head taller than me, his arms are muscular and there's a tic in his neck.

My eyes become glassy with fear; time stretches. Probably no more than a few seconds have passed, but it feels like minutes, minutes in which I know I'm in serious danger.

Thick fog in my head. Reason, Lydia. Talk. I need to talk. Start up a calm conversation. Show him this isn't the solution. Show him I'm taking his feelings seriously.

After letting out a dry cough, I find my voice. 'Put the knife down, Bilal. You really don't want this and it won't get you anywhere. Why are you so angry?'

'Why am I so angry?' he shouts. 'Why do you think, bitch? You just stood there, all full of yourself, and told me to leave school!'

'That's not what I said—' I begin, but the denial is a mistake. His face contorts and I fly into the corridor. There's a clamour in the classroom, but I don't stop.

I run to the headmaster's office and throw open his door. Jan van Osnabrugge has the phone in his hand, but one glance at my wild appearance is enough for him to put it down.

'Lydia! What is it?'

I close the door behind me – Bilal hasn't followed me – and lean against it. For a few seconds I can't speak. 'Bilal. He pulled a knife on me.' I indicate the size of the knife with my hands and Jan's eyes grow even wider.

'You look pale. Are you all right? I'll get you some water.'

2

He gets up, but I shake my head – I don't want to stay here alone while he fetches water.

'Sit down for a bit,' Jan says. 'Tell me what happened.'

Shaking, I sit down in the chair opposite him, but I can't remember a single thing. I can't recall anything of what happened beforehand or how the argument progressed, all I can see is the knife. I bury my face in my hands and weep hot tears.

Jan crouches next to me and puts his arms around me. 'Have a good cry. Don't worry. We'll handle this. Where is Bilal now?'

I shrug, still shaking.

'I'll send someone to your classroom to look after the other students.' Jan strides out of the room and I want to call out to him to stay, but no sound emerges from my throat.

I sit there in a daze, looking out of the window that opens onto the playground. Rotterdam College offers various types of education, but most students are doing some kind of technical or professional training. Generally they're pleasant, reasonable young people. They do need keeping an eye on, but you can have a good relationship with them. Just like at any other school. And just like at any other school, we have students with learning difficulties such as ADHD, autism, Asperger's or dyslexia. In the old days they would have gone to special schools, but not now.

I've always invested a lot in my students – I do a lot of over-time, making home visits or popping into the McDonald's where they hang out, so we can have a chat. Mostly, my students appreciate this. Plenty of them have told me so; others have demonstrated it by sharing secrets, big and small, or telling me about their home lives. Believe me, this is not easy for them. In general, a child's shame runs deeper than their need to talk about their problems.

In the beginning, if I turned up unannounced at their homes, they'd refuse to let me in, but little by little I've gained ground. I've been in most of their living rooms by now and, yes, I'll admit that I'm proud of it. Why shouldn't I be?

I wouldn't have been able to get up in front of a class and teach if it didn't inspire me. I feel responsible for my students; I might not be the driving force of their existence, but I do have some kind of influence on their future.

If I call a student to my desk to discuss their behaviour, we can have a conversation without them storming out, as they often do with my fellow teachers. The other teachers haven't gone to the trouble of attending the inter-cultural coaching sessions – they take up a lot of time in the evenings but give important insights into immigrant children. Every teacher there has come because of troublemakers in their class, and Bilal Assrouti has always been a troublemaker.

Bilal has been in my class for almost two years and we have clashed from the start. He's the kind of domineering child who rules the roost at home and thinks he can act that way at school too. But the idea that he'd draw a knife…

I've been teaching Dutch for seven years now and I've never come up against a problem with a student that I couldn't solve, but every day Bilal gives me the feeling that I'm a failure as a teacher, that I fail at all those things I'm desperate to do well. I've tried from the start to get through his armour-plating of defensiveness and scorn – the problems that he has with me as a female teacher – but in vain. And on a sunny morning at the end of April, it's come to this.

The noise of the school bell pierces the corridors and makes me jump. There's an instant uproar and shortly afterwards the playground fills up with students. Dark hair, caps and head-scarves everywhere. Is Bilal among them or has he gone? Would he really have stabbed me? I shunt restlessly backwards and forwards on my chair and decide not to leave the school premises before I've seen Bilal being carted off by the police.

2.

The door opens and Jan comes in and closes the door behind him. 'Bilal's friends say he's left. I'll get in touch with his parents presently and let them know about the incident.' He sits down at his desk. 'Lydia, we'll address this without delay.'

I let out a sigh. 'Thank you, Jan. Do you think the caretaker could take me to the police station in a little while? I daren't go out while Bilal is still on the loose.'

My words are met with silence. Jan coughs and stares at the pen pot on his desk. 'I'm wondering whether it makes sense to report this. Of course I can't stop you, but I don't think it's worth it. There's a large chance the case will be dropped due to a lack of evidence.'

'A lack of evidence? With twenty-four witnesses?'

'Most of whom are Bilal's friends,' Jan argues. 'Don't rely on your students too much – they'll either be loyal or scared of repercussions. I'd rather not have them drawn into this, you understand.'

I stare at Jan as though I'm seeing him for the first time. 'I don't understand at all. I've been threatened with a knife and you propose we act as though nothing has happened. Why is that?'

I already know the answer. If I report him, Bilal will be arrested and it will generate negative publicity for the school. Rotterdam College has been losing students for years, despite merging with two other schools, and it's not the first time we've made the news in this way.

My disgust must be evident because Jan raises a hand. 'It's not about the school, Lydia. The situation will only get worse if you make a big deal out of it. Bilal's in his final year, there's no way we can expel him. He's legally entitled to take his final exams. We've all just got to get along for the rest of the year. Reporting him to the police would be like throwing oil on the fire.'

I hesitate. The mere idea of seeing Bilal in my classroom again makes my heart race.

'I don't want to run into him in school. I don't want him in my class anymore, I don't want to bump into him in the corridor and I don't want to see him hanging around the assembly hall.'

Jan folds his hands. 'I swear that Bilal won't get away with this lightly.'

'What are you planning to do?'

'I don't want to come across him in the corridors either,' Jan replies. 'I'll suspend him for a while and after that he can finish the rest of the year at the other site. That way he can take his exams and you won't have to be confronted with him. I'll inform his parents and arrange an appointment with them for this afternoon. How do you feel about that?'

I rub my forehead, trying to massage away the beginning of a headache. 'I'm not sure. Christ, Jan, he could have stabbed me!'

'But he didn't,' Jan says in the tone of someone reassuring a child. 'Why don't you take the rest of the day off. Take as long as you need. Get over the shock, make sense of things and let me know when you're ready to get back in the saddle. You're too upset to teach right now.'

I shove my chair back and stand up. 'Fine, but as far as the police go, I'm not promising anything.'

Jan says quietly, 'If there's another negative article in the papers it will cost us twenty new students next year and just as many will decide to change schools. That'd mean two jobs on the line, two teachers unemployed. Please, Lydia.'

3.

As I stand in the corridor, amid the bustle of students, I'm overwhelmed by exhaustion. I walk back to classroom no. 209, unlock the door and go inside. My eyes dart to where I was standing when Bilal threatened me. I picture him stabbing me, see the knife in my throat, a big slash across my face. I see the blood pouring out and suddenly I'm shaking uncontrollably.

I gather my papers into the bag I'd left on the small podium and hurry out. I want to go home but my need to talk to Jasmine is stronger. The lunch break is almost over, but I have to tell her what has happened. Jasmine is my colleague and friend; we both joined the school seven years ago, fresh from teacher-training college. We have been through the same problems with discipline and difficult students. In the beginning she lived outside Rotterdam, but as soon as she got a permanent position at the school, she and her husband Lex bought a house in the same street as Raoul and me in the Hillegersberg area. We'd always been friendly, but after they moved into the street, we began dropping round for cups of tea, and looked after each other's children. Not that either of us have got much time for tea-drinking. We've both got families and a busy working week, so we mainly see each other at school.

'My god, what happened to you? You look dreadful.' Jasmine is in the staffroom drinking coffee and a quick glance at my face was enough to alarm her. The bell goes and the teachers around us pack up their bags, put their empty mugs into the plastic crate and leave the staffroom, chatting and laughing as they go.

'Do you have to teach now?' I ask.

Jasmine nods, frowning. '2E. Why? Tell me!'

'Bilal,' is all I say. 'He had a knife.'

'What?!'

I look at Jasmine; her expression of horror has made me feel better already. 'A knife. And not a small one. A long, thin blade. He held it to my throat.'

Jasmine's jaw drops. 'You've got to be kidding.'

My hands are trembling and I'm close to tears again.

'We have to talk about this, but I've got a class now.' Jasmine is flustered. 'Hold on, I'll set them an essay, then I'll be able to leave them for a while. Sit down and have a coffee, I'll be back in a minute.'

She puts a cup of coffee down in front of me, then is gone, and I'm alone in the staffroom. I read the announcements on the noticeboard without taking them in. All I can think about is whether or not I should go to the police.

When Jasmine rushes back in, I jump.

'Well, this really is the limit!' she cries out. 'We shouldn't have to put up with this kind of rubbish. Tell me exactly what happened.'

'We had an argument,' I say, 'but the crazy thing is, I can't remember what was said.'

'That's the shock,' Jasmine says. 'It doesn't matter. You had an argument and then what?'

'He got up and came towards me. His face was all contorted, it was horrible. And then he pulled out a knife and pointed it at my throat.' Three sentences and I'm crying again.

Jasmine puts her arm around me. 'It must have been so terrifying.'

'I really thought he was going to stab me,' I sob, choking back the tears. 'All I could think was, not my throat, not my throat, because I knew I'd have no chance of surviving that. But then I realised that he could also cut my face and I imagined spending the rest of my days with a big scar, or just one eye.' I cry even harder.

Jasmine strokes my hair; her face is pale. 'Where is Bilal now?' she asks. 'Have you already spoken to Jan?'

'I ran out of the classroom and went straight to Jan's office.'

'And? What did he say?'

I pick up a plastic spoon and toy with it. 'He would rather I didn't report it to the police. He said he'd get in touch with Bilal's parents this afternoon, and he'd suspend Bilal immediately.'

'Okay. And what else?'

'Legally speaking, Bilal's got the right to take his final exams here, but he'll be barred from entering this building. He'll take classes at the other site.'

Jasmine nods. 'The sooner they get him away from here the better. That does seem the best solution to me. Jesus, just the thought that he might pull a knife on me! I'd die of fright!'

I bend the plastic spoon, making a white crease in the plastic. 'But I wonder if I should go to the police.'

Jasmine frowns. 'You should really, shouldn't you?'

'It wouldn't do much for the school's reputation, but on the other hand...' I look at my friend despairingly. 'What kind of signal would that send out, that a student can threaten a teacher with a knife and the only punishment is being sent to work in another building?'

'And a suspension.' Jasmine adds.

'A suspension?' The spoon snaps. I put the pieces down. 'He'll get a week's holiday, watch a bit of MTV.'

'That's true,' Jasmine says, 'but what do you expect the police to do? The most they'll do is caution him. If we reported every threat that was made in this school, we'd all be out on the street in no time.'

'That might be true,' I say heatedly, 'but what kind of school is this then? Not reporting him means that the students have the upper hand, that they can do whatever they want.'

'They can,' Jasmine says soberly, 'and you know it.'

I do know it. The power of the students, protected by their parents, is growing and growing. When I was at school, just the threat of being sent to the deputy head's office was enough to stop me in my tracks if I was fooling around in class. These days they just laugh at you. Once, a student I'd sent out stood outside the classroom windows and dropped his trousers.

If you telephone the parents to ask them in for a chat, they never have time and they aren't interested. If they do turn up, they barely understand what you're saying because their Dutch is so poor – or they promise they'll give their son or daughter a good hiding which you then desperately try to talk them out of. Often, they're defensive. How dare you?! Are you saying they aren't good parents? Isn't it the school's job to sort out problems? Isn't that what they're paying taxes for?

Victor, one of my colleagues, was once punched by a father.

'What should I do, Jasmine?' I ask. 'What would you do?'

'I'd sleep on it.' Jasmine gets up to make another coffee. 'Think it over.'

We sit there together, drinking our coffee in silence. I look at Jasmine over the rim of my cup. 'I've got a headache.'

She rests her hand on mine. 'Just go home,' she says. 'I'll call you this evening, all right? And whatever you decide, police or no police, I'll stand by you.'

4.

I'm glad I never cycle to work, even though the weather's lovely for the end of April. I can't take my bike because I have to rush off at the end of the day to pick up my six-year-old daughter from school. To my shame, she is sometimes there waiting for me, holding the teacher's hand. But not today. It's Monday, early in the afternoon, and I've got plenty of time to tell my story to the police.

If I decide to.

As I cross the playground on my way to the car park, I catch myself looking around. The sight of every dark-haired, broad-shouldered boy gives me a jolt and I only feel safe once I'm in my car with all the doors locked.

As I join the busy Rotterdam traffic, it all comes back to me, piece by piece.

From the moment the lesson began, Bilal had been looking me up and down. I was wearing a skirt – not a mini-skirt, it was to the knee – and high black leather boots. Slouched in his chair,

Bilal looked from my legs to my breasts and then back again.

Ignoring things is always the best approach, so I carried on with the lesson. Until Bilal raised his hand.

'Miss?'

'Yes?'

'You look really hot today. Are you going somewhere?'

There were some repressed giggles, but most of the room gave Bilal a cold stare.

'I'd appreciate it if you'd keep such thoughts to yourself, Bilal.'

'I bet you would,' Bilal said. 'You know what we call women in Morocco who walk around like that?'

I gave him a warning look. I'd recently made clear to the class the consequences of swearing, specifically of using the word 'whore'.

Bilal sat up straight, leaned towards me as if in confidence, and said, 'Prostitutes.'

Anger coursed through me but I managed to control myself. 'Do you have chewing gum in your mouth? Do be so kind as to put it in the bin.'

Bilal worked his long body out from under the desk and walked, with the same sly grin, to the bin. He spat out the gum and went back to his place. As he prepared to sit down again, he stared leisurely, suggestively, at my breasts.

That's when I did something wrong. I should have told him to leave the classroom and report to the headmaster, but instead I looked at his crotch, my expression scornful. It happened so quickly – I shocked myself – I realised I was making a mistake, but it was too late. Bilal had seen it. His expression changed from sly to hard, his lips thinned and his eyes filled with a threat that set all the alarm bells in my body ringing. I stepped backwards and that's when he pulled the knife.

The memory fills me with a burst of confidence. I'm going to go to the police; of course I'm going to go to the police.

I head back towards the centre, brave the traffic along the Coolsingel Canal and turn off into a side street called Doelwater Alley. I park there and look over at the 'swimming pool', as the mint-green tiled police station is known.

But I don't get out of my car.

My eyes sweep the alleyway and the square in front of the police station, searching for Bilal. He isn't here. Of course he isn't here, but he might come out from behind a parked car once I get out of mine.

I don't really expect that to happen, but my heart pounds away all the same and I wonder whether I'll be able to get any words out once I'm inside.

I need to get a grip on myself. A glass of iced water would do me good, but all I've got is a mouldy tangerine lying next to the gear stick.

I take a deep breath. Would Bilal really have stabbed me? I've known him long enough not to believe that. Yet, that look in his eyes when I provoked him…Who knows what I triggered in him? Even though I have a good relationship with most of the students from immigrant families, I'll never truly understand them.

I imagine Bilal being interrogated – he might have to spend some time in a prison cell – and then I see the Bilal I've always known, an arrogant but intelligent boy who is probably already regretting what he did. Maybe Jan is right and I'd only make it worse by reporting it.

I don't know how long I sit in my car, but at some point I wake up from my stupor and drive home.

5.

I've always felt the need to make the world a better place. As a five-year-old, I took the new kids at school under my wing, and this protectiveness carried on into middle and high school. For the bullied kids, my support made the difference between a quiet, unremarked existence and being the butt of classroom jokes. I was popular at school and other children followed my lead.

When I was fifteen, I started working on the school magazine. Before that, no one read the magazine; afterwards I'd see copies in school bags and on the tables in the canteen. My complaints about teachers discriminating against the immigrant students made me a kind of school heroine.

I'd take on anyone, whether it was about headscarves being tolerated in the classroom or smoking on school grounds.

I've only ever wanted to help.

As I drive home, I remember Bilal's face as I fled the classroom, the aggression in his eyes, the complete arrogance of his manner. What I usually see with my Moroccan and Turkish students is that they've lost all sense of direction. These kids are born in the Netherlands, they grow up watching *Sesame Street* and Disney cartoons, but feel that they're considered second-class citizens. They don't feel Turkish or Moroccan, but don't feel Dutch either. Caught between the culture of their parentage and the country they live in, they're wrestling with their identity, anxious because there are no jobs to go to when they leave school, angry because they feel discriminated against.

If a student is having problems, I offer to buy them a drink, sit down with them, and discuss what's going on, while respecting their social codes. We almost always find a solution. My teacher training didn't prepare me for today. We were taught pedagogy and maintaining discipline, not how to handle aggression or violence.

I'm almost home when I think of how empty it will be there: the silent rooms, nobody to tell my story to. Should I go to Raoul instead? It's ten past three, he'll be in a meeting right now. To Elisa's then? If she's busy she'll make time. You can always drop in on her.

Elisa is my twin sister. We're identical twins, but I'm fifteen minutes older; perhaps that's the reason I've always protected her – first from the school bullies and later from a crowd who liked to spike your drinks with ecstasy and cadge money from you.

When Elisa set up a photography studio, I soon realised that her lack of business acumen would stand in the way of success. She wasn't assertive enough to get new clients and she let the clients she did have barter her prices down. In any case, the studio didn't attract much custom. Not that it really mattered, neither of us has to work. We come from a wealthy family; wealthy and old and noble. It's not something that particularly interests us – we never talk about it.

But money can't buy everything. Our parents always impressed on us that we should study and get jobs, that it was more comfortable to have wealth, but that shouldn't be the guiding principle in life. We weren't spoilt as children; we got the same pocket money as the others, did Saturday jobs and had to take on a paper round if we wanted extra money. It was an education I feel deeply grateful to my parents for.

I would have got by on my salary, but my husband's company would never have got off to such a flying start without the cash injection from my parents. I wonder whether Elisa could actually make a living from her photography.

To help her along I regularly have a series of portraits of Valerie taken. She never wants to charge me, but of course I pay the going price.

My husband has a successful software company and I asked him to give Elisa as many advertising commissions as he could. It turned out he'd been doing that all along, which I should have known because Raoul and Elisa get on really well.

I'm happy about that because Elisa is just as important to me as Raoul, perhaps even more so. The idea that identical twins have a special connection is true for us.

I'm often asked what it's like being a twin. It's a curious question. It's not that I'm unaware of how unusual it is to have an identical twin, but other people's reactions always remind me of how disarming our likeness is. I do see the physical resemblance, of course, but we are so different in nearly everything else. For example, Elisa is sportier than me. I rarely wear trousers, and she rarely wears a skirt. I'm extroverted, energetic and spontaneous; Elisa is relaxed and self-contained. I like shopping and going out, she'd rather go for a long walk in the countryside, and I could go on…

Elisa's studio is on Karel Doorman Street, next to the Coolsingel Canal and Raoul's offices. I park at Software International because finding a parking space in the centre of Rotterdam is nigh on impossible. When I get out of my car, my eyes follow the fire escape up to the third floor, to Raoul's office. I half expect his face to appear at the window, as if he might have sensed that I need him, but he's not there. Should I text him? Perhaps the meeting has finished or was cancelled.

I hesitate for a moment and then decide not to. Even if Raoul isn't in a meeting, he doesn't like to be disturbed at work. We made a deal about sharing the household chores and looking after Valerie and he never breaks it. If it's my turn to do the shopping and I forget the milk, I have to go back to the shop to get it, I mustn't bother Raoul. If I have a problem picking up Valerie from school, it's not his problem. It works the other way too though: I can always count on him getting Valerie to school on time each morning, with her gym kit, a boxed drink and a biscuit. She's just turned six and is in the second year of primary school. Two weeks ago she went on a school trip with her class. I was on a course that day, so Raoul was the one who carefully read the instruction sheet from the school and made sure that Valerie had everything she needed. They were first in the queue at the playground waiting for the bus, and when I got home from my course, she'd already had her bath and was eating her dinner. That's what Raoul is like. You know exactly what you're getting with him. Right now I only want one thing – to tell him what happened, and for him to comfort me and reassure me that I did the right thing by not going to the police.

I cross the Coolsingel in low spirits and walk towards Karel Doorman Street. Elisa occupies the ground floor of a small, narrow building with Elisa's Photographic Studio painted on its window in pretty black lettering. It's not a very imaginative name for someone as creative as my sister, but she thinks it works.

I push open the door and a bell tinkles. I always feel like I've wandered into an old-fashioned grocer's shop, like the ones in the television adaptation of *Pippi Longstocking*. When we were children, Elisa and I used to be mad about *Pippi Longstocking*. For at least a year I got up to the same kind of tricks as Pippi, with

Elisa following in my wake like a second Annika. Whenever I hear the theme tune, I get the urge to do something rebellious.

The front room of the studio is empty. That's to say, the walls are covered in photographs, but Elisa isn't here.

'Elisa?'

'I'm out back.'

I make my way out the back. She's at her computer, dressed sportily as usual, wearing khaki trousers and a white sweater. Her brown hair is gathered up in a ponytail and she pushes one escaped curl away from her face.

'Hey, sis,' she says. 'Don't you always finish much later on Mondays?'

'Yes,' I say simply.

My twin looks at me in alarm. 'Has something happened?'

Elisa

6.

The emptiness is waiting for me after the funeral, a terrible, apathetic emptiness. In the first few weeks after her death, I was too dazed for it to really sink in. It was as if I'd run full speed into a wall and just stood there swaying, too stunned to feel the blow.

I didn't hear a word of my father's funeral address, which made me more keenly aware of his pallid face and quivering voice. I tried to listen, leaning against my mother, mute with distress. She gripped my hand; her other arm was wrapped around Valerie. Raoul sat doubled over, his face buried in his hands.

Every pew in the church was full. And the sea of flowers! Lilies everywhere, giving off their heavy, sweet smell. The procession to the grave crossed a sun-drenched yard. It was early May and already twenty-five degrees.

We stood around the coffin, Raoul in his black suit, holding Valerie's hand. She wasn't crying; she didn't seem to understand.

She clutched a lily, Lydia's favourite flower, which she didn't want to leave behind at the grave. We let her take it. She'd already done a drawing which we'd put inside the coffin.

I remember the warmth, the birdsong, the fresh green leaves on the trees, and Raoul's tears when he threw the first shovel of soil onto the coffin. My father's contorted face, and my mother, who appeared impassive, a heavy dose of valium helping her get through that day.

I was wearing an orange and pink skirt and a matching sweater, and the boots Lydia had bought for me. Both inside the church and in the graveyard, I'd been conscious that I looked like I was going to a party and I felt many shocked glances directed towards me, which made me feel ill at ease. Should I have worn black?

It was only after the funeral, at the restaurant, as I caught my reflection in the window, that I understood the real reason behind those glances. I looked so much like Lydia right then. It shocked me too.

The last time I saw my sister, I was aware of the irreversibility of each passing second. I studied her dead face through a mist of tears – my twin sister.

They sometimes say that people who have died look like they're asleep, but it's not true. Lydia looked like what she was: dead. Her eyes were closed, her hands were folded and her skin pale. But the most shocking thing was the rigid way she lay on that white satin.

Suddenly the meaning of the expression 'deadly silence' sank in. And of the word 'forever'.

Before the funeral I was numb. Afterwards my new reality began to take shape. Despair overwhelmed me and dragged me under. For the first few weeks, I barely felt like I existed. May had promised a beautiful summer, but I spent the month in bed, staring at the white walls and ceiling. White is a comforting colour: so calm, empty and pure.

21

I found myself in a state that could be called neither sleeping nor waking. In any case, real sleep was elusive. The nights were only distinguishable from the days by a paper-thin film. Sometimes I barely knew whether I was awake or dreaming. I listened to the silence, to the indescribable lull in which I found myself, safe in my own little world.

Before her death, I had felt that something was about to happen, something that would have far-reaching consequences for me and for those dear to me. Something unnameable, but nevertheless unavoidable. The feeling had been strongest when I woke up in the mornings.

When I woke up that Monday at the end of April, I remained very still and didn't open my eyes. As if my childish refusal to look at the day would have any influence! Of course I did have to open my eyes eventually. My gaze went first to the alarm clock – it was still early – and then to the ceiling. For a quarter of an hour I looked at that white surface and tried to rationalise my feeling of discomfort. Where was it coming from?

Lydia.

Something had happened to Lydia.

I could have thought about any number of people who were dear to me: my parents or Thomas or Raoul. But Lydia's name was the one that burned itself into my mind and, in a fit of panic, I grabbed my mobile from the bedside table and called her. There was no ring tone, it wasn't switched on.

But of course it wasn't, it was a quarter past eight, her first lesson had already begun.

Had I dreamed something that had made my head so full and heavy? It was possible; if only I could remember the dream, it might explain the feeling that something was wrong.

That day I was going to Capelle aan den Ijssel, to photograph a wedding with Thomas. Thomas is a photographer as well, and his sister, Laurien, was the bride.

By the time I got out of the shower, I was late. I raced out of the house dressed in green combats and a white sweater, my hair still wet. I grabbed my stuff, it was all there ready – my camera, tripod, light reflector. I was soon in the car; it belonged to my friend Sylvie. She lives and works in Rotterdam, where she can walk everywhere, so she lends it to me at times.

If you are a photographer, there's always some family member with something to celebrate and they remember you just in time. Because of course you don't charge them the full rate – you wouldn't do that to family. You'd be invited anyway, so while you're there, you might as well take pictures, right?

I'm positive that another professional photographer wouldn't get as many requests for 'just one more shot with Uncle Jim' or of the five girlfriends of the bride with their children, who look so pretty in their new clothes.

A commissioned professional records only the official events: the church, registry office, reception and a few posed pictures in the park. They wouldn't be asked to stay until the bitter end, because that would be much too expensive. But you, dear friend or family member, you can't leave until the grand finale – the guests standing in a ring around the married couple, waving their lighters in the air, bellowing 'You'll Never Walk Alone', which you can't join in with because you're supposed to be taking pictures of it.

I hate weddings and so does Thomas. That's why we go together. We've agreed never to shoot them alone.

So off we went together that Monday, which was a good distraction from my vague sense of dread.

'Do you think you'll ever get married?' Thomas mumbled.

We'd greeted the bride and the rest of Thomas's family in his parents' house and were drinking coffee while we waited for the groom to arrive. We sat a little apart and barely had to lower our voices through the constant chatter of Thomas's mother and grandmother.

'I don't know,' I said.

'I can imagine you in a white dress,' Thomas said, a touching seriousness in his brown eyes.

I looked away with a smile on my lips, it was something I couldn't imagine at all and for various reasons the subject made me feel embarrassed.

'It would suit you.'

'I'm not getting married.' My voice sounded a little too harsh and the crash as I put my cup down on its saucer was perhaps a little over the top, but Thomas didn't seem bothered.

'I know that,' he said calmly. 'It doesn't mean that much to me either. Why shouldn't you just live together? That's much simpler, isn't it?'

'But our society is set up so that it's easier if you get married,' I said. 'If you just live together there's a lot more red tape to get the same rights.'

Something that looked like pain flashed across Thomas's face. 'Red tape? Rights? What on earth happened to romance and being faithful until you die?'

'They don't exist. You've settled down until you die, that's all.'

Thomas glanced at his sister. 'But Laurien looks really happy.'

'Wait and see whether her fiancé turns up,' I said, and he had to laugh.

I didn't really think the groom would fail to show up, that's just the kind of conversations Thomas and I have – a little rebellious, kicking against the establishment. If we'd been young in the seventies, we would have fitted in quite well. I pictured Thomas cycling to the registry office, dinking his bride-to-be. Or even better, Thomas carrying his bride on a delivery bike, swerving along the canals. Only I didn't see myself as that bride, though for some time I'd been getting the impression that Thomas did.

We'd been hanging out together for years because we'd both gone to art college in Amsterdam; even back then we'd been really close.

'There's Cyril. Thank god!' Thomas winked at me and stood up. He took his camera from the table and walked outside. I began to mount my camera on the tripod.

7.

Thomas is a great guy, but he's difficult, a real artist. You wouldn't call him handsome; his eyes are a bit close together for that and his face is long and thin, but his dark eyes and athletic build make up for quite a bit. If he had a more cheerful personality, he might be really attractive, but Thomas and light-heartedness don't go together. When we were students, he was a loner. He suffered from depression and he didn't make friends easily. During his depressive episodes, which could last for weeks, he would withdraw and become unreachable. I only discovered that when I got to know him better, and it was years before he told me that his father had had similar mood swings. His father committed suicide. Thomas wasn't as bad as that, thanks to drugs and intensive therapy, but you would never call him carefree.

I didn't like him at first. I thought he was a grouch, an egoist, uninterested in other people – but then one day he came to my rescue. I was in a crowded tram, blocked in by the crush of people and unable to get away from the man behind me, who took the opportunity to make a grab at me and have a feel. People around me saw it happening, but nobody said anything or intervened, until Thomas pushed his way over to me. I hadn't known he was on the tram. At the next stop he pressed the button to open the doors, punched the guy in the face and threw him out, shouting after him, 'Go fuck your mother, you prick!'

There was a round of applause in the tram, but Thomas sat back down with a miserable look on his face. When the tram was less packed, I made my way over to thank him, and that afternoon we worked together on a project at the art college. It was the beginning of our friendship.

It was an unusual kind of friendship, none of the other students understood why I hung out with Thomas. I didn't really understand it that well myself. I'd probably felt sorry for him at first, until I got to know the real Thomas and made a friend for life.

'If you go back and process the pictures we've taken, I'll take care of the reception and the party,' Thomas said to me early in the afternoon. The lunch was over, the guests were leaving the restaurant and the bride's curls had already dropped out of her hair.

'I don't mind helping you. I've still got space on my card.'

'It's fine. You look a bit tired, are you feeling all right?' Thomas's eyes glided over my face in concern.

'I didn't sleep very well last night.'

'Well, get an early night then. I'll see you tomorrow.' Thomas put his arm around my shoulders and pulled me towards him, holding me tighter and for slightly longer than was strictly necessary. Not that it bothered me, but I wondered if he considered every instance of bodily contact as a point in his favour.

I knew the feeling, only it wasn't Thomas who inspired it.

I drove back to Rotterdam, to Sylvie's, and left a note of

thanks under the windscreen wipers, then caught the tram to Karel Doorman Street. I'd have preferred to go home and settle down on the sofa with a cup of tea and packet of fudge – my addiction – but I'd promised Thomas I'd get to work on the pictures straight away.

I unlocked the studio door and went through the exhibition space to the back where I've got an office and a small kitchen. The kitchen opens onto a badly kept garden. It's overrun with weeds, which always winds my father up. My father loves gardening and made several attempts to tame the plants shooting up in all directions, but each time he came back, he had to start all over again. Finally he had to accept that this garden would never amount to much unless he spent more time in it, and he already looks after the garden of my summer house in Kralingen, as well as Lydia's, which is huge. And his own garden.

I looked over my computer screen at the garden and sighed. First a cup of tea.

I made a pot of camomile tea – I swear by herbal tea when I'm anxious – and took it out into the garden.

It's actually quite nice. I don't like stylised flower beds and themed areas. Just give me a garden that's alive, even if it's so exuberant you can hardly get into it. Lawns with a few rickety bistro chairs are not really my thing.

I wandered through the jungle, pulling out a few random stalks, and finally went inside to do some work.

For a while I concentrated so hard that I forgot everything else. Even my tiredness slipped away. When the doorbell rang, my concentration was shattered and the uneasiness rolled over me again. I didn't need to get up to see who it was.

'Elisa?' Her voice was higher pitched than usual.

'I'm out back!'

Lydia's footsteps came towards the office, dragging a little. I swivelled around in my desk chair and got up. Lydia appeared in the doorway, groomed from top to toe as usual, with a tight

28

black skirt and a fairly sexy black wraparound top. She seemed tired and irritated.

I pushed my hair back out of my face.

'Hey sis,' I said cautiously. 'You don't usually finish until much later on Mondays.'

'Yes,' she said simply.

Then I knew for sure. 'Something has happened,' I said softly.

Lydia

8.

I'm no longer surprised that I don't need to explain much to Elisa. A single word, a single glance at my face is enough for her to know that I'm not paying a social call.

'Lydia? What is it? Here, have my chair.' She pushes me into her place and strides into the kitchen. Within a few seconds she's back with a glass of cold water, exactly what I need. I drink deeply while my sister stands there with her arms crossed and peers down at me.

'What happened?' she says again, as soon as I've emptied the glass.

'Bilal Assrouti.'

Only my parents – who've both taught difficult children in the past – can understand what it feels like to matter to another person, to make a difference, and what you have to go through to get there. Apart from my parents, Elisa and Raoul are the closest people to me, but they've never understood what drives me to work in a profession that takes so much energy and delivers so few rewards. That's my own fault for being so open about how bad it can be. I don't tell them enough of the nice things that happen: the flowers my class gave me on my birthday, how they sing the national anthem in the proper Dutch way, with their arms around each other, to prove that they've picked up something from my lessons.

When I talk about my work, the most memorable things are the bad things: one of the students punching Vincent in the jaw, or the attitude of some of the students when I wear a short skirt. I'm afraid I've dropped the name Bilal more than once because Elisa reacts immediately. 'Bilal? What's he done?'

I look at her for a while without speaking and she crouches down next to me. 'You're not hurt, are you?'

'No,' I whisper. 'He only threatened me. With a knife.'

Elisa takes my hand, but she doesn't have to do that for me to know that I'm not on my own in this. I feel some of her life-force and energy flowing into me and I take a deep breath.

'Tell me about it,' Elisa says gently.

I tell her. Every detail, every minor and major incident of the day. I don't even leave out my own ill-advised reaction to Bilal's provocative behaviour and Elisa listens without interrupting. When I've finished at last, she says, 'Lydia, this is not your fault. Please understand that. I'm wondering why you're here instead of at the police station. Or have you already been?'

'No, that could have enormous consequences for the school.'

My sister gives me a look of incomprehension. 'For the school? And what about you? This has enormous consequences for you too!'

'Bilal is going to be suspended and transferred to the other site,' I say. 'I won't have to see him anymore.'

'Is that all?' Elisa says in astonishment.

'He didn't stab me,' I remind her. 'He only threatened me.'

'Only threatened!'

'We have to deal with worse things at school, you know.'

31

'And so it's normal? I don't understand this.'

'I've never had a problem with that boy, Elisa. Not of this magnitude, in any case. In some ways, I've only got myself to blame. If I hadn't looked at his crotch, he wouldn't have flipped. A thing like that is an enormous provocation in the Moroccan culture.'

'So what. We live in Holland, and it's not normal here for a teacher to be called a whore because she's wearing a short skirt.'

'I do know that, but I have to work with these boys day in, day out. You still have to take their views into consideration.'

'I suppose it's easier to blame yourself.' Elisa shrugs. 'Would you like a cup of tea?'

She goes into the kitchen without waiting for an answer and I stare out of the window at the neglected back garden. She's right, of course, it is much easier to blame yourself. If you blame yourself, you feel less powerless.

Elisa returns with two steaming mugs of tea.

'What next?' she asks. 'Does Raoul know already?'

'No, he's in a meeting. I'm not going to bother him with this now. He can't do anything about it, after all.'

'I suppose not,' Elisa says.

The doorbell tinkles and we look at each other.

'Hi-i!' A voice with a rather exaggerated sustained note rings out in the exhibition space.

Sylvie.

'Hiiii,' I imitate quietly.

'Shut up,' Elisa says, and then in a louder voice, 'I'm out back.'

There's a click clack of high heels on the wooden floor and then Sylvie Roelofs appears in the doorway. Sylvie is quite a good friend of Elisa's, though I'm not sure why. It's not that Sylvie is unpleasant, but she's…fake, that's the word. And instead of keeping any kind of distance, she does her best to please me, which is even more irritating.

She once came on to Raoul while I was there. Luckily Raoul doesn't go for women like her so she had little success. Since then she's behaved more normally, but we'll never be friends.

'Oh,' Sylvie says. 'You're here too, are you? How are you?'

'All right, thanks.'

She looks me up and down critically. 'You don't look that great.'

'Why, thanks.' I say.

'Lydia's had a bit of a difficult day,' Elisa says. 'She's been threatened by one of her students.'

'Really? How dreadful! What happened?'

'He pulled a knife,' I say.

'Lord! What did you do? I think I would have died of fright, wouldn't you?' Sylvie says, directing a look of horror at Elisa.

'The only thing I could think of doing was to leave the class-room,' I say.

'Well, that was probably for the best,' Sylvie says. 'You know, something like that happened to me once. I was on the tram and a man sat down next to me, right up against me. I moved towards the window and he shifted too so that I was clamped in. And then he opened his legs wide so that our knees were touching. I couldn't sit anywhere else because the tram was full, so I pretended not to notice. And then, I swear it, he put his hand on my leg!' She shudders.

'Oh gross,' Elisa says. 'What did you do then?'

'Nothing. I should have hit him, but I was completely over-whelmed. I wriggled around in my seat to get rid of his hand. Then he gave me a really letchy look. "I've never seen such a beautiful woman," he said. "You've really made my day." I had no idea how to react!'

Sylvie gives me a glance that suggests that now we have a shared trauma, we might become better friends.

'Wow,' I say simply, because I only ever half believe Sylvie's stories. She's always experienced everything you mention herself, although the similarity with your own story is usually quite hard to find. Worse still, she always finds it necessary to give a very detailed account, which means that you can't finish your own story. People like that drive me insane.

'I have to go.' I get up from my chair.

'No, stay a while,' Elisa says at once. 'We've hardly talked.'

'It's important to talk,' Sylvie comments. 'It helps you get over things. I once—'

'Another time.' I get my bag, give Elisa a wave and I'm gone.

9.

At half past three, I'm standing in the playground at Valerie's school, waiting for the bell to go and for her to come running out. I usually chat with the other mothers and the odd father, but today I keep to myself.

There it is, the shrill noise of the bell and the first children come streaming out. Valerie is often the last one, I don't know why. She comes sauntering out at her own cheerful pace when all her classmates are already on the back of their parent's bike, or strapped into the back seat of their car. I couldn't find my beaker, I lost my scarf, I had to go to the toilet, I wanted to tell the teacher something.

It's not something that bothers me today, but if I'm waiting in the rain it's a different matter. And there's rarely a parking space near enough to wait in the car.

She comes ambling out at twenty to four today too, drawings in her hand and her beaker stuffed into her coat pocket.

'Hi Mummy!' she says, standing on tiptoe to greet me.

I bend down to kiss her warm, red schoolgirl's cheek. 'Hi darling, have you had a nice day?'

'No, what are we going to eat tonight?' she says in a single breath as we walk to the car.

'I'm not sure yet. There's lots of things in the fridge, we'll look when we get home.'

'I want chips.'

'Maybe we'll have chips then.' I open the back door so that Valerie can climb in. She fastens the seatbelt herself and says, 'I've made some nice pictures, Mummy. Do you want to see them?'

She passes me a couple of scribbled drawings that I admire at length.

'They're for Grandma.' Valerie checks my expression. 'Do you mind?'

'Well, maybe a very tiny bit,' I admit. I once said that I really didn't mind and had to spend the next hour making up for my lack of interest.

'I'll do another one for you at home. A really pretty one.'

I slide behind the wheel. 'What did you do at school today, sweetheart?'

'Played in the standpit,' Valerie says, without taking her eyes off her artworks.

I can't help laughing at her corruption of sandpit, but her second remark wipes the smile from my face. 'And I bit Christian.'

'What?' I look at Valerie in the rear-view mirror. 'What did you do that for?'

'He wanted to play cops and robbers,' Valerie says. 'But I didn't want to. I always had to be the robber and he kept poking me with his sword, like that' – she makes a stabbing gesture and pulls the kind of face that over-enthusiastic boys make when playing 'and then he wanted to tie me up and then I bit him.' Valerie folds her arms.

36

'You can always go to the teacher,' I suggest as I turn out of the street.

'You know what I don't understand, Mum?'

'What?'

'I've been going to school for ages and I still can't write.'

'You're only in your second year,' I say. 'Nobody learns to read and write until the third.'

'That's too long!'

'It's soon enough,' I say. 'Cutting and gluing things is nice too, isn't it?'

'But I've been able to do that for ages! I could do that in crèche!'

I study my daughter's defeated face in the mirror. She's quick for her age, always trying to do things she's a little too young for. I recognise that – it's exactly what I used to be like.

'Shall I teach you to write a few letters?'

'You can't do that,' Valerie giggles. 'You're not a teacher!'

'Yes, I am. For big children.'

'Oh yeah,' she says. 'Well, all right then. When we get home?'

'When we get home,' I promise as I turn on the radio. Valerie joins in with Robbie Williams' latest hit. 'Sing, Mummy! Sing!'

We sing until we turn into Juliana van Stolberg Avenue in Hillegersberg and park in front of the house. And then I realise that I'd managed to forget about Bilal for the past fifteen minutes.

'I've told you enough times that you should leave that place! This cannot happen again!' Raoul says.

I didn't make chips, but a curry dish as a treat. Raoul got home at half past five and it was really hard not to assail him immediately. I waited until we had finished dinner. Afterwards we stayed at the table chatting as usual, while Valerie watched TV, leaving us to talk in peace.

'How many times have I told you to look for a better school? That bunch aren't worth wasting your time on. I hope you've finally realised that. You've got a child of your own here who needs you, you know.' Raoul leans back a little, one hand on the table, one on the arm of his chair and looks at me with a mixture of compassion and exasperation.

'Excuse me, are you trying to say that it's my fault? That I asked for this?'

'No, of course not.' Raoul leans over the table towards me and places his hand on top of mine. He asks if I can deny that I work in the kind of environment where this kind of thing happens. He's always been worried about something like this, he says, and he hopes I'll finally see sense.

'See sense?' I repeat.

'You can start at Software International right away if you like.'

I sigh and study the congealed curry on my plate, the grains of rice on the white tablecloth, and the yellow stains around Valerie's place. I've never managed to convey the satisfaction I get from teaching to Raoul. He only seems to see the problems. He calls my work 'farting into the wind'. If I were to transfer to Saint Laurens College, a private school in Hillegersberg, he might be able to understand it, but a poor, state school…

'It's not all trouble at school,' I say. 'I have a great time with most of the students. I feel like I can affect their lives in a positive way, and I don't just mean in terms of their education. You know that.'

Raoul doesn't look like he does know. He remains silent.

'So you're just going to carry on,' he says eventually. 'Despite the students you're working your ass off for coming at you with knives. Are you surprised that I find your logic hard to follow?'

'I do understand your point, but every profession has its risks,' I say. 'If you were a policeman, I wouldn't keep banging on at you to find safer work, would I?'

'I sell software,' Raoul reminds me.

'But you wanted to be a pilot and you would have been if your eyesight had been good enough,' I say. 'That's not a job without risks.'

Raoul raises his hands in the air and lets them drop. 'Fine! Go and teach those half-wits tomorrow. Pretend that nothing has happened. But tell me how I'm going to explain it to Valerie when her mother gets seriously injured one day.'

'Don't exaggerate, Raoul. You're acting like this happens on a daily basis.'

'Once is enough as far as I'm concerned.'

I'm bewildered. I'd have been better off saying nothing. Instead of being worried and supportive, he's twisted it into proof that I shouldn't teach. Don't get me wrong, I love Raoul dearly, but sometimes he's got the sensitivity of a grizzly bear. A memory flashes through my mind: Valerie wanting to cycle without training wheels and being too impatient to wait for Raoul after he'd unscrewed them. She rode off and of course she crashed. There she was on the ground with a bloody nose and grazed knees. The first thing Raoul did was to ask her why she hadn't listened to him. He picked her up and consoled her afterwards, but I would have done it the other way round.

I stack up the plates and dishes and take them to the kitchen where I rinse the scraps of food off the plates. I finish clearing the table with agitated movements and shake out the tablecloth outside. Raoul doesn't get up or come over to me until I've put the vase of peonies back on the table and pushed the chairs in. He wraps his arms around me and pulls me towards him. I let him kiss my neck, but don't react to his tenderness.

'I'm upset by it, don't you understand that?' Raoul says softly.

I lean back against him and feel his body warmth through my clothes.

'I'm upset too,' I say. 'A bit of understanding and support would be nice.'

'Sorry,' Raoul says, his cheek against mine. 'Have the police already done anything?'

I take a deep breath. 'I didn't report it.'

'Oh?'

I hear the amazement in his voice and brace myself, but his reaction takes me by surprise.

'Oh well, I don't suppose there's much they could do.'

Raoul pulls me even more tightly towards him, 'If he'd really stabbed you, he'd have gone to prison, but I think they'd only caution him and let him go for this.'

I study the bright peonies on the table. 'Yes,' I say finally, after my day of turmoil, reflection and changes of mind. 'That's what I think as well.'

10.

We go to bed late. I have a hot, soothing shower and as I dry myself and apply night cream, I hear Raoul checking the locks more attentively than usual and I'm glad that he's here to make me feel safe. I snuggle against him in bed and close my eyes with a deep sense of security.

'Sleep well.' Raoul kisses me on the forehead.

'Sleep well,' I murmur.

I'm exhausted, but after an hour I'm still curled up against Raoul, waiting to fall asleep. I roll onto my other side. Raoul is snoring lightly and I tap him before it gets any louder. I know what's coming next.

'What is it?' Raoul mumbles, drunk with sleep.

'You're snoring,' I say quietly. 'Lie on your other side for a bit.'

'I'm not snoring.'

'You were snoring, I could hear it.'

'I'm not even asleep,' Raoul says.

'You were asleep.'

'So why didn't I hear anything if I was awake then?' Raoul asks, also irritated.

'Because you were asleep! You were asleep and snoring!'

Raoul mutters, turns over and after a few minutes is asleep again. And snoring.

I sigh and get some earplugs from the bedside drawer. But even my earplugs can't combat the number of decibels Raoul can produce at night. After fifteen minutes I give up and take my pillow to the spare bedroom. I set the alarm clock on the bedside table and close the curtains with a single swipe. As I'm doing it, my subconscious registers something strange. I open the curtain a chink. Someone is standing outside our house, on the other side of the street. A dark figure with a cigarette in his hand. I presume it's a man – I can't imagine that a woman would stand there smoking a cigarette in the middle of the night.

Bilal comes to mind.

I try my hardest to make him out, but I can't from this distance. Finally the figure moves off, with the slouchy, indifferent walk so typical of my students. Shivering in the cool night air, I watch until he has disappeared. What should I do? There's no point calling the police – even if they find him, there's nothing illegal about staring at a house in the middle of the night.

I turn back the duvet and slide into bed, but the chances that I'll fall asleep now are virtually nil. The image of the sharp point of the knife forces itself into my mind and is amplified many times in the darkness.

I'm up at the crack of dawn the next morning and leave the house half an hour earlier than normal. Raoul and Valerie are usually getting up when I put on my coat, and I give them a quick kiss before I get into my car. This morning they are still asleep, but I enjoy the quietness of my departure. Thoughts race through my mind: I want to go to school and yet I'm dreading entering the building. What am I going to do if I come across Bilal? Jan might have suspended him, but that won't necessarily keep him away.

I drive through the misty Rotterdam rush hour with a sense of foreboding. A grimy figure jumps out in front of the car at a red light. He holds up a sponge and a bucket. I nod, and he washes my windscreen with sweeping strokes. It only takes him a minute. I gaze sympathetically at his neglected appearance, his long knotted beard and worn-out army jacket. I let my window down slightly and say, 'Hi, Tom!'

Tom gives me a smile that's missing at least two teeth and holds out his hand.

I press five euros into his hand. 'Get yourself a good meal for once, Tom.' Sometimes I give him one euro, others two and occasionally even a ten euro note. It depends how cold it is outside and how bedraggled he's looking.

'Thank you, miss,' Tom says. 'You've got a good heart.'

I smile because he always says that and I suspect he uses the same line on everybody.

'I mean it,' he says. 'There are enough people who spit in my face or try to run me over. It's dangerous work, lady. Dangerous work for just a few euros.' Before I can say anything back, he's walked off, still talking loudly.

Tom is always at the same crossroads. He usually walks along the queue of cars with a bucket and gets a bit of loose change without having to get his sponge out. I find it impossible to drive on and ignore Tom. In fact I can't ignore anyone.

A while back, the action group 'Keep Rotterdam Safe' called on Rotterdammers not to give money to beggars. The morning before that, I'd given Tom ten euros, a bag of currant buns and Raoul's windproof ski jacket. I can still picture him standing there with them.

'Now I'm all set!' he'd said.

The following day he was at the crossroads, wearing the red

jacket. I've never dared tell Raoul about it – he's not that keen on beggars and tramps – but he's never missed the jacket.

'No one has to live like that in Holland,' he always says. 'They could look for a job, and if they don't want to, I'm sorry, but they shouldn't hassle people who do work for their money.'

The topic keeps cropping up in our conversations and occasionally causes rows. But it's also how we met in the first place.

11.

I was twenty-two and still a student. Raoul was twenty-six. I was in my final year of teacher training at college in Rotterdam and travelled in from Berkel & Rodenrijs, where I lived with my parents.

My train was a commuter train, full of passengers who were delighted if they could find a seat and doze unashamedly or open up their morning newspaper. But the majority went through the daily torture of standing, packed together.

It was usually quite quiet when I got on and I'd be fortunate enough to get a window seat, safely out of reach of the pointy elbows in the central aisle. Engrossed in a book or course material, the time passed quickly and I barely noticed my fellow passengers.

One bright spring morning in March I was staring out of the window at the cows in the meadows and the clouds that seemed to rise up out of the mist. A loud shout broke my reverie. It came from the area next to the doors, where a few people were standing. Two young men stood facing each other. One was wearing a tracksuit, he was bald and had a nose ring; the other was dressed in a smart coat and had neatly combed hair – the picture of decency and good sense. But that must have been just show because the bald guy was shouting, 'What did you say? Mind your own business, you prick!'

Everyone in the carriage was pretending not to have noticed.

The well-dressed man said something back, at which point the bald guy flew at his throat, pushed him against the corridor wall and punched him in the head.

I pushed past the man sitting next to me and rushed towards them.

'Stop that!' I threw open the glass doors. 'Both of you!'

I threw myself between their fists. That stopped them momentarily – the scruffy guy looked at me in amazement, then irritation, and gave me a harmless shove. The well-dressed man seemed to be wondering if I was in my right mind. The scruffy guy tried to push me aside, but I didn't let him. I grabbed his arm, looked him in the eye and said, 'Stop! Please! Can't you just discuss it?'

His expression was so full of fury I was frightened he'd hit me, but at that moment someone behind me said, 'She's right. Come on, lads, this isn't the way.'

I looked around and saw the tall, dark-haired man who'd been sitting opposite me in the carriage. The fight was stopped, the two parties separated with final hateful glances at each other and I returned to my seat.

The man who'd come to my assistance sat back down opposite me. 'That was brave of you,' he said, 'but also a bit foolish.'

'Everyone pretending not to notice is the obvious solution, isn't it?' I snapped back, my cheeks flushed.

'One of them could easily have had a knife.'

'Don't be silly, not everyone walks around with a knife.'

The man looked like he doubted that. 'It can't get much worse than it is.'

His words turned out to be prophetic. At the time knife-incidents were on the rise – these days the ticket inspectors won't get involved in arguments on the trains.

Nowadays every suspect character who comes into Rotterdam is preventatively searched, street shootings have become banal, many secondary schools are equipped with surveillance cameras and metal detectors, and children who witness crimes are shot dead when they're out playing. The violence is mounting and paralysing us all.

'Why did you get up then?' I asked my rescuing knight.

He shrugged. 'I could hardly have stayed in my seat while a girl was sorting it out, could I? They might have stabbed you.'

'They might have stabbed each other too.'

'Yes,' he agreed, in a way that suggested it wasn't something he would worry about.

We got out together at Rotterdam Central Station, said goodbye and went our separate ways. Then he came back towards me.

'I'll walk with you a while,' he said. 'We don't know where those guys are now.'

He accompanied me to the tram and I began to suspect ulterior motives. But he didn't ask for my phone number or suggest we meet for a drink. He put me on the tram, the tram moved off and that was that.

At least, for that day. I saw him again the next day, standing on the platform, and happiness swept through me. He came over as soon as he spotted me.

'Hey,' he said. 'It's me. You know, from yesterday.'

'Yes, I do remember. Sometimes, if I really try hard, I can even remember things that happened the day before yesterday.'

He laughed and we took the train together. His name was Raoul and he'd just set up his own software company in

Rotterdam. From the way he told me all of this, I could tell that he was single.

I was telling him about my course when three scruffy-looking musicians entered our carriage. Two played a brisk off-key tune on the guitar while the other one went around with a smelly cap. Raoul shook his head, but I gave the man some small change. Quite a few people gave me irritated glances.

'See those dirty looks,' I muttered to Raoul.

'Some people find it annoying, they want to read their papers in peace in the mornings,' Raoul commented. 'Giving money only encourages begging.'

'I'd rather they asked for money than pickpocketed my purse,' I replied.

Raoul grinned. 'I bet you give a euro to those people who don't have quite enough cash for their train ticket.'

I blushed and Raoul shook his head pityingly. 'You'd have been better off training to be a social worker.'

The train came to a standstill. The conductor announced that we'd be delayed for an indeterminate period of time, regretfully. I didn't find it at all regretful.

As we continued talking, I studied Raoul. Was anything unattractive about him? By the time we pulled into Rotterdam station, I still hadn't found it.

We went out a couple of times and during the course of one of those evenings, Raoul told me that he never usually took the train to work. The morning we'd met, smoke had poured out of his car engine and he'd had to take the train. A few days later his car had been repaired, but he'd kept taking the train to see me.

He was lodging temporarily with his parents in Berkel & Rodenrijs because he'd been able to get a good price for his house and hadn't found a new one yet. He wanted to move to Rotterdam to be closer to his work.

A few dates later, I invested my feelings in him and six months later I invested my money in his company. We moved in together and two years after that we got married. Raoul's business went well, particularly well, so that after we got married we could move into the chic Hillegersberg area, into a beautiful, spacious house with high ceilings and old wooden floors.

Raoul wanted me to be at home far more than I did – he didn't want me to work, especially not in a teaching job. But I didn't study education for four years to sit at home. His complaints got worse when Valerie was born. She'd been going to the crèche for two years, and was very happy there, when Raoul came home one evening and threw a letter down onto the work bench, where I was making pizza.

'Look what I've got for you! An invitation to have a chat!' His smile was broad.

'Do you need to write me an invitation? Are things that bad between us?' I joked.

He laughed and kissed my throat. 'No, you idiot. There's a vacancy in our PR department and it's made for you.'

'Public relations? Why would I want to do that?'

'Don't you like the idea? I think it would be perfect for you,' Raoul said. 'It's a shared part-time job, you can choose between two or three days a week.'

'Raoul, I've got a job.'

'But you're not going to be a teacher for the rest of your life.' Raoul spread his fingers, a gesture that expressed his incomprehension.

'Why not?' I turned the oven to 200 degrees and took two purple placemats out of the cupboard. All the accessories in our home are purple; it's my favourite colour.

'Come on, Lydia! You don't mean that Rotterdam College is your goal in life, do you?'

'Any school is all right,' I said, 'as long as I'm making a difference for my students. And I don't just mean in terms of their education. Do you get it?'

Raoul didn't say anything, but he didn't look like he got it. He stood there staring at me, his hands in his pockets.

'So you're not coming to work at Software International?'

'No,' I said. 'I know you don't like Rotterdam College, but I'm happy there.'

'I'm not so sure,' Raoul said. 'You always look so tired. I'd rather you didn't work at all.'

I smiled at him. 'Darling, I am always tired, just like you. But I don't suggest that you sell your company, do I?'

He didn't buy it. 'I just don't think it's good for Valerie.'

My smile disappeared. 'I'm always home when she finishes school.'

'But she has to have lunch at school four days a week.'

'She really likes having lunch at school!' I shouted. 'Why are you pulling a face? You knew beforehand that I wanted to keep on working. I don't understand why you keep complaining about it. Why don't you resign from your job?'

We're still having this kind of conversation. Raoul is a modern man who will help with the housework and believes in sharing the load equally. He likes modern women who work for a living and contribute to society, but it's something he appreciates in other women, not me.

12.

I drive into the school car park at twenty past seven. It's still very empty. I don't get out immediately; first I look around. There's no one to be seen, the playground is deserted. The beautiful wisteria covering the fence is blossoming early this year.

I walk across the playground. The door is still closed to the students, but Dan, the caretaker, unlocks it for me.

'You're early!' he says.

'I just couldn't wait any longer,' I say with a weak smile.

'I can imagine,' Dan chuckles. 'I find the silence at this time of the morning difficult too.'

'It won't last much longer.' I glance at the clock in the corridor. 'Shall I fetch us some coffee, Dan?'

'Lots of milk, lots of sugar.' Dan goes back to his caretaker's office where the phone is ringing.

I watch him with affection. Dan Riemans could have retired long ago, but instead he's still faithfully guarding his post. He's a small, plump man with light blue eyes that usually sparkle with fun. He's often telling jokes to the students; they like him. But if he's angry, it thunders through the corridors. The students aren't afraid of him, but they like him too much to want to cause trouble. With a few exceptions, of course.

'If you want to skive off, you'll have to do a better imitation of your mother's voice, Ayesha,' I hear him say as I bring our coffees back from the staffroom. 'I'll be expecting you at exactly five past eight. Bye, Ayesha, see you soon.'

He hangs up and smiles at me.

'Thanks, lassie. Sit down and tell me what that was all about yesterday.'

'Did you already hear about it?'

'The school's buzzing with it.'

Dan sinks into his comfortable chair from where, with a swivel, he can survey the corridor as well as the playground.

I sigh and blow onto my coffee, then tell him all. Dan listens in silence, shaking his head from time to time. I also tell him about my conversation with Jan. When I get to our disagreement about whether to go to the police, Dan looks up.

'And? Did you go to the police?'

I shake my head and think I glimpse something of relief in Dan's eyes.

We drink our coffee and gaze out at the playground where the first children are arriving on their bikes.

'Assrouti won't get in here anymore, don't worry about that,' Dan says.

'Did Jan ask you to make sure?'

'Yes, very clearly. You just go and teach, lass, and I'll personally make sure that Bilal Assrouti doesn't set a foot inside this school.'

I smile gratefully at him. Dan once had to face a student with a knife and I know that it made a deep impression on him. Bilal will have to use all his resourcefulness if he wants to force his way in.

At seven-forty-five I see Jasmine approaching. I finish my coffee, ready to leave, then pause in the doorway.

'Dan?'

'Hmm?'

'Do you think I should have gone to the police?'

Dan looks at me. I'm expecting him to say 'no', but he doesn't. 'For you, personally, perhaps you should have.' He pauses. 'But I'm glad you didn't for the school.'

I wait for Jasmine in the corridor and as we go to the staff-room I find myself talking about it again. I once read that people who have had a traumatic experience need to remember every detail of the event and find an explanation for it. Coming up with answers is a way of processing the trauma.

'I hardly dared get out of my car once I'd parked,' I tell her. 'That's bad, isn't it? And I'm constantly looking at the play-ground. Do you think Bilal would have the nerve to simply show up, as though nothing had happened?'

'I don't think so,' Jasmine says. 'No, we won't see him again, Lydia. Don't be scared.'

I'm not scared, I want to say, not here with my colleagues in the staffroom where there's a large cake box in the middle of the table. We arrive just in time to see people wishing Hans, an older colleague, a happy birthday. I join in, but before Hans has finished cutting his cake, I tell everyone about Bilal.

'Hey you, can't it wait?' Jasmine says, but I won't be deterred. It's weighing down on me too much, it has to come out.

The atmosphere changes immediately. Not everyone knows about it yet and the consternation among my colleagues is great. Everyone is talking at once. Hans sits there with a plate of cake and a surly look. He's one of the old guard on the staff. He's not usually the most cheerful person, but now he looks like one of his test tubes has exploded and covered him in whatever type of acid corrodes a good mood.

I realise I'm ruining his birthday, but I can't help it. It's important that all my colleagues know what has happened. More important than singing happy birthday to one person.

'I really wouldn't have expected that from Bilal,' Nora, my departmental head, says, shocked.

'Didn't he once throw a chair at your head?' Luke asks.

'That wasn't Bilal, that was Ali,' Nora says. 'He's gone off the rails. And he can't aim either, that chair missed me by miles.'

'Quite a feat,' I say, not thinking anything of it until I catch Luke's reproving look. Nora's quite large. She gives me a cool look too. I'm about to apologise, but then a couple of colleagues come in and are immediately filled in on the Bilal situation by others.

Luke moves closer and smirks, 'Ouch.'

'It just popped out,' I whisper. 'I'll make it up to Nora later.'

'Don't worry about it. She's not that tactful herself,' Luke says. 'And another thing, why didn't you just have a nice day at home today?'

'What would I do at home?' I say. 'It would only make it harder to come back afterwards. If you fall off a horse, get back in the saddle.'

Luke nods understandingly. He teaches Dutch as well. He came to the school halfway through last year, replacing a colleague who'd had a serious burnout. In the beginning, I thought he was ten years younger than his thirty-two years, and I wondered whether the students would accept him. To my astonishment, he's had no discipline problems at all and has even given me tips on how to keep my class quiet.

As well as being attractive, Luke is also gay, which thankfully he told me in the early stages of our friendship. That slammed a few doors shut in my mind – just as well. His preference is definitely a loss for womankind. I used to pigeonhole all gay men as pink-feather-wearers, dancing on boats on the Amsterdam canals during Gay Pride. I've got over that now. If Luke hadn't told me, I would never have guessed, and I don't think anyone else knows either. He'd rather keep it that way. At other schools he worked at, his contracts were terminated without clear reason and while he'd rather just tell people he's got a boyfriend, this time he's going to keep it quiet until he's got a permanent contract.

Our shared secret quickly forged a bond between us and I've met his boyfriend Sven a few times. I've never told anyone. Apart from Jasmine, but that doesn't count. Jasmine is my best friend and I know she can keep her mouth shut.

'If you have any problems, just come to me,' Luke says.

I smile at him and thank my lucky stars that he came to work at this school.

Elisa

13.

The school entrance was a sea of flowers. They set up a make-shift altar, with Lydia's photo in the middle, surrounded by candles and flowers. The teachers and students held a minute's silence for her.

The police investigation is still in full swing. Bilal Assrouti was questioned and released. Everyone Lydia knew has been questioned, including me. For the first few days, the newspapers were full of the brutal murder, and my sister's photo was on the news.

Detective Noorda called around all the time after Lydia's death. I would hear him ringing the bell, but I never opened the door. I didn't answer the telephone either. Finally I let him in and heard him out. He asked me all kinds of questions and assured me that they'd find the murderer. He talked about gunpowder spores, ballistics and cartridge cases. In the beginning he'd talk to me for a long time, but now he gets up faster to leave and the intervals between visits are longer.

Sylvie and Thomas pulled me out of the black hole. They come round every day with shopping, and they talk to me even though I barely respond. They cook for me and open the windows from time to time so that the fresh spring air blows away the stale smell in the house.

Today Thomas is visiting.

'Have you done anything recently?' he asks.

I tell him that I've been keeping busy, that I don't lie in bed the whole day. That I've made a collage of pictures of Lydia and myself, a collage covering a whole wall. I've used recent photos as well as ones from our childhood so that in the morning when I open my eyes our whole life stretches out before me.

Thomas goes into the bedroom and looks at the wall, speechless. Then he says that we're going out to eat tonight.

Later I go out to dinner with him, dressed in my pink and orange skirt with the matching top. Thomas looks at me in surprise when he comes to pick me up, but all he says is, 'You look…different.'

Once we're seated in the restaurant, he says, 'That's what you wore for Lydia's funeral.'

I nod without looking up from the menu.

'Are you going to wear skirts now because Lydia wore them?'

I close the menu and put it down on the table. 'Of course not. Why are you saying that?'

'Because you've got one on now! Those are the clothes you bought with Lydia – that last time you went shopping together?'

I sigh and look to see if the waiter is coming. I should never have told Thomas about the shopping trip. It was a lovely afternoon – I've got precious memories of it – and it's annoying that he's bringing up that one false note. What does it matter if Lydia wanted to give me a makeover? What does it matter that she wouldn't take no for an answer, that I was more or less forced to buy these clothes? She meant well. And I'm wearing the clothes a lot now.

Thomas had come round that evening after I'd been shopping with Lydia. The clothes were spread out on the sofa.

'What's all this?' He held the bright skirt and top up, his eyebrows raised.

'I bought them with Lydia.'

'Aha,' Thomas said.

That was all, but his voice was layered with many different things.

'I like them,' I said. 'I'm not used to wearing skirts, but I don't have to wear trousers my whole life, do I?'

'No,' Thomas said. 'But you also don't have to wear exactly what Lydia likes.'

Thomas used to make comments like that a lot. Of course I wasn't blind to the fact that things hadn't clicked between him and Lydia. It was a shame, but Thomas and Sylvie – who Lydia didn't like either – were my friends and it wasn't the end of the world if Lydia didn't like them.

'What do you like about Thomas?' Lydia once asked when we were sitting in her back garden. 'He sticks to you like a limpet. It'd drive me crazy.'

It was a hot day last year. Valerie was in the paddling pool and I was explaining how I'd helped Thomas to photograph a disgraced politician for the *Rotterdam Daily*. That's to say, I was planning to tell her about it in detail, but Lydia didn't give me the chance.

'He might be a bit different,' I said, 'but he's a very good friend.'

'A bit different?' Lydia's manner was disapproving. 'He's a weirdo. He doesn't look at you, he leers at you. And when he smiles it's like his mouth is twitching.'

She was exaggerating, but the grain of truth in her words made me uncomfortable. Instead of defending Thomas or telling Lydia how horrible I felt when she attacked him, I kept silent. I turned my head away, in exactly the same way as she always did. I saw the movement reflected in the window of the house and Lydia did too. You could say a lot about her, but not that she didn't pick up signals.

'I guess you form a bond when you've known each other as long as you have,' she said. 'And you've never had that many friends.'

As if I was socially handicapped. But I didn't feel like a fight, so I didn't let my irritation show. Instead, I looked over at Valerie, who was stretched out on her stomach in the pool, and I pretended to be shocked every time she splashed me. When I looked up again, Lydia was studying me.

'Elisa,' she said. 'You're not in love with him, are you?'

'Certainly not, we're just friends.'

'It just worries me. I don't think Thomas is good for you, not even as a friend.'

I frowned and wanted to snap at her, which is unusual for me, but she changed the subject.

'How do you like Valerie's new bikini?' Valerie stood up proudly. 'Nice, isn't it? She chose it herself!'

Lydia should see Thomas now. A warm tide of affection washes over me. So many people have tried to console me: some have tried to talk me out of my grief, others have ignored it. I've heard so many meaningless expressions – 'life goes on', 'you've still got so much to be thankful for'. Thomas and Sylvie have never made that mistake. Well, Sylvie sometimes, but she's also been so supportive that I forgive her. But Thomas has always been able to adapt to my mood. If I don't feel like talking, he doesn't either. If my tone is light, so is his. And if I need to cry, he wraps his arms around me and I see that his eyes are brimming.

I look on with some sympathy while Thomas pulls a beer mat apart, searching for something to talk about. I feel sorry for him through my grief. It's the first time since Lydia died that I've worried about what another person is feeling. Perhaps that's a good sign. I make an effort to chat, but after a while the inevitable silence descends. I look into Thomas's eyes. Warm, brown, with a small splash of yellow-gold in the middle.

'How's the police investigation going?' he asks.

The question sends us back to the subject he was just trying to avoid. 'I don't think the police are any further than they were at the start. First they cross-examined Raoul, then me, then my parents, Lydia's colleagues and students, but I don't know what they're doing now. Bilal Assrouti has an alibi.'

'That he was at a night club with a group of friends?' Thomas says, his voice doubtful. 'Don't the police keep you informed about any new developments?'

'If there's been any.'

'Perhaps it was random after all – a mugging gone wrong,' Thomas says.

'Someone lay in wait for her, someone who knew what time she'd get home, someone who waited for their chance and…' My voice breaks and Thomas looks at me with concern. I swallow, take a sip of water. 'You know what…'

Thomas looks at me.

'Sometimes I get the feeling…' I fall silent, but after a while I go on, choosing my words with care. 'Every now and again I get the feeling that Lydia is here. Like she's standing behind me and looking over my shoulder.'

Thomas involuntarily looks at the spot behind me.

'When my grandfather died, I didn't really feel like he was gone for good and I was just a child then. I had intense dreams about him and sometimes I got the feeling that he was in my bedroom.'

'Really?'

I know what he's thinking. Thomas is a down-to-earth person, he's not that into mystical experiences.

'You don't believe in all that, do you?'

'No,' Thomas says, and I laugh. That's why I like him so much. He'll never agree just because he's afraid of upsetting me, he always stays true to himself. It's good. I don't need my friends to be acting differently right now.

Thomas sips his beer. 'There are so many of those stories. People have regression therapy and think they once lived in the time of the Pharaohs, people say they see spirits and communicate with them…'

'Have you ever seen that program with Char?' I ask.

Char is an American medium who claims to be able to contact the dead. I always watch her, but Thomas is clearly less impressed with her paranormal gifts. He pulls a face and does a good impression of Char, bending towards me, taking my hand and reciting all the letters of the alphabet in a serious tone. Then he imitates the client bursting into tears after a session with Char and sobbing, 'Yes, M! My mother's name is Johanna but her fourth middle name is Maria!'

I can't help but laugh.

'It's all guesswork,' Thomas says in his normal voice.

'Yep.' I survey the last piece of steak on my plate. After a long pause, I look up and say, 'But I still believe in it.'

Thomas looks at me, his expression troubled again. 'Well,' he says at last, 'it might be good for you to believe in that.'

14.

Raoul is the only person I feel comfortable with at the moment. He's the only one who knows how it feels. And my parents, of course, but their grief is too large to leave room for me.

We go for a walk in the Bergse woods and end up having coffee on the outdoor terrace of a restaurant. Valerie's spending the day with Raoul's parents.

'How are you getting on now?' I say. 'Are you coping?'

I'm asked that question so often myself that it makes me feel ill. How do people expect you to be getting on? And of course you're coping, you have to, you can hardly give up breathing. But my own grief gives me the right to ask such a clichéd question and I have to because Raoul looks dreadful. So dreadful my stomach bunches up.

Raoul stares at the black liquid in his mug as if he's wondering why he would have any need for it now. Why carry on eating, drinking, and all those other trivial acts when so much emotion and pain is racing through your body?

'Do you know what kills me?' he says. 'All those people who say "time heals" or that I should be "grateful" for all the lovely memories I have of Lydia. That she's gone to a "better place". She's lying under the cold ground!'

I remain silent, not at all taken aback by his outburst.

'I don't know,' I say. 'I constantly get the feeling that Lydia is close by.'

The very second I say that there's a gust of wind. We should be sheltered by the restaurant building.

'I keep dreaming about her,' I continue. 'About earlier, when we were little, and our childhood. We had so many rows…'

Raoul looks up from his coffee. 'I always argued with my sister too.'

'I know it's normal, but I regret it now. Every nasty word I said to her, every mean thought.' My voice quavers.

Raoul puts his hand on top of mine.

'You mustn't start thinking like that, Elisa, or you'll go under. Do you think I don't suffer from regrets?'

I avoid meeting his eyes.

I take a tissue from my handbag, blow my nose and sit there holding it. When I look up, Raoul is staring straight at me and for a couple of breathtaking seconds our eyes lock.

'We've all got something we could reproach ourselves for,' he says. 'I was always nagging her – about not being home enough, about the school taking over her life, about there not being enough time left for me.' He laughs briefly and joylessly.

'Well, that was true,' I say. 'She was always going out in the evenings, or having to telephone one of her students…I found it irritating, but at the same time I admired her for it. If Lydia dedicated herself to something she did it body and soul.'

Raoul's hand balls into a fist. 'And to think that one of her beloved students put a bullet through her head.'

'You don't know that,' I say.

'I do know that!' Raoul rages. 'I should never have let her go out on her own. I should never have left her alone for a second! Damn, damn, damn!'

People around us look up in surprise. He hides his face in his hands and makes choking noises.

I shunt my chair closer to his and put my arm around him.

I can still remember the day Lydia brought Raoul home for the first time. We were twenty-two. She was still living at home and I was living in Amsterdam. It was Sunday and we'd arranged to have lunch at our parents' house.

Lydia had gone away for the night with Raoul. I came alone and waited with my parents for them to return. We were in the garden. It was a warm spring day – much more pleasant to be in my parents' park-like garden than in my tiny, roasting apartment.

'It's so beautiful here.' I looked around in admiration. 'It's so green. And Dad, your flower beds!'

My father sipped his beer and surveyed his garden, his great love. 'Thanks, doll,' he said. 'If you need any more cuttings for your balcony, just let me know.'

'I can't fit anything else on it,' I said. 'But one day I'll buy a house with a garden and then you can get to work on it, okay?'

'You've got a deal.'

'Have you already met this boyfriend of Lydia's, Elisa?' my mother asked.

'No,' I said. 'I think she's only just met him herself.'

'What's only just?'

'A few weeks at the most,' I said. 'They met on the train, I believe.'

'I wonder what he's like,' my mother said.

I wondered too. Despite the fact that Lydia and I are twins, we didn't like the same type of men and we'd often criticised each other's choices. Or to be more accurate, she'd criticised mine.

But the moment Lydia strolled into the garden with Raoul, I knew that it was different this time. And when he shook my hand and looked into my eyes, I knew that I had a problem.

Initially I hoped that he'd be a total asshole, but he wasn't. As well as being gorgeous, Raoul was also considerate, witty, affectionate and warm-hearted. At first, I avoided him as much as possible. I arranged to meet Lydia when I was sure that Raoul wouldn't be there. But there was no avoiding him on occasions like birthdays. Then I'd withdraw into a corner and listen to my sister's happy chattering. Lydia had always been more outgoing and over time I got the impression that it annoyed Raoul a little. Lydia's impulsive, lively character meant that she sometimes cut other people off when they were talking. Once I saw Raoul looking at her in a way that made me wonder, and that night, his eyes rested on me for a few seconds.

When it was time to say goodbye, he pulled me tightly to him. I couldn't help but feel nourished in his embrace. I smelled him, heard his heartbeat and tried to imprint every second into my memory, so I could think back to it later as I lay alone in my bed.

Did Lydia ever notice anything? Did she see how I looked at Raoul when I thought I was unobserved? Did it ever occur to her that Raoul and I were drawn to each other at birthday parties or nights out with friends? Did she suspect anything when Raoul sent job after job my way when I started work as a photographer?

I never acted on my feelings, but ran headlong into a series of relationships that had nothing to offer, could never have anything to offer. I never broached the subject with Raoul and he's never said anything to me. But those feeling are there…still.

15.

Wouldn't I like to go home with him for a bit? We could eat together, perhaps even go to a restaurant. The house is so quiet and there's no one to talk to.

It doesn't seem like a sensible thing to do. I can't help Raoul with his loneliness and I don't want to. I'm not afraid of the silence of my own home, perhaps because I'm used to it, perhaps because I don't really feel like I'm alone. Lydia tells me what to do, still. Every time I make a decision I know what she would have said about it, and nine times out of ten I hear her saying it. In a way she interferes as much in my life from beyond the grave as she used to when she was alive.

Only now do I realise how tightly Lydia and I were bound together, though our whole lives we tried to be individuals.

When Lydia decided she liked jewellery, I refused to have my ears pierced. If Lydia wanted to go somewhere hot and sunny for our holidays, I got travel brochures for Scandinavia. Once when I was about fourteen I had my hair cut so short my scalp shone through the stubble.

However much I emphasised our differences, there were always many similarities. I quite liked skirts and beach holidays, but after a while I found myself trapped in a pattern of behaviour I'd chosen and from which there was no escape.

When we were ten, Lydia got appendicitis and had to go to hospital. When my father brought her home after the operation, it was raining hard and he carried her inside from the car with great tenderness and concern, covered in his new suede jacket.

That evening I had a sore stomach too. My parents called the doctor, but it turned out there was nothing wrong. The doctor said it was solidarity pain, common in twins. I cried when he went away again without sending me to hospital.

'Why are you crying now?' my father asked.

'Probably from relief,' my mother said, stroking my hair. 'She was scared she might need an operation too, of course.'

I let them console me, pulled on my father's suede jacket and refused to take it off for the rest of the evening.

Lydia took charge from a very early age. I remember playing ball with her in between the parked cars on our street. Finally we'd had enough and I had to cross the street back to our side of the road, where Lydia was, only I couldn't see between the parked cars very well. Lydia couldn't either, but she still beckoned to me. Trusting her blindly, I ran into the road and found myself in front of the screeching tyres of a car. The car managed to stop just in time – the skid marks stayed on the road for at least a year afterwards. I ran home in shock and threw myself crying into my father's arms.

'Why didn't you look?!' he cried out.

'Lydia said it was all right,' I sobbed.

My father sighed and stroked my hair. 'You're going to have to learn to think for yourself.'

We both liked music. I had piano lessons and Lydia played the violin. I was talented and enjoyed performing for other people, but the applause was never for me alone – Lydia was just as good at playing the violin.

Sometimes I fantasised about being an only child. I was jealous of friends who could be completely themselves.

My wish came true. I'm on my own now.

Lydia

16.

It's almost impossible to teach that next morning. News of what happened with Bilal is buzzing through the school and during my first lesson, everyone wants to vent about it. Hafid and Jeffrey shout that we should get tough on him, Yussef makes a couple of philosophical comments and Niels punches the air, pretending it's Bilal. Abdel is the only one who doesn't engage; he's turned away, looking outside. That doesn't surprise me – Bilal is his cousin, which is another reason I'd rather not spend too much time talking about it, but the class has other ideas.

'Bilal is scum,' Elvan says. 'He's not a good Muslim, Miss. He's always doing bad things, like drugs and stuff.' Her friends and a couple of the boys back her up.

Abdel gives them a dirty look.

'It's time to move on, now,' I say. 'It happened, it's been resolved.'

'We think it's horrible for you! We want to know how you are!' Funda calls out, her eyes large.

I'm sure they do, but I also know that they'll clutch at anything to turn a boring Dutch lesson into a juicy conversation, and the minutest details will be spread through the school afterwards. I begin the lesson.

After that I've got Bilal's class, the final year students. They are older and less unruly. They don't seem to need to talk about the incident so much. Only a few students, mainly girls, have something to say.

'Bilal always feels insulted, Miss,' Naima says. 'You can't do anything about it. You only have to blink for him to think you're making fun of him.'

'It's true.' Mohammed is a quiet student and the sound of his deep voice is so unexpected that I look up at him in surprise. 'It wasn't your fault, Miss. We're all really impressed that you stayed so calm.'

The rest of the class agrees and I'm moved.

'Thanks, Mohammed. I appreciate you saying that.'

We set to work. I'm so pleased I started teaching again right away. The support of my colleagues and students does me a world of good.

I write everything to be copied down on the board. From time to time I look over my shoulder at the bowed heads behind me and feel warm inside. This is the reason I teach: it doesn't just require energy, it also gives me energy. I love my students, well, most of the time I love them. When it's Ramadan and they're hungry and thirsty, I feel for them. I do my best to help them get good grades, a good report and, ultimately, a qualification. Nobody can take away the joy I feel when the future of an apparent no-hoper looks promising. Not even Bilal can take that away.

I bump into Jan on my way to the staffroom afterwards. Rather than ask me how I'm doing, he says that telling everyone my story is causing unrest and suggests I be more discreet.

I ignore him. Telling it over and over again reduces the chaos in my mind. But during the lunch break, I do feel the need for some quiet time.

'I'm off for a wander,' I say to Jasmine. 'Do you want to come?'

She shakes her head and points at her pile of test papers. 'I still have to get through these.'

'Can't they wait?'

'Sorry.'

'All right.' I put on my coat and get an apple from my bag.

Jasmine turns to the test papers again, but then looks up and says, 'You'll be careful?'

The note of concern in her voice touches me. We look at each other. 'I'm only going to walk round the school.'

It's wonderful to be outside. It's always so stuffy in the staff-room during the breaks. As I cross the playground, I toss my hair back and take a bite of my apple. Students nod shyly at me here and there or wave and come over.

'Miss! Miss! Have you marked the tests already?'

'I can't do my talk today, Miss. I didn't get much sleep and I don't feel very well.'

I keep the conversations short, promise to give their tests back this afternoon and tell Fatima that she simply has to give her talk, whether she's got her period or not. I up my pace and walk around the school. The sun has broken through and I'm enjoying its warmth and the fresh greenery.

And then I see him.

Bilal is standing on the other side of the street, wearing a hoodie, surrounded by friends. The shock is acute. He stares at me. My heart hammers in my chest and my step falters. What to do? Go back? Walk on? Show him that I'm not afraid of him?

But I'm almost rigid, rooted to the spot, and my eyes are locked on him. It's more than obvious that I'm terrified.

A smile spreads over his face; there's no warmth to it. He

71

nudges one of his friends and points to me. Four faces turn towards me. One of them is taking into his mobile, but cuts the call off immediately.

I look at my watch, pretend to start, as if I've realised I'm late for something and spin on my heels. I walk straight into someone. He grabs my arms and I scream.

17.

'It's me! Don't panic!'

Luke.

I take a shaky breath. 'I almost jumped out of my skin.'

'I didn't mean to scare you. Come on, the bell's about to go.'

'Were you having a walkabout too, or…?'

'No,' he says. 'I heard that Bilal had been spotted in the area and then Jasmine said you'd gone outside.'

'You're so sweet, you really are,' I say. 'I wonder what Bilal and his friends would have done if you hadn't turned up.'

'To be honest, I don't think I'd have deterred them if they were planning something,' Luke says. 'They were probably just trying to provoke you.'

'I hope they aren't going to make a habit of it. I was really scared.'

'It might be better if you don't go outside on your own for the time being.'

I give him a sideways glance. 'Do you think it's that serious?'

'Bilal Assrouti is bad news,' Luke says. 'I once made him clean the classroom as punishment and got a brick thrown through my window every night for a week.'

'Really?' I say, shocked. 'Why didn't you ever tell me?'

'You had your own stuff going on.'

'Did you report it?' I ask.

'I didn't want to make things worse.' He sighs and runs his hand through his blond hair. 'So all he learned was that he can get away with anything. That's why I think it's better if you report it. The more complaints the police get about Bilal, the more they'll have on him. But I'd keep quiet about getting them involved.'

Luke knows that I'm in turmoil about whether or not to go to the police. He gives me a gentle pat on the shoulder and says that he'll always be there for me if I want to talk. We walk through the chaos of bags and knocked-over chairs. The bell goes as I enter the staffroom.

'Blown away the cobwebs?' Jasmine puts a pile of corrected papers into her bag and smiles.

'Bilal was there,' I say. 'On the other side of the street.'

'No! What did he do?'

'Nothing. He was about to cross the street when Luke turned up.' I stroke Luke's arm; he's standing next to me rummaging around in his pigeon hole.

'Accidentally on purpose,' he says.

Jasmine frowns. 'I don't like this at all.'

'Me neither,' Luke says.

'What don't you like?' Nora is walking past. Hans, who is leafing through a teaching magazine, follows the conversation with his usual frown.

'Bilal was outside waiting for me,' I say – a slight exaggeration.

Nora looks at me, worried.

'Nothing happened. But I don't feel very relaxed about him hanging around here.'

Nora nods. 'I'll have a word with him.'

'I've never had a problem with that boy,' Hans says.

It sounds like an accusation and I swivel to face him. 'I'd never had any problems with Bilal before either. It could happen to any of us, Hans.'

'I wouldn't have provoked him,' Hans says.

Count to ten. Just count to ten before sinking your nails into his face. Jasmine is quicker.

'Don't be stupid, Hans. You know those boys are provoked by anything these days. If I remember right, Bilal accused you of being racist because you wouldn't bump up his exam mark by ten per cent.'

'And then I explained that marking the exams didn't have anything to do with racism. You just have to know how to handle them.'

'Oh, and I don't know how to?' I flare up.

'Looking at someone's crotch isn't the approach I'd recommend.'

I feel myself flushing. How does Hans know that? Who's helped that rumour into the world? Hans and Nora leave – her expression has turned sceptical.

As Luke and I walk to our classrooms he says, 'You look worried.' He's broken into my thoughts – I'd forgotten how perceptive he can be.

'I'm worried they'll be waiting for me at my car.'

'I'll walk with you,' Luke promises. 'It's not a problem. From now on I'll go everywhere with you if it's necessary.'

I hesitate, but not for long. I'm not easily frightened, and I don't like accepting help – being helped feels like a kind of fail-ure. I'm used to solving my own problems. Nevertheless, Bilal's predatory gaze follows my every step.

'Okay?' Luke asks. He knows me by now.

I give a very slight nod.

18.

I wait at the door for my students before each lesson, making comments, cracking jokes or telling one of them off for misbehaving. This afternoon I've got a pleasant but restless class of first years.

'Saïda! How long have you been wearing a headscarf?' I ask as she walks past me and into the classroom.

'Since now,' she says, raising her chin.

'Was that your choice or did your parents make you?'

'I decided myself.' She responds fast, too fast.

'All right,' I say. 'As long as that's the case.'

'Don't you believe me or what?' Saïda asks, annoyed. She takes out her mobile and checks her make-up in the reflection of the screen.

'Of course, if you say so. Put your phone back in your bag, please.'

Saïda rolls her eyes, punches in a number and walks to her seat, phone to her ear.

'Yeah. What's up? I've got Dutch now. Yeah, with her. Shall I send a photo?' She watches for my reaction out of the corner of her eyes.

I tap the board, the lines the previous class were given as punishment and Saïda hangs up. Not straight away, but still, she hangs up.

I've got a difficult relationship with Saïda. She's precocious, assertive, not openly rude, but cuttingly scornful. Her group blocks me by speaking their mother tongue – Turkish.

As I begin the lesson, Saïda says something to her friends. All four of them burst into loud giggles.

'Saïda, please repeat what you just said in Dutch.'

'You wouldn't want to know what she said, Miss,' Zahra says.

Saïda gives her a poisonous look and immediately gets one back from Zahra. I let out a silent sigh. At moments like these I'm fed up with teaching, tired of being by turns prosecutor, defendant, educator, referee, confidante and enemy.

'The next person who speaks any language other than Dutch, gets fifty lines. I've got a thumping headache so please bear that in mind.'

They're quiet. I don't hear a peep out of them for the rest of the period. I give them a reading assignment so that they can work independently, and walk between the desks, offering assistance here and there. Looking at their bowed heads softens my mood. Even Saïda is working hard, and every now and then one of them will look up at me, as if to check that I'm all right.

I'm always filled with satisfaction if I can keep my students under control without raising my voice. My classes used to be chaos. I'd get the kids quiet only for them to be disturbed a few minutes later by latecomers. After a lot of backchat, I'd send the latecomers to get a note, and then they'd return ten minutes later and disturb the class all over again. One way or another, I could never keep them fully quiet, but I got used to the gentle murmur which always hung in the room and which could blow up into a storm at the most unexpected moments. The art was in circumnavigating the storm or quickly dampening it. During my first year of teaching, all my energy went into maintaining order.

My father was responsible for the turnaround. One day I'd gone over for dinner, exhausted and burnt out, and had poured my heart out to my parents. If there was anyone who'd understand, it was them.

My father asked what kinds of punishments I gave and I explained that I sent students out to fetch a note from the deputy head – later they'd be made to mop floors or pick up rubbish, that sort of thing.

Neither of my parents thought this was a good idea. 'Doing chores just earns a troublemaker respect from their friends,' Mum said. 'You'd be better off punishing them by taking away something that's dear to them – their free time.'

'Detention?' I said with little enthusiasm. 'That takes away my free time too.'

'Lines,' my mother said. 'Give them lots of lines.'

I tried not to let my thoughts show – their approach seemed old-fashioned and backward to me. My father read my mind, though. He gave me a book, which turned out to be recent, not from the 1950s. It argued for the return of the authoritarian teacher. No more negotiating, no more endless discussions with mouthy students, no equality between students and teachers – instead teachers who set clear boundaries.

How antiquated, I thought, as I read the book. I'd been used to calling my teachers by their first names at my secondary school. My students didn't do that, but the things they did say sometimes rendered me speechless.

But I read the book and gave out lines. I had nothing to lose. After a couple of weeks I was convinced that the approach worked. No more softly-softly. Lines! Fifty times: I must not call anyone a bitch because it is unnecessarily crass and insulting and comments like this don't achieve anything.

It worked. They found writing lines such a waste of time that they cut their losses and shut up.

Even with this new-found quiet, I never quite manage to get through the curriculum. There's always something going on in Rotterdam that affects the children from immigrant families, and if it isn't Rotterdam, it's Amsterdam: a disturbance involving Moroccan kids, a bag-snatcher who gets run over, Theo van Gogh's murder. There's always something to be discussed. And these discussions are the reason I went into teaching in the first place.

19.

The afternoon drags on, filled with lessons and breaks and, as an encore, a drawn-out departmental meeting. No one mentions the incident with Bilal. I bring it up a couple of times and Nora, the department head, cuts me off and says that there's not much that can be done about it.

'Why not?' Luke steps in. 'As a school we could speak to him about it.'

Nora looks at him over the rim of her glasses. 'I think it would be wise to ignore Bilal Assrouti as much as possible. There was an incident, it's been resolved now, let's move on to the business of the day. There's no point blowing it out of proportion.'

My mouth falls open. 'And if I was to tell you that he was loitering outside my house last night?'

'Was he?' Nora asks.

Everybody looks at me. 'There was someone there. He had the same build and height as Bilal,' I say. 'And he was standing there staring in such an obstinate way…'

Nora raises her eyebrows ever so slightly.

Luke comes to my assistance. 'There's no proof it was Bilal, but you'll have to admit that it's not implausible. It was certainly no coincidence that he was hanging around outside the school, I can assure you.'

Nora pushes her glasses up higher on her nose. 'And? Did he do anything? Make any threats?'

For a moment I almost wish we could say that Bilal was waiting for me with a knife. The fact that he was there at all hasn't made any impression on my colleagues.

Jasmine shrugs, to make it clear that she supports me but can't do anything about it. I notice that she doesn't try to either. Nora taps the paperwork with her pen and announces that we're moving on to the official agenda.

At three fifteen, I push my chair back. 'I have to pick up my daughter from school.'

'Just a little longer, Lydia. We're almost done, another five minutes,' Nora says, raising her hand.

'Sorry – we'd set aside an hour for this meeting, it's now gone on for more than an hour and a half and I don't get the feeling that we're going to make any major decisions in the next five minutes, so I'm off. See you all tomorrow.'

Hans mutters to the person next to him. A few others also have something to say about it.

'Wait a minute, Lydia. I was going to walk you to your car.' Luke's voice breaks through, calm and decisive. He looks around the circle and says, 'You'll cope without us, won't you? I want to make sure no one's hanging around the car park.'

To my surprise, Nora nods.

'Wow,' I say as we walk along the corridor. 'No comeback?'

'She probably thinks it's better to ignore it.'

'I don't understand why the others don't get involved.' Even I can hear the disappointment in my voice. 'This affects us all. We should present a united front.'

Luke sighs. 'No one wants to rock the boat. Things aren't going that well for Rotterdam College, Lydia. We've had fewer enrolments than last year and I've heard on the grapevine that they'll be cutting jobs.'

'Who told you that?'

'Dan. He overheard a conversation between Jan and Harry.'

Harry van Zuylen is the deputy head. He's a nice guy and, at thirty-eight, quite a bit younger than Jan, but he has the same narrow-minded attitudes.

'Do the others know there are going to be redundancies?'

'I can't believe I'm the only person Dan would have confided in.'

'He didn't say anything to me.' I'm slightly piqued.

'You weren't in the danger zone until now. The new teachers and the ones who can't keep their classes under control will be the first to go.' Luke holds open the cloakroom door.

'Nora then,' I say. 'And Hans, and you?'

'And you too, if you keep going on about Bilal.'

I pull my coat on. 'But what should I do then?' My fingers fumble with the buttons.

'Stop talking about it,' Luke says. 'That's if you want to continue working here.'

I wait for Luke in the corridor, his words troubling me. Is it worth it? Should I carry on? Through the window I see a group of fourth years. One of them spots me and waves. I smile and wave back. There's my answer.

Tarik is a Turkish boy who came into my first-year class three years ago. He was very intelligent, but didn't lift a finger at school and fell asleep in class. One day I came across him in town, sitting on a wall in the pouring rain. I bought him a coffee and began to get a picture of what was going on in his life. You didn't have to be a psychologist to figure out that he had trouble at home; he was covered in bruises.

I invested a lot of time in Tarik. It would have been easier to refer him to social services, but I spoke to his father instead. The man turned out to be a real emotional mess. His wife had left him a couple of years previously, he was having difficulty settling into Dutch life and he vented his sorrows on his son. I organised for Mr Kaplan to be seen by a psychologist and other professionals, and little by little things improved for Tarik. Since then I've had a special bond with him.

Luke and I pass Tarik and his friends in the playground.

'Miss!' Tarik walks over, his hands in his pockets, cap down over his eyes. 'Miss, I just wanted to say I think it's terrible what happened. I mean, that shit Bilal pulled. It's unreasonable, man!'

'Thank you, Tarik.'

'I'd watch out if I was you, Miss,' Tarik says, with concern. 'Bilal is really angry. He says he's going to get his revenge.'

His friend Ali breaks away from the group and nods in agreement. 'That guy is flipped, man.'

We keep walking. I have no idea how to react to their warnings.

'It's all bluffing,' Luke reassures me. 'Bilal's been boasting to his friends to save face.'

Perhaps, yet still the blood races through my body. What if we've misjudged the situation? What if Bilal really is out for revenge?

'You've gone pale,' Luke says, touching my arm. 'Maybe it's not too late to tell the police.'

The car park lies abandoned in the afternoon sun. There are only a few cars left and I spot mine instantly. Not because it's conspicuously red, but because of the damage.

The broken antenna.

The smashed side window.

The scratches in the paintwork.

A broken sound falls from my mouth. I don't breathe, I can't move. My brain has trouble processing and interpreting what I'm seeing.

'Shit,' Luke says quietly.

He walks ahead of me and after a moment my body reactivates and I follow him with leaden steps. I survey the damage in silence. The paint on the bodywork has been treated with a sharp implement and the mirrors have been snapped off. The word WHORE is scrawled large across the bonnet.

20.

The short journey home is dreadful. I can't help but think that the damage, the word, is glowing like neon, apparent to every driver, cyclist and pedestrian around me. Even though that may not be the case.

It's only once I've parked in front of the door that I realise I shouldn't have driven like this and that I've forgotten to pick up Valerie.

I let my forehead sink onto the wheel. It's gone half three, school has finished. If I went on foot, I'd be even later. There's no other option, I have to get Valerie in the car.

Valerie is waiting at the school entrance with her teacher. I toot and she runs across the playground towards me, her coat open, her hair coming loose from its pigtails. The teacher glares at me then disappears into the building.

'Sourpuss,' I mutter.

I'm not that keen on Valerie's teacher. Yvette is in her mid-fifties and I'm guessing that she longs for retirement. But Valerie loves her, so she must act differently towards children than she does towards the parents. Or towards me. That might be due to me 'parking' my child in lunch-care, as Yvette calls it, or because I never volunteer to help with the craft lessons or after-school parties.

At one parents' evening, Yvette made a few sly digs at parents whose behaviour 'demonstrated a worrying lack of involvement or interest in their child's development'.

Anger flared up in me. In front of everyone, I told her what I thought. A toxic silence fell over the room. Later, a few cowardly parents came over and said that they absolutely agreed with me.

'You should have said so, then,' I told them.

Since then I haven't been that welcome in most of the playground mafia circles. Not that it bothers me.

'Hi Mum,' she says, climbing into her car seat. 'What happened to the car?'

'It's a bit damaged. Do up your belt and we'll go.'

Valerie fastens her seatbelt and looks for her teacher out of the window so that she can wave.

'Oh, she's already gone inside,' she says. 'Why?'

'Why is she inside?'

'No-ho, the car!'

'One of mummy's naughty students did it,' I say lightheartedly and hope that's enough information. It is.

'I was in a play,' Valerie tells me. 'Do you know what I had to be? A cat!'

'Oh, how nice,' I say, relieved. 'Tell me about it.'

She talks about it in great detail until we arrive at home. She gets out of the car miaowing, and once I've opened the front door, she crawls along the hallway.

'Get up,' I say. I know what's coming next. After seeing *Aristocats*, Valerie pretended to be a cat. She was a cat that wanted to lap up saucers of milk rather than eat her greens.

And a cat that wanted to lie in the sun in the sitting room. As I fetch the post from the doormat, Valerie crawls into the kitchen on her hands and knees and, when I offer her a glass of cordial, she shakes her head, miaows and points at the milk.

I roll my eyes, and put a glass of milk on the table. The cat can get to it and sticks her tongue into it. Naturally this works for exactly five seconds before the glass gets knocked over and milk streams all over the table.

'Oh Valerie, please!' I restrain her when she goes to lick the milk from the table. 'It's been a difficult day, the car is broken, I've got a headache, please try to behave. Get a cloth and help me clean up.'

The cat fetches a cloth, mops up the milk and sorrowfully says, 'Miaow.'

When Raoul gets home, I've laid the table and the potatoes and cauliflower are cooking. I wait for the inevitable outburst from Raoul when he sees the car. But the door opens, closes, and Valerie crawls over to his legs, miaowing.

'Hello poppet,' Raoul says. 'We're back at that again, are we?'

'She was a cat in a play,' I call out from the kitchen. Spatula in hand, I join them in the sitting room and look out of the window at my poor, battered car.

'Have you seen it?'

Raoul puts Valerie back down on her feet. 'What?'

'My car. Haven't you seen what's happened to it?'

Raoul looks outside in alarm. 'Have you dented it again?'

'What do you mean "again"?' I snap. 'I've never damaged the car.'

'I didn't really pay any attention to your car.' Raoul walks over to the window and shouts out, 'Jesus!' He runs outside.

I turn down the gas, get rid of the spatula and follow him outside in my apron.

'Would you look at that! Covered in scratches! Who did it?'

I shrug. 'It happened at school.'

Raoul takes a deep breath. It seems he's on the verge of saying something, but doesn't.

'And you just drove round in it like that?' he enquires.

'What else could I do? I had to pick up Valerie, remember?'

Raoul doesn't speak. He's spotted the scrawl on the bonnet.

'Jesus,' he says again, then puts his arms around me.

'Was it that Bilal?' he asks.

I shrug.

'We've had enough of this,' Raoul says.

'Yes.'

'This has to stop, Lydia. It's going to cost a couple of thousand euros to get this resprayed.'

I look at him in complete astonishment. 'What kind of a reaction is that?'

Raoul doesn't respond. He always goes silent when I've said something that makes him think. He goes back inside. I follow him and close the door behind us.

'Don't you think it's a crying shame? That car is only a year old!' he says.

'The car's the least of my worries,' I reply. 'I'm just pleased that I wasn't the one to be worked over with that knife.' I bang the lids of the pans, checking to see how the vegetables are cooking.

'Listen, Lydia,' Raoul says. 'I've been worried about you ever since you went to work at that school, and you know it. You were coming home with stories that made me think things would seriously go wrong there at some point. I advised you to leave, to look for a safer school, or to come and work at Software International, but you wouldn't. Now you're angry because I'm not pacing about wringing my hands. Of course I'm happy that nothing happened to you. But if I tell you what I think, you get angry. Then I'm the egoist who won't let you have a career. So, if you must know – yes, I'm worried sick, I'm happy that you're safe, but I'm really pissed off that the car is fucked up.'

Now it's my turn to be quiet.

'I'm not sure if it was Bilal,' I say, finally.

'If it was a different student it would only make this worse – you'd have two guys to watch out for!' The words poured out of him: school management should take better care of its staff. Aren't weapons regularly found in pockets and lockers? Why haven't they done anything against this? Why haven't they installed walk-through metal detectors? He rages on and on.

'I don't know what to do! I only know that I don't want to lose my job. And it would be nice if I had a bit of support instead of blame.'

I wasn't intending to, but I burst into tears. Naturally Raoul isn't immune to that. He might seem tough but he isn't impenetrable. He pulls me to him and enfolds me in his arms.

We stay like that for a long time.

21.

At dinner, once we've calmed down, I tell Raoul about my row with Nora and the speed with which Bilal's actions were wiped from the table during the departmental meeting. Raoul shakes his head, but doesn't comment.

Then I tell him about Bilal on the street.

Raoul's expression is grim. 'That little bastard.'

'What's a little bastard?' Valerie asks.

'Nothing,' Raoul says, because Valerie tends to put every word we do explain into use. Preferably at school, in the group discussion with her teacher.

'I'm not a little bastard, am I?' Valerie says. 'I'm a big bastard.'

Our fit of laughing clears the air.

That evening, when Valerie is in bed, Raoul and I sit down together. We have a glass of wine and watch a film on television, but my thoughts are elsewhere. I get up halfway through the film. Never mind Nicholas Cage, I'm going to have a bath and go to bed. Raoul's coat is lying on the tiles underneath the rack in the hall. I pick it up and hang it on the peg. There's a small box where it was lying on the floor. Elongated, dark blue and unmistakably from a jeweller's. A silver swan announces a Swarovski trinket. I pick it up in wonder. A sparkling, crystal bracelet is nestled inside. At that moment Raoul comes into the hall.

He stops abruptly, shocked. His expression turns to regret. 'Ah, so now you've found it,' he says. 'I wanted to give it to you on our wedding anniversary.'

'That's two months away.'

'I know, but I saw it and thought it was perfect for you.' Raoul takes the box from me and with a tender, almost dutiful gesture, fastens the glittering bracelet around my wrist.

'Now that you've found it…' he says with a smile.

The crystals conjure up new colours with every turn of my wrist. 'It's beautiful,' I say. 'Thank you.'

Raoul holds my wrists at my side, kissing me. Then his hand slides to my breasts.

'If we're going to celebrate our anniversary, we might as well do it properly,' he whispers.

I hesitate, but it would be silly to go to bed alone now, with this beautiful bracelet on my wrist.

'Champagne?' Raoul says, his lips to my ear.

Champagne. Why not. Raoul goes to the kitchen to open a bottle as I sink into the sofa and hope with all my heart that the bracelet was intended for me. The jewellery around my wrist is as fragile as my confidence.

Do women sense when they're being cheated on? Is it possible that I've got a sixth sense for it?

All I know is that Raoul is not always honest. He lies to me. The problem is that I don't know when he's lying. All those meetings and appointments out of the office, those business dinners and trips…A man who is that attractive to women is exposed to a lot of temptation.

That sixth sense tells me that some meetings aren't the same as others, and neither are some telephone conversations. For the last few weeks, Raoul has been making calls on his mobile in the evenings when he goes outside for a smoke, and in February he received an anonymous Valentine's card. I wouldn't have been so suspicious if he hadn't played up his own surprise. He was too adamant that he didn't know who had sent the card.

Raoul returns with the champagne and proffers me a glass with a flamboyant gesture. I'm not ready to accept it.

'Why did you buy that bracelet again? We usually choose something together, don't we?'

'This time we didn't.' Raoul clinks his glass gently against mine. He's sitting very close, but suddenly pulls back. 'Don't you like it?'

'I do,' I say. 'It's stunning.'

But I wouldn't have chosen it myself. The bracelet is too delicate, it's not practical. I like jewellery that can take a knock, that can be worn every day. I'm not that into bling. Raoul knows that. I've said it to him often enough.

I pretend not to notice that Raoul is getting more affectionate. He sits with his arm around me, stroking my upper arm.

It's at least a month since we last made love and just as long since we cuddled. Men seem to take these moments as a sign that sex is on the cards, but I'm often content not to take it further. I can't face the thought of being stroked all over and having to get into the mood. The only thing I want is a hot shower and then to fall asleep with Raoul's arms around me. One glance at his face tells me that I'm not going to get away with it.

When he announces that he's going to bed, much earlier than normal, I know what that means. He takes his empty glass to the kitchen, returns to the sitting room and asks, 'Are you coming?'

'Just a bit more TV.' I turn on the television and look at the screen as if I'm immersed, as if what he's really asking has passed me by.

Raoul looks at the screen where two politicians are arguing.

'Politics?' he says. 'I thought it always sent you to sleep.'

'Not always.' I turn up the sound.

'So you're coming soon?' Raoul says.

I look at the clock. 'Fifteen minutes.'

'I'll go and shave.'

Raoul's gaze lingers on me, then he leaves the room. When the program has finished, I tidy the room so thoroughly it looks immaculate. I empty the dishwasher, put everything away and lay the table for breakfast.

Finally I go upstairs. I can hear Raoul's snoring from the landing. It will disturb me all night if I sleep beside him. Instead, I make my way to the guest bedroom.

There once was a time, not that long ago, when Raoul and I slept close to each other. We even shared a single bed comfortably. My pregnancy put an end to that and Valerie's arrival marked the beginning of a new chapter. For the first two years, sleep was a luxury that only childless people knew.

Valerie was a poor sleeper. As a baby she cried all night, but we got through it by telling ourselves that all babies did, that the phase would pass. It didn't. By the time she was two, she still didn't fall asleep until late in the evening, and we were dragged out of our bed several times a night. At first we'd let her get into bed with us, but she'd lie crossways and push us to the edges. So we decided she had to stay in her own bed. When she tried to sneak in we'd push her away, literally, with our elbows, our arms, our legs. It felt like something bitter had been poured over my heart, but my need for sleep was more acute.

It worked. Finally Valerie stayed in her own bed, but all that time spent defending every square centimetre of the bed had an effect on our relationship. The time of spooning was long past.

If Raoul invaded my side of the bed, I'd push him away. He'd do the same – it had become a reflex.

I don't know when the bottom fell out of our sex life. Of course there comes a time when you no longer claw the wallpaper off with excitement when your beloved comes home, but it's not that I've gone off Raoul. I still enjoy sex with him. Just not late at night when I've spent the evening marking tests then struggled up to bed semi-conscious after a consolatory glass of wine.

The urge usually takes me at inappropriate moments. We'll be walking hand in hand through the amusement park as our daughter runs ahead to the fairytale woods. Or we're in town on a Saturday morning and I see other women looking at Raoul. Recently, we were in the car on a warm spring day and Raoul rolled up his shirt sleeves to reveal brown, muscular arms. I wanted him so badly I nearly told him to pull over. We could have; we didn't have Valerie with us. But the thought of moving the child seat and tidying up all the dolls on the backseat ruined the moment before it had even begun. Instead I just fantasised about it.

But it's not just my fault that there's been so little to report on that front these past two years.

Elisa

22.

At the bottom of a drawer, tucked away in an envelope, there's a photograph. It's an enlargement of Raoul and me taken during a Software International company outing. We're not gazing into each other's eyes and we're not hand in hand on a beach backlit by the setting sun. We were on a survival weekend in the Ardennes: a team-building exercise. As I took so many photos for the company, I was invited. Naturally I went.

I'd expected Lydia to be there, but I wasn't surprised she stayed home. Survival is not really her thing.

Raoul and I spent every minute together. It was a relief to be by his side without feeling Lydia's eyes on my back.

I take out the envelope.

It's a good photo. We're in a canoe in high spirits, riding the rapids. The foam splashes around us and we may capsize at any moment, but we're both smiling, paddles in hand. I'm up front and Raoul is behind me. He looks tanned and burly, in his element. He sits diagonally of the lens and smiles over my shoulder, his face close to mine, at whoever is standing on the riverbank taking the picture.

Later, when I saw the photo it struck me that we were smiling in exactly the same way, high on adventure and danger. If Lydia had been in my place she'd have had a poor facsimile of a smile. Her expression would be anxious. That's what I tell myself.

The picture is so precious to me. I wish I could hang it in a nice frame and look at it all day.

I put the phone down and stretch. These days I force myself to go to my studio, but all my work is backlog. I don't take on any new projects. I can't focus. Will I ever regain that tingling feeling I used to get when I was busy doing my job? Will I ever enjoy doing anything again?

Sunlight falls through the window, onto my computer screen, bleaching out the colours and text. The layer of dust stands out even more than usual. I draw a line in it with my index finger, then a downwards arch, and another, until a large L appears in the dust.

'Lydia,' I whisper. 'Where are you?'

In the middle of the night, somewhere between sleeping and waking, a voice whispers inside my head.

'Do you remember,' the voice says, 'do you remember the holiday at Benidorm? All those drunken idiots there. You taking photos of them striking poses for us. How we laughed. We were happy then, weren't we?'

I'm dreaming, I must be dreaming because then we're in Benidorm, swimming in the sea, the sun bathing us in a bright warm light. Every evening we have dinner on the terrace of a small restaurant, a ceiling of vines above us.

Even after Lydia was married and had Valerie, we still went away together once a year. To the Maldives, the Canary Islands, Crete, Curaçao…

'This is so wonderful,' I say as I float on my back in the warm sea. 'Why can't it stay like this forever?'

Lydia swims in circles around me. I feel the water shifting with each stroke, I hear her breath.

'One day it will be like this forever,' she promises. 'Nothing can separate us.'

She talks some more, but her voice fades away. I try to catch her words. By then I'm fully awake.

It's 1:20. My skin is gooseflesh and I'm shivering.

The duvet, which seemed too thick when I got into bed, is no longer warm enough.

I switch on the lamp, get out of bed and put on flannelette pyjamas over my thin nightdress. I even put on a pair of socks, but under the duvet I'm still not warm enough. Could I be getting the flu?

The clock turns 2:00. It turns 2:45.

I push thoughts of Lydia away. Think of something else. Raoul. Walking through the Bergse Woods. Apple tart with cream in the restaurant. The way we consoled each other. But then I feel his hand on mine again and Lydia looks at me accusingly. I don't want to think about Lydia.

I drift off. A noise wakens me again, an unexpected and insistent noise in the darkness. I'm confused for a moment, registering the noise but not understanding it. And then I do.

A door is creaking open.

23.

Steeling myself to sit up, I turn on the light and get out of bed. On the way to the bathroom, I switch on every light I come across, the standing lamp in the bedroom, the main light in the hall and then the bathroom light.

My familiar house appears reassuringly from the darkness and I sigh with relief. I sip cold water from the tap, then return to the bedroom. And then there's someone standing in front of me.

Lydia.

I scream, my hand in front of my mouth, until I see my own likeness screaming back.

What I'd thought was Lydia is nothing more than my own shadowy reflection in the dark window.

I go downstairs, my legs shaking. The sitting room door is half open, and I can't remember whether I closed it. All the doors upstairs were open too, so which door did I hear opening? Did I hear it, or did I dream it?

I hesitate at the bottom of the stairs, listening to the night. After a while I go back upstairs. In my bedroom, I have a curious feeling, as if somebody is waiting for me.

'Lydia…' I whisper. 'Is that you?'

My bedroom is quiet and familiar. There are no noises, nothing stirs.

Less sleepy than ever, I get back in bed, leaving all the lights on, and crawl under the duvet. There are many different kinds of loneliness, but being on your own at night, awake and worried, is the worst.

When I wake again it's still dark outside. It takes me a while to remember why my bedroom light and the hall light are on. It all seems a little unbelievable now.

I look at the time – 5:33 – and throw off the duvet. My god, what thick pyjamas I'm wearing. They're completely damp with sweat.

In the shower, warm water streams over me, comforting me. I raise my face, eyes closed, to catch the drops and rinse the night away.

Gradually the bathroom fills with steam; it clings to the mirror and the shower cubicle. I should have left the bathroom door open.

I squeeze some shower gel onto a sponge and run it over my body. I hold onto the taps with one hand and wash my feet. When I straighten, I see something through the clouds of steam in the bathroom. A dark shape, next to the sink. I'm so shocked I almost slip. I grab hard onto the doors and peer into the bathroom. The dark shape has vanished. But it was there.

I get dressed. On the stairs, I think I hear something behind me as I descend, but there's nothing there. As I bend down in the kitchen to get out the toaster, I feel something brushing past my back.

At that moment I'm certain I'm not alone in the house.

24.

Sylvie is dumbstruck.

'What?' she says, as if she hasn't heard correctly.

'Lydia is here,' I repeat. 'I keep feeling her behind me, like a shadow, but when I look around she's gone. I know it sounds weird.'

We're in the kitchen clearing up after dinner. Sylvie looks at me in alarm then her eyes glide around the kitchen. 'Why do you think that?'

'I've just told you. Because I can feel it.'

'Oh…' Sylvie wipes the bench with a cloth. 'And can you feel it now?'

'No. I mean, not here in the kitchen, but I know she's nearby. I keep hearing noises.'

There's a silence during which Sylvie avoids my gaze. 'Noises? What kind of noises?'

I can't blame her for not believing me. I can hardly believe it myself, but the need to share it with someone is greater than my fear of seeming ridiculous. 'As if someone was walking around the place,' I say quietly. 'Last night I heard a door open, but when I went to look there was no one there at all.'

'And the door was open?'

'Yes, but I'm not sure whether I closed it or not.'

Sylvie takes a deep breath and exhales slowly. 'You should call the police. If you think there's someone in your house, they should come and look around.'

'There isn't anybody here but Lydia. I can't see her but she's here with me. I know it sounds crazy and I won't blame you if you don't believe a word of it, but…' I break off the sentence, empty the sink and wonder whether I should go on.

'Are you paranormally gifted or something?' Sylvie asks.

I shake my head. 'No, it's not that. At least, I don't think so. I don't see ghosts, I don't hear ghosts and I don't expect to either. But my mother has always said that I'm very intuitive.'

'Oh, I am too,' Sylvie says. 'Sometimes I'll be talking to someone and I'll know that they're lying, or hiding something from me. It's the way they fiddle with their clothes or avoid my gaze.'

That is not at all what I meant. 'In those instances it's revealed in people's behaviour, but I also get it when I'm talking on the phone.'

Sylvie nods in agreement. 'Yes, when they want to cancel a date. Then they get a bit stuttery or come up with excuses. Men in particular are so transparent.'

'Yes, but I get it as soon as I pick up and say my name,' I say. 'I often know who's calling before they've said anything.'

'Oh yes, sometimes you know even before you've picked up,' Sylvie laughs. 'One of my friends always used to call me at exactly half past eight, once the news had finished. Then I'd pick up and say, "Hey Manon" straight away. She never understood how I always knew it was her.' She grins. 'These days I have caller recognition, but I didn't then.'

I remain silent and begin to understand why Lydia always got annoyed with Sylvie. It doesn't bother me because I know Sylvie better than anyone else. It's not that she's told me that much about herself, but her history comes across in what she doesn't say. I know that she didn't have an easy childhood, that she's alone in the world.

Sylvie brings me back to earth. 'What is it?'

'Was I staring?' I say with an apologetic laugh. 'Sorry. I was just thinking that I know very little about you, for such a good friend. I know that you haven't had it easy and that you're not in touch with your family anymore, but you've never told me why.' I fill the coffee machine with water and put a filter into the holder. 'Ever since Lydia died, I find it very easy to imagine how lonely you must be. And I've still got my parents, and Raoul and Valerie.'

'Yes.' The smile has disappeared from Sylvie's eyes and her voice is flat. 'I've always been quite jealous of you. I'm always jealous of people who have families.'

I spoon the coffee into the filter. 'Do you really not have anybody? No one at all?'

'Yes, but I don't see them anymore,' Sylvie says. 'I'm an only child and my father walked out on us when I was six. You might think I was too young to remember much about him, but I can actually remember quite a lot, and it hurts. I've never been able to understand why he left us. He never tried to explain it. Before he left he was such a good dad. I missed him so terribly, and then some.'

Her voice breaks and I reach out my hand and touch her arm to comfort her.

'Sorry.' Sylvie's smile is weak. 'I came round to help you.'

'Perhaps it would help me more to know that I'm not the only one who has it hard,' I say. 'Not that I want you to be unhappy, but I'm tired of people's sympathy. I'm a good listener too, you know.' I touch her arm. 'Tell me, is your mother still alive?'

102

'Yes, but we're not in touch anymore. After my father left, my mother and I were on our own for years until she met Bert.' A shadow passes across her face. 'He moved in with us when I was thirteen. I couldn't stand him at first. The idea he might think he could take my father's place made me furious. But that wasn't Bert's plan. He left my upbringing to my mother and treated me like a friend. We were close.'

Sylvie is silent for while, sinks into a kitchen chair and continues. I can barely hear her. 'A bit too close. One night he came into my bedroom and tried to get in bed with me. I kicked him away and threatened to call the police. That shook him. He never tried it again, but he'd stare at me if I was walking around in my nightie, or if I was sunbathing in my bikini in the garden. Try to imagine what that was like for a growing girl. What a creep he was!'

I'm horrified. 'And your mother? Did you tell her?'

'She didn't believe me,' Sylvie says. 'She thought I was imagining things and said that she'd never noticed anything. If I had a problem with him looking at me, I shouldn't go wear a bikini or parade around the house in mini-skirts. Parade! That was the word she used, as if I was inviting him to keep accidentally brushing against me whenever we passed each other in the hall.'

Sylvie stares ahead without speaking and I feel deep sympathy for her. No wonder she never reveals much about her childhood. I pour the coffee.

'How long did it go on for?' My voice is full of repressed anger.

'Until I was sixteen. I left school, got a job and moved out. I was too young of course, but they made no attempt to stop me,' Sylvie says. 'So you understand why I don't visit them.'

We go into the sitting room carrying our mugs and sit down on the sofa.

'Did you ever see your real father again?'

Sylvie shakes her head. 'As far as I'm concerned he can stay away. I've managed without him all this time, the rest of my life should be possible too.' She straightens her shoulders and smiles. 'Enough about me. Let's talk about something else.'

I nod, but the silence that falls stretches out.

'How's it going with your studio?' she asks.

It's a difficult change of tack, but Sylvie clearly doesn't want to talk about herself anymore.

'I haven't been doing much, but I can allow myself not to work for a while.'

'That makes a difference,' Sylvie says. 'It must be useful, having so much money. But both of you went out and got jobs, didn't you?'

'What else were we going to do? The money has never been that important,' I say. 'It made it easier to study, that's true. We didn't need weekend jobs and we could afford to live in nice places, but neither of us would have been happy doing nothing. I've invested a lot of my money in my studio, and in my house, of course.'

'And Lydia?'

'In Raoul's company. I think she owns half of the shares. That was smart, Software International is going to be big some day.'

I realise that I'm talking about my sister in the present tense, and the reality undoes me. I struggle for breath and close my eyes in an attempt to master the pain.

'Are you all right?' Sylvie's voice is gentle.

I nod, even though I'm not really. 'When I talk about Lydia, I keep forgetting that she's gone.'

I can't hold it back anymore and Sylvie puts her arms around me. She lets me cry until I've calmed down, which takes quite a while. I'm embarrassed about crying, but Sylvie doesn't seem to mind. She rubs my back, makes consoling noises and says all kinds of things that barely get through to me.

Finally I wipe the tears from my face. 'How could she just die,

Sylvie? One minute she was here and the next she was gone. She can't be gone, she just can't. How can you just suddenly stop existing?'

Sylvie looks at me helplessly. 'I don't know.'

Another silence falls. After a while I wipe my hair out of my face, look at her and ask, 'Do you believe there's life after death?'

Sylvie hesitates. 'I don't completely rule it out, but I don't really believe in it either. I've never had a reason to believe there's anything more.'

I get up and fetch a box of tissues from the cupboard. I pull one out and blow my nose. Crumpled tissue in my hand, I say, 'Lydia and I always used to go and look for chestnuts in the graveyard in the autumn.'

Sylvie looks at me expectantly.

'The chestnut trees were enormous. At the end of September the conkers would be pouring off them and we'd cycle there with big plastic bags.'

'Didn't you think it was scary?'

I shake my head. 'Not at all. Lydia certainly didn't, she wasn't afraid of anything, and I felt more respect for all those graves than fear. I didn't see the graveyard as a place full of dead people, but as a sort of…spirit realm. It's not that I saw anything in particular, but I could feel the presence of all those souls.'

'Really?' Sylvie shivers.

'I was just a kid, so I didn't really think about it, but I knew exactly which graves we could get chestnuts off and which we'd better leave alone.'

Sylvie's fingers tap against her mug. 'And now you think that Lydia is visiting you.' Her voice is cautious.

'Well, maybe she is. Just because I don't have a sixth sense doesn't mean it doesn't exist.'

She takes a sip of coffee and adds, 'I'm happy I don't have a feeling for paranormal things, it seems dead creepy.'

My eyes wander around the room and come to rest on the chair where Lydia liked to sit when she visited. I picture her there, one leg crossed over the over, chatting away.

'It's not creepy, it's reassuring,' I say gently. 'It means that she hasn't gone completely away.'

25.

She hasn't gone. Most of the time she's with me. She goes away when I sleep, work or when I'm momentarily distracted by my grief. I can sense it immediately when she's not there and I try to summon her back

On a sunny, windy day, I catch the train to my parents' house. I know they aren't home and that's why I've chosen to go today. I haven't been home since Lydia's death; I'm afraid of the memories.

On the path up to the house I contemplate the imposing white manor. It looks so familiar, so unchanged while everything else is in pieces. Part of me expected the trees to have lowered their branches, the leaves to have withered and the sun to have disappeared from the place where I was once so happy. I stand there for ages, my hands buried in my pockets, until my feet take me further along the garden path. I follow it past the house and, once again, I feel a shadow joining my own. It comes to stand next to me when the back garden opens out in front of us.

'Papa made that picnic table so that we could eat outside in the summer,' a voice says.

'Yes,' I say quietly. 'And we turned it into a den.'

'Do you remember how we wanted to spend the night in it?'

'We weren't allowed to.' I smile at the memory.

'No, we were upset about that, weren't we?'

'We were furious!'

I go deeper into the garden and feel Lydia close to me. She moves within each gust of wind, she envelops me in the sunlight that dances over the grass. Together we summon up the memories hidden in every nook and corner.

Here we…there we…do you remember…?

I stay in the garden until the shadows grow longer and the sun sinks behind the fence. I'm reluctant to leave my childhood home, afraid I'll lose Lydia again if I do. But she fills every corner of the train back to Rotterdam with her presence.

When I get home, Thomas is waiting for me in the back garden. I see him through the kitchen window when I go to inspect the fridge for possible dinner ingredients. He's sitting in a garden chair, smoking a cigarette and reading the paper.

I repress the urge to knock on the window and instead decide to observe him for a while. How long has he been there? He must have climbed over the gate to get into the garden, but why didn't he go away again when he realised I wasn't in?

Because Thomas doesn't mind waiting, I know that. He's the most patient person I know. Elisa isn't home? Then I'll just wait until she gets back. His body is not as busy as his mind, my father would say.

And what he doesn't see doesn't exist is something else I'd add. When we were students I had a couple of relationships. Whenever I was in love, Thomas acted like he didn't know me. He walked right past me in the corridor and sat next to me in the photo lab without saying a word. He only looked at me if I said something to him, with an expression difficult to gauge.

I don't know if Thomas had set his sights on more than friendship back then. I still wonder whether he isn't in love with me. He's never said anything, never tried to kiss me, but I wonder.

After all these years, I still don't really understand his behaviour. Perhaps that's why Lydia didn't like him. Understanding people was vital to her job, but she could never pin Thomas down. Right from the start she told me to avoid him, which was a good reason for me to keep inviting him to my birthdays and to see him more often.

All of a sudden Thomas looks over and our eyes meet. I gesture as though I was about to knock on the window, but I know he saw me standing there, staring at him.

I open the door with a wide grin. 'You been sitting here long?'

'About an hour.' Thomas puts the paper down, stubs out his cigarette and comes inside. He starts to set up the coffee machine. 'Want one too?'

'I was about to make something to eat.'

'First coffee.' Thomas spoons the coffee into the filter and fills up the water container. 'What were you going to eat?'

'Pasta maybe.' I lean against the counter and watch Thomas's preparations. 'Are you staying for dinner?'

'Sure.'

'Then I'll start cooking.' I get out a packet of macaroni and a jar of sauce.

'First coffee.'

Thomas watches the water running slowly, spluttering like an engine having trouble starting. He stands there until the very last drop has fallen and fills up a mug. In the meantime, I've put a pan of water on the stove and I'm frying a mixture of minced meat, herbs and onions.

'Why didn't you open the door right away?' Thomas asks without looking at me.

That's what Thomas is like, he cuts to the chase, no messing around. We've always been like this with each other and so I give him a straight answer.

'I thought it was a bit strange that you were sitting there like that. I was wondering why you were waiting.'

'Because you weren't here,' Thomas says matter-of-factly. He gulps the coffee. It must be burning hot, but he drinks it as though it's a pint of beer. In between sips he looks at me, then says, 'You were thinking about something, weren't you?'

'About you and Lydia.'

'Me and Lydia? What do you mean?'

'I just think it's a shame that she never got to know you like I do.'

Thomas shrugs. 'You mustn't worry about that. What other people think really isn't important.'

'She is, was, my twin sister. It was important to me.'

We are standing quite close, facing each other, Thomas with his coffee and me with the frying pan. The kitchen is filled with the smell of caffeine, herbs and meat cooking. And with Lydia's presence. It's as if the air solidifies, like she's wormed her way between Thomas and me. Without thinking I step back.

'What is it?' Thomas asks at once.

'I…nothing. It's nothing. Would you lay the table?'

I turn around to the counter and get out a tin opener. My confusion must be visible because Thomas looks at me with concern.

'You looked odd suddenly. What is it? Did it feel like Lydia was nearby again?'

I'd told him about it over the phone a few days before. It doesn't sound as if he thinks I'm crazy, but still I nod with some hesitation.

'She came and stood between us. That must sound idiotic.'

Thomas sits down at the dining table and pats the wood. I sit down opposite him.

'Elisa, I know you need to think that Lydia is nearby. I also understand that you'd like to go on believing it for the rest of your life, but it's time to face up to reality.'

Cold, empty disappointment. 'What do you mean by that?'

'I mean—' Thomas begins but I don't let him finish.

'You believe that everything stops with death. That the world is only for the living, and that one day you simply stop existing.' My voice sounds shrill.

'Yes,' he says. 'When you die your blood stops circulating and everything stops, indeed. Death is death. Lydia isn't here anymore, Elisa. You have to get on with your life.'

'I am doing that. I am getting on with my life. I—'

'You're walking around in a dream world,' Thomas interrupts. 'I understand that it's a survival mechanism, but it has to end some time. When your sister was alive she had too much influence over you and I can't bear to see her carrying on controlling your life after her death.'

'Where did you get that idea from? She's not controlling me, she's consoling me!'

Thomas leans forward over the table and rests his hand on mine. 'It's normal to deny that you've lost someone for good. Believe me, I know what it's like. I went through the same thing when my father committed suicide. It's not a bad thing to convince yourself otherwise, or you risk going mad with grief, but you're going too far. Do you know what I think the problem is? That you got so used to Lydia telling you what you could and couldn't do that you don't know what to do with your freedom.'

I don't get angry. I don't yell. The only thing I feel is disappointment. I'd hoped that Thomas would be open to this kind of thing.

'I didn't make it up, she really is there.' My voice shakes slightly and because Thomas is looking at me with such an exhausted pity I leave it at that. I should have kept it to myself.

'Are you angry now?' Thomas asks quietly.

I look up at him, into the warm brown eyes of a friend who only means well.

'No,' I say with difficulty.

'I had to say it.' Thomas spreads out his hands, a gesture of helplessness.

I nod.

'So we're still good friends?' Thomas takes hold of both of my hands.

I nod again and he smiles.

'One question,' I say.

'Yes?'

'Do you really think that Lydia dominated me?'

Thomas looks into my eyes. 'Yes.'

Of course he's right. It's not the first time it's been said. But actually, Lydia's domineering personality didn't really bother me. It was always well intentioned and when it came down to it, I always did what I wanted. Some people interpreted my silence as submissiveness, but it wasn't that bad.

Lydia didn't like Thomas or Sylvie, although I did my best to convince her that she was wrong. I tied myself in knots trying to keep them away from each other at my birthday parties. I defended one to the other and worried about everyone's welfare but my own. I stayed friends with Thomas and Sylvie despite Lydia. I made my own decisions.

What did Thomas say just now? That I'd become so used to taking Lydia into account that I don't know what to do with my freedom?

That was a nasty comment.

Lydia

26.

'Do you feel like going into town?'

It's Saturday morning before ten, and I'm still wearing my dressing gown when Elisa calls.

'I'm not even dressed, you madwoman.' I yawn.

'Not right this minute, this afternoon maybe,' Elisa says. 'Have you looked outside? The weather's beautiful. Weather to sit out in. I think you need a bit of that.'

The sun is shining in full force and I have to admit she's right.

'Raoul and I have to do the shopping first. Shall we meet at one?'

'In front of De Bijenkorf?' Elisa says.

'See you there, sis.'

I bump into Raoul on the landing, he's already washed and shaved.

'Who was that?' he asks.

'Elisa. We're going shopping this afternoon.'

Raoul frowns. 'Shopping? But I have to go out this afternoon.'

I walk past him into the bathroom and turn on the shower. 'Where? You didn't mention it before.' I step under the warm stream and raise my face in enjoyment.

Raoul stands in the bathroom doorway. 'To the gym. I train every Saturday, remember?'

'You haven't been going recently. I thought you were going in the evenings instead,' I shout above the sound of the splattering water.

'That's right, but I wanted to go at the weekends again as well.'

I feel the storm coming and begin to feel miserable.

'Go when I get back then.'

'I can't, I've arranged to go with someone.'

'Me too, and I said it first so you look after Valerie.'

'She can go with you and Elisa, can't she?'

'You can't be serious,' I scoff. 'Have you ever tried going round the shops with a child of six? Why don't you take Valerie with you now to the supermarket, so that I can go into town. I'll give Elisa a quick call. What time do you want to go to the gym?'

'Three o'clock,' Raoul says.

'We'll be back before then. Is that all right?'

'That's not going to work. I've got to drop into a client's beforehand.'

I turn the shower off and open the cubicle doors. I don't believe it. 'On a Saturday?'

'It's a customer from abroad. He arrived late yesterday and is going to Germany this afternoon. If I don't speak to him before then, I'll forfeit a very good deal.'

I wrap a towel around myself and observe Raoul silently.

'What's this customer called? Do I know him?'

'No, he's a new one. Ernst Riebe. He's the owner of a big food manufacturing company. It would be really nice if we could get him on board, Lydia.'

I dry myself and brush my hair, stark naked. I see only worry in Raoul's eyes, not desire.

'You say it like Software International will go bankrupt if you don't get this contract.'

'Things haven't been going so well with the business recently, Lydia,' Raoul says.

I look at him, uneasy. 'How bad is it?'

'We can hold out for a while, but we do need a couple of big earners soon.' Raoul sighs.

'Why didn't you tell me this before?'

'I'm telling you now. And you've had other things to worry about the last few days.'

My thoughts return to Bilal. The rest of the week passed without incident. It's over, it's in the past. He probably just wanted to get me back. Hopefully he thinks he's even now and he'll leave me alone. I'm going to have a nice time shopping this afternoon and no one is going to spoil it, not Bilal and not Raoul. On the other hand, if Software International isn't going so well…I've never seen Raoul so worried.

'Should I talk to my father? I'm sure he'd give the company a financial injection if worst comes to the worst.'

'No,' Raoul says abruptly.

'Well, all right then.' I walk past Raoul into the bedroom.

'Off you go to your client then,' I say as he watches me get dressed. 'We'll take Valerie with us. She does need some new clothes.'

Raoul's face brightens. He pulls me to him and kisses me. 'What did I do to deserve such an understanding wife?'

'As long as you appreciate it. And you realise that I'm going to have to go to the supermarket on my own as well now.'

'I'll cook tonight,' Raoul says at once. 'I'll cook all week long.'

'Deal,' I say, because I really hate cooking. 'Do you have time for a coffee?'

'A quick one. I have to leave in fifteen minutes.'

'In your jeans? Shouldn't you wear a suit?'

'Not on a Saturday,' Raoul says. 'Ernst Riebe isn't that formal.'

Only once we've had coffee and Raoul has left do I realise that Ernst Riebe may well be a casual dresser, but that would never have been sufficient reason for Raoul to go to a business appointment in jeans before.

27.

When we arrive at De Bijenkorf, Elisa's waiting for us outside. I see her through the tram window, wearing dark green combat pants and a shirt in the same colour, as though she might be called up to defend her country at any moment.

Shaking my head slightly, I take Valerie by the hand, cross the Coolsingel Canal and wave to Elisa. A tramp is talking to her, pulling up his trouser leg to show her an unsavoury bandage.

'I don't want to bother you, madam, and I don't want to frighten you,' I hear the beggar say, 'but I can't work and I wanted to ask you…'

Elisa looks to me for assistance. I examine the fake blood colouring the bandage. 'If you don't want to bother anybody then don't. You can see she's frightened.' I push two euros into his hand, link my arm through Elisa's, grasp Valerie's hand and lead them through the revolving doors of the department store. We walk into a world of refined perfumes and expensive sunglasses.

'That wasn't real blood, was it?' Elisa wonders out loud.

'Of course not, you could see that. Hello sis!' We pause to give each other a kiss. 'Do you mind that I brought along Valerie? Raoul had to go out so I didn't have a choice.'

'Of course not, what difference does it make?' Elisa smiles down at Valerie's blonde head. 'Hey shrimp! You've got nice pigtails today,' she says and Valerie smiles back.

'I don't think she'll be able to handle too much shopping,' I say.

'Me neither,' Elisa says. 'I can hardly keep up with your pace either, so it's a good thing Valerie has come along.'

She winks at Valerie, who has heard every word, of course, and tries to return the wink, blinking with both eyes.

'I need new clothes, Elisa,' Valerie says. 'Do you too?'

'Not really, so we'll do some nice shopping for you,' Elisa answers.

'And for Mummy,' Valerie says.

'Mummy doesn't need anything either, she's got wardrobes full of clothes,' Elisa says. 'That way we'll be done quickly! Shall we find a nice cafe right away?'

'Yay!' Valerie shouts, but I intervene.

'Absolutely not, we're going shopping first. And where do you get the idea you don't need anything, Elisa? You haven't got a stitch to wear. I always see you in those army pants.'

Elisa shrugs her shoulders. 'They're comfortable.'

I sigh and continue through the store with my daughter and sister trailing behind me. We take the first escalator and as we zoom upwards, I turn back to my sister. Suddenly, in a split second, I think I see Bilal downstairs among the shoppers. A grim face with dark eyes stares up at me. I'm so startled I have to cling to the rail, but when I try to get a better look, he's vanished.

'What is it?' Elisa turns her head and follows my gaze.

'Nothing.' I recover quickly. There's no reason that Bilal shouldn't be in the Bijenkorf. It doesn't have to mean anything.

Two Muslim girls are walking towards us, covered from head to toe. One of them is wearing a pair of white linen harem trousers, combined with a pale-blue long-sleeved shirt and matching headscarf. The other has on a long pink flared skirt with a pink jacket, a white handbag from Guess and, of course, a matching headscarf. They look fresher, more modern and attractive than my sister.

I nudge Elisa. 'Shall we look for a skirt for you?' I suggest. 'You know what, Elisa, let's give you a makeover! New make-up, a different hairstyle, a whole new look!'

I look at my sister with excitement, but I can see that my enthusiasm isn't infectious. But she's not getting out of it that easily. It's already quite an event that I'm in town with her, she really doesn't like shopping. The only reason she called me this morning was to cheer me up after my horrible week. I appreciate it, but I'm also going to take shameless advantage of it.

As soon as we arrive at the fashion floor, I set off towards the racks of a collection I'd personally kill for. I pull everything out and hold it in front of me, so that Elisa can see how well it would suit her. That's the advantage of having an identical twin.

'I never wear that kind of thing.' Elisa looks dubiously at the pink and orange patterned skirt.

'Then start now.' I pull a matching sweater from the rack and push her towards the changing room.

'Lydia!' Elisa protests.

'You could try it on at least.'

Elisa disappears, sighing, into the cubicle. 'This sweater is far too tight,' I hear her complaining.

I lean against the wall next to the curtain, determined not to let her escape. 'That's because you always wear baggy clothes.'

Elisa comes out. She looks so sunny and feminine that even Valerie claps her hands in delight.

'I think pink and orange is pretty,' Valerie says, stroking the soft fabric with one finger.

'Oh, is that what you think, shrimp?' Elisa asks. 'I feel like one of your Barbie dolls.'

'You look fantastic,' I say. 'Come on, let's pay. Pull the tickets off, then you can keep it on.'

Elisa makes a move to return to the cubicle and take everything off again, but I bend down and with a couple of quick jerks, pull the tickets off and hurry with them to the till.

'Lydia!' Elisa cries.

Of course, Elisa still disappears into the changing room and comes out again in her camouflage trousers, but I've already paid.

'Call it a gift,' I say as we go towards the escalator, 'and don't give me such a nasty look. You looked terrific.'

'Mummy, I need to pee,' Valerie says.

'Can you hang on, otherwise we'll have to go all the way upstairs.' I help my daughter off the escalator. 'You can go to the toilet in McDonald's.'

'Are we going to McDonald's?' Valerie asks in delight.

'Just to pee. We're going to buy clothes for you now.' I lead her towards the exit. Elisa follows, frowning, the bag containing her new clothes in her hand.

'Can I have an ice-cream?' Valerie asks.

I promise her that we'll sit outside the Italian ice-cream parlour once we've finished and she can choose something big, but of course that's not enough. Valerie insists that she needs an ice-cream right now, at once. I ignore her and slow down until Elisa has caught up with us.

'Do you still need shoes?' I ask her.

It's a rhetorical question because of course she needs shoes to go with the new skirt. Open shoes for when the weather's nice and boots for when it's cooler.

'We could have a quick look in Manfield. I saw some lovely orangey-brown leather boots in the window recently. They'd go perfectly. I've already tried them on, so you'd only have to pay.'

'And to like them, perhaps?' Elisa says. She's not usually sarcastic.

'You will like them,' I assure her.

When we get to Manfield, I point to the dream boots in the window display. The leather is soft and smooth, they have a slender heel, nicely finished…

'They are nice,' Elisa admits. 'Perfect for you. I don't like heels, I can't walk in them.'

'But the heels are so low! You'd just have to get used to them.' I pull Elisa into the shop.

The saleswoman who has been discreetly observing us, comes forward. 'Can I help you?'

'She'd like those boots in a size 39,' I say. 'She doesn't need to try them on.'

I set off towards the till, followed by Elisa, who is hissing at me that she doesn't want the boots, and that she's not going to buy them.

'I'll buy them for myself then.'

As we leave with the shoebox, I say, 'If you ever want to borrow them, just say so.'

Of course, I have no intention of keeping the boots. At the first opportunity, I'll leave them at Elisa's house, perhaps even this afternoon.

Elisa shakes her head, half in exhaustion, half in amusement. 'Shall we go and get a drink?'

'Let's go to Bambino's first,' I say. 'It's really close, otherwise we'll have to walk all the way back here.'

As soon as Valerie hears the word Bambino's she begins to complain that she's got 'tried legs' and she needs to pee. I promise her that we'll only go into one shop and that's all, but Valerie shakes her head so that her pigtails swirl round and round. I bribe her by promising her the newest Barbie, Cali Girl. Valerie follows me into the shop.

28.

In retrospect we'd have been better off stopping at a cafe right away. Getting a six-year-old into new clothes is always difficult, but a six-year-old who doesn't like trying on clothes at the best of times and who is highly sensitive to my own irritation about Elisa's behaviour…But if I quickly kit Valerie out now, we won't have to do this again for a while. That's what I keep telling myself. So we go into Bambino's.

Elisa and I gather together a few things for my daughter and go into the changing rooms. Despite the promise of being the owner of Cali Girl shortly, Valerie doesn't behave. She doesn't want that itchy jumper, she wants a top that shows off her navel.

'You're not getting a tiny top. You're six, not sixteen. You need a couple of T-shirts and you need a jumper for when it's colder.' I force a T-shirt over Valerie's head. 'Look what a pretty colour. Pink's your favourite, isn't it?'

'No, I hate pink!' the smothered Valerie says, the T-shirt

already halfway back over her head.

'Put your arms into the holes.'

'It prickles!'

'That's not possible, there's no wool in it. It's a hundred per cent cotton.' I grab the yellow summer trousers that go with it and hold them up to Valerie. 'Step into these.'

'Mummy, I need to pee.'

I know that trick. Unfortunately for Valerie I'm not going to fall for it. She becomes redder and more peevish while I do my best to get her leg into a yellow trouser leg.

'Are you all right?' Elisa pokes her head around the corner of the cramped cubicle.

'I'm desperate!' Valerie cries.

'I think she really needs to go,' Elisa says in concern.

Flustered, I glance at Valerie and her anxious face tells me that we indeed do need to find a toilet. I pull her leg out of the yellow trousers again, let her step back into her skirt and try to convince her that it doesn't matter if she doesn't wear her vest to look for a toilet.

I come out of the changing room with a sobbing child and hurry to the till.

'I'm sorry to interrupt,' I say in an apologetic tone to the saleswoman as much as to the customer at the till, 'but could she please use your toilet?'

The saleswoman looks at Valerie, who has turned red from holding in her pee.

'I'm sorry, but the toilet isn't for customer use, we can't make any exceptions,' she says.

I look at her in disbelief. 'You can see she's desperate!'

'I'm sorry,' the saleswoman says, though it's obvious she's not.

'I spend hundreds of euros on clothes here every year,' I snarl at her. 'What fantastic customer service! Come on, Valerie, we'll have to run.'

I have a fleeting wish that Valerie will let everything out here, in front of the till, but she's much too well behaved for that. She'd rather die than let a drop leak out.

'We'll be back in a sec,' I say to Elisa and dash to a small diner down the street where I take Valerie out the back and put her on the toilet. The door has a large sign on it: 'Use of toilet: 1 euro. Paying customers, free.'

'One euro? Are they completely crazy?'

Valerie sits on the toilet, her legs dangling. I don't hear much happening so I ask her if she's finished.

'I suddenly don't need to anymore, Mummy.'

'What do you mean, you suddenly don't need to? You were desperate!'

'Yes, but the pee has gone away now.'

'Did you pee your pants?' I check them and her shoes, but they're dry.

'No, it's gone. That's funny, isn't it?'

'Yes, it's very funny. Have you been joking with Mummy?'

Valerie shakes her head and looks between her legs as if she expects that someone is playing a joke on her. She gives me an uncertain smile, because she can see from my face that I'm not amused.

'Get down then,' I sigh. We leave the diner hand in hand.

'Using the toilet costs one euro, madam,' a waiter informs me.

'She didn't go,' I answer, without stopping.

Elisa is waiting for us in Bambino's with a resigned look on her face.

'Sorted?' she asks and I grimace. The clothes are still piled up in the changing cubicle, so we go back in. The saleswoman comes over to us, 'Can I be of any assistance?'

'No, thanks. You've done enough,' I say, drawing the curtain in her face.

I lift Valerie into the yellow summer trousers and turn her to the mirror. 'They fit well. Do you like them, Val?'

Valerie looks at me with downcast eyes. 'Mummy…'

'What's the matter?'

Suddenly Valerie's eyes widen in shock, she pulls her knees together and puts her hand to her mouth. We both look down.

'What are you doing now?' I cry out.

Valerie doesn't look at me. She keeps her knees together, her cheeks bright red, her hands covering a big wet patch.

I can't do anything about it, I'm bursting with laughter. 'Take them off quickly,' I whisper between giggles. 'Throw them in the corner and put your own clothes back on.'

Valerie hurries to obey and I go to the till with a couple of other items of other things.

'So, you were successful in the end?' the saleswoman asks.

'Absolutely.' I drag my card through the machine. 'The things we don't want are still in the changing rooms.'

29.

Weak from laughing, we cross the road and go to the cafe terraces on Karel Doorman Street. We install ourselves, our shopping bags at our feet, rummage around in our handbags for sunglasses and giggle a bit more.

Our order is taken, two lemon teas, two apple tarts, and a fruit sorbet for the little miss, and then we raise our faces to the April sunshine and don't talk at all for a while. I haven't felt this good in ages, spending time with my daughter and my sister on a sunny terrace. A group of Muslim girls parade by, their hair caught up in flattering headscarves. A couple of girls with them wear their hair long and loose, tossing it around as they pace up and down, stomachs bared, glittering navel piercings on show.

It's like being in the playground at Rotterdam College.

'Hey, should we get something for the barbecue tomorrow?' Elisa asks.

'The barbecue at Mum and Dad's tomorrow! Shit, I'd totally forgotten.'

'You haven't prepared anything?' Elisa asks. 'I thought you were going to make a quiche.'

I groan. 'Do I have to go to the supermarket again?'

'No, we're going past the deli later. They've got the most delicious things.'

I sink down again. I'll get something from the deli. My mother has probably done the same herself. In any case, I've never seen her prepare any of the exquisite dishes she serves up.

Our order is brought and Valerie sits up with a cry of joy. 'What a big ice-cream!'

'If you can't finish it, just let me know,' Elisa teases her.

Valerie shakes her head. 'I'm going to eat it all myself!'

We drink our tea and take a couple of bites of the apple tart.

'It will be nice to have a barbecue,' I say. 'The weather forecast for tomorrow is good, too.'

'Are you going to tell Mum and Dad about that boy at school?' Elisa asks.

I spread whipped cream on my tart. 'I don't know, probably not. It will worry them and they can't do anything about it.'

'You don't know that. They do have experience of those things.'

'Of children with behavioural problems, not violence,' I say. 'Shall we talk about something else, Elisa? I'd just managed to take my mind off it.'

'Sorry. What do you want to talk about?'

'Thomas. You're not going out with him, are you?' I ask.

Elisa sighs and puts her teacup down on the table. 'Can't you just stop with that? You've been bellyaching about my friends for years without knowing what you're talking about. You might think that Thomas is an oddball, but he's had a difficult life.'

'What happened to him?' I ask, but of course I don't get to know because Elisa is discreet when it comes to her friends. It's a quality I appreciate, but which always makes me feel a bit hurt. As if I might gossip. As if anyone else would be interested!

I really don't care what Thomas went through as a sullen child or adolescent. I can't imagine that he was ever a ray of sunshine.

'Has he ever had a girlfriend?'

She shrugs. 'Sylvie is crazy about him.'

'Sylvie? About Thomas?'

'Yes. I'd suspected it for quite some time, but she admitted it recently.'

'Strange.' I picture the dollish Sylvie and have difficulty imagining her with scruffy, long-haired Thomas.

'I was surprised too, but she really likes him.'

'And Thomas is only interested in you. Poor Sylvie. She can't be used to not being able to get a man.' I feel a sense of redress, after all her flirting with Raoul. She had the wrong man there – Raoul doesn't go for those artificial types. Just to be sure, I asked him what he thought of Sylvie. 'Admit you find her attractive,' I challenged him.

'If you like implants,' he said. I'm certain Sylvie overheard. It was at the party for the opening of Elisa's studio. For the rest of the evening she avoided us. It's never been right between us, but that's fine by me.

It's warm on the terrace. I doze off as I listen to Elisa and Valerie talking about school and Valerie's friends. Now and then a dark shadow falls across my face as somebody passes by and I look up. The sunlight conjures up red and yellow spots on my retina and I have to blink to see clearly.

My eyes clear. Bright colour returns to the world. Something catches my attention. It's not the passers-by; it's a persistent shadow in my field of vision. Someone is standing on the other side of the road, in front of the Pathé cinema. I can't have seen him clearly in those couple of seconds, but warning signals pulse through my body.

Bilal.

Elisa

30.

'My mummy is dead,' says Valerie. She's sitting at the kitchen table colouring and looks up at me. It's approaching five on a Wednesday afternoon, my parents are looking after her and I've just dropped round on my bike.

It's strange to be in my sister's house and to watch my mother making coffee without Lydia being here dominating the conversation. Her absence fills every nook and cranny.

'Mummy is in the clouds,' Valerie says.

'Yes,' I say, 'and that's not nice for you.'

'Why not?' Valerie asks. 'Papa says it's lovely there and Mummy comes back often.'

'Oh darling,' my mother says with a strangled voice, adding to me in a subdued tone, 'She always talks about Lydia in the present tense, have you noticed that?'

'It's true, you know,' Valerie continues her colouring. 'She comes to visit me, and then she goes away again.'

Her hand hovers over the coloured pencils, in two minds as to which colour the roof of the house should be.

I rummage around the pencil tin. 'Red?' I suggest.

Valerie shakes her head, takes a purple pencil and sets to work. She immerses herself in her task, making the grass blue, the sun red, the sky green and the roof purple. My father stands over the kitchen table and admires her picture.

'That's very pretty, Valerie,' he says. 'You're using happy colours, aren't you? What a lovely roof. Why is it purple?'

'That's what Mummy likes best,' Valerie answers without looking up.

My father's eyes meet mine over her head. My mother comes in with the mugs of coffee shaking in her hands.

I'm worried that my parents will never get over Lydia's death. Particularly my mother. Every day she writes a letter to Lydia.

I don't think Lydia was ever aware that she was our mother's favourite. I've heard that favourites never realise it. In their experience they get the attention they deserve, without really thinking that another person might be damaged by it. It's not that I blame her for having a deep bond with my mother, they had so much in common. They both liked nice clothes and shopping. They both made their own jewellery. I can still picture them sitting at the dining room table, with all those boxes of beads and fastenings. I had no desire to join them, but at the same time I felt excluded when they were together, talking and laughing.

I directed my attentions towards my father instead, but that was a different kind of relationship to the one Lydia and my mother had. Neither of us are real talkers, but we would take photos together or go for a bike ride.

Now we're all sitting together and I have no idea how to reach them. We chat a little, about the daily grind, things like my studio. I tell them that I don't go there much anymore.

'That's not good,' my father says. 'You have to go back to work, it'll help you.'

I shrug and sharpen a few pencils for Valerie.

'All in good time, Maarten,' my mother says. 'She'll pick it up again presently.'

'I hope so.' My father runs a hand through his white hair and looks up. He nods at the bay window and says, 'Someone's coming. Looks like that policeman.'

We all exchange a look. The doorbell rings and my mother gets up first, brushing down her jeans and saying, 'What do you think he wants? Maybe there's news?'

The thought that Lydia's murderer is still on the loose is frustrating. An arrest wouldn't bring her back, but we'd be able to cope better if we knew that the perpetrator was behind bars.

The front door opens and Noorda's voice fills the hall. An instant later, he comes into the sitting room with my mother.

'Good afternoon.' He pats Valerie on the head.

'Good afternoon, Inspector,' my father says, and I mumble something similar.

'Is there some news?' My mother searches the detective's neutral face, as if hoping to read on it that the murderer has been hung, drawn and quartered.

'We have a new lead,' Noorda confirms. 'It's a small lead, but worth following. That's why I came round, to ask a few questions. It was my understanding that Mister Salentijn always came home early on a Wednesday.'

'Not today,' my father says, 'we're looking after our granddaughter so that he can stay longer in the office.'

'That doesn't matter, I wanted to talk to you too. It's lucky to have found you all together.' Noorda nods at the table. 'May I sit down?'

'Yes, of course!' my mother pulls out a chair and heads towards the kitchen. 'Would you like a coffee?'

'That would be nice,' Noorda responds. He turns to me.

I'm uncomfortable under his scrutiny. I feel myself blushing.

'You studied in Amsterdam, didn't you?' Noorda asks.

'Yes,' I say, surprised at the direction the conversation has started off in.

'On the Korte Prinsengracht, if I'm not wrong,' Noorda says as he consults his notebook.

'Yes.'

'That's not far from the police station on the Prinsengracht.'

I exchange a look of incomprehension with my father.

'What do you want to know, Inspector?' he enquires.

'I'm looking for a certain Hubert Ykema. You don't happen to know him?'

'No,' I say without a moment's thought.

'Are you sure?'

'Yes. I've got a good memory. I still know all the names of the kids I went to primary school with.'

My mother returns with a cup of coffee and sets it down in front of the inspector.

'Thank you, madam.' Noorda looks at her, nods and smiles. 'I wanted to ask you the same question.'

'What was it?' my mother asks.

'If we knew anyone called Hubert Ykema,' I say.

'Hubert Ykema? No, never heard of him,' my mother says. 'Maarten?'

My father shakes his head and stirs his coffee. 'Unless it was a former student…My wife and I were both teachers, you see. I'm afraid that I've forgotten most of the names of my students by now.'

'Ah, so you were a teacher too,' Noorda says.

'Yes, at a school for difficult children,' my mother says. 'Tough work but rewarding.'

'Hmmm.'

There's silence while we drink our coffee, until Valerie holds up her picture. 'Finished!'

We admire her work with appropriate seriousness, even Noorda pays attention to it, which is very kind of him. It's still quiet and I wonder who Hubert Ykema is and what he's got to do with us.

'Where did you get the name Hubert Ykema?' I ask when still nothing is said.

Noorda looks away, and when he begins to talk, he sounds almost casual, as if he's making an offhand comment. Only he's not.

'Hubert Ykema is a policeman who worked on the Prinsengracht in Amsterdam. Years ago he reported his service gun missing, a Walther P5. The weapon was never recovered, but the ballistic analysis has revealed that the bullets that killed Lydia came from that same gun. Hubert Ykema's Walther P5.'

31.

Silence descends.

'So you'll understand,' Noorda continues, 'that I'm trying to find out what the connection might be between an Amsterdam policeman and Lydia Salentijn.'

'Does there have to be one?' I ask. 'The gun could have ended up anywhere.'

'That's true,' Noorda admits. 'There may not have been a direct link to your sister. The gun was probably flogged on the black market. But of course we need to investigate it. There's also the possibility that Hubert Ykema registered his gun as missing when it wasn't. These things happen, but we can't find any reason for him to have done that. We have questioned him, but he was at work on the evening of the murder. Several colleagues can confirm that Ykema didn't leave the police station in Amsterdam. He claims not to know Lydia, and none of his colleagues recognised her, which doesn't mean he and Lydia didn't know each other.' He directs his question at nobody in particular, 'Do you know if Lydia knew anyone in the police force?'

'I wouldn't know,' I say.

'A boyfriend or an ex-boyfriend, perhaps?' Noorda proposes. 'Or someone she met recently?'

'I don't have a clue,' my father says, and my mother shakes her head.

'You should ask my son-in-law,' she says.

Noorda nods. 'If I might wait for him here…?'

'Of course,' my mother says.

Noorda turns to me again. 'You're the only link I've been able to find.' He gives me an almost apologetic look, which he should, because what he is suggesting is not pleasant.

'Because I used to live in Amsterdam?' I say with raised eyebrows.

Noorda shrugs. 'It's not much, I'll admit it. Your college was on the Korte Prinsengracht. Hubert Ykema worked at the police station on the Prinsengracht. That's not far away.'

I stare at the inspector, wondering if he's lost his mind.

'And so?' I ask.

'Have you ever been to that police station?'

I reflect. 'Once. My purse was stolen and I reported it.'

'And did you meet Mr Ykema on that occasion?'

'Certainly not. Well, at least not that I know. As I said, I don't know the man.'

Noorda sighs. Every wrinkle and groove in his weathered face expresses doubt.

'But there has to be a connection,' he says as he taps his notebook on his knee. 'You and your sister look very alike.'

'Yes,' I say, 'that's often the case with identical twins.'

'Undoubtedly you've often been mistaken for each other,' Noorda hypothesises.

I nod.

'I used to be friends with identical twins,' Noorda says in a confiding tone. 'We had so much fun together, especially when they swapped classes with each other at school. They weren't in the same class, you know. One was good at maths, the other at English. They took each other's place in tests. It was wonderful!'

I smile. 'Lydia and I did that once or twice as well.'

'Only as children, I presume,' Noorda says. 'Or did you do it as adults too?'

'No.'

'Never?'

'Never.'

Noorda seems disappointed by this reply. 'So it's not possible that someone mistook one of you for the other.'

'Well, yes, of course it's possible. But we wouldn't have intended them to.' I look at my parents and see that they are feeling as uncomfortable as I am. My father puts his coffee cup down on the table with more force than necessary.

'Do you think someone wanted to shoot Elisa instead of Lydia, Inspector?'

'We do have to take that into account. I'd like you to think about that, Miss van Woerkom.'

I nod, but I suspect that my face says it all. Who on earth would want to murder me? On the other hand, who would want to murder Lydia…?

Raoul doesn't know who Hubert Ykema is either, he's never heard of the man, and so Noorda leaves none the wiser. I wonder what he'd expected. That gun must have been sold on the black market and passed from hand to hand. Try tracking down the murderer that way. But it strengthens my feeling that some kind of criminal was settling accounts with Lydia, and that leads to just one person: Bilal.

As I'm seeing Noorda out, I ask him why they've let Bilal go, why it's so difficult to build a case against him. We stand in the sun in the front garden and I light up a cigarette. It's a lovely evening in early June and a light breeze shakes the heavy foliage of the trees lining the street. I'm surprised when Noorda lights up a cigarette too.

'If you bring someone up before the judge, you have to have enough evidence to be able to convict them,' he says. 'We don't have any evidence, only suspicions. Assrouti would certainly get off and then we wouldn't be able to charge him a second time if some evidence did turn up, Miss van Woerkom.'

'Call me Elisa. Do you think Bilal managed to get hold of Hubert Ykema's gun?'

'I'm not ruling anything out.'

I sigh and tap the ash from my cigarette. 'Are you having Bilal followed? I mean, he might not have done it himself, but he's got friends who could have done it.'

'I'd like to, but I just don't have sufficient manpower.'

'What's going to happen now?' I persist.

Noorda stares out at the sunny street. His silence continues for so long that he doesn't need to give me an answer. Anger and a feeling of impotence flare up inside me.

'I don't understand this!' I burst out. 'That boy threatened my sister with a knife, which makes him not just guilty of intimidation, but also of carrying an illegal weapon, and the police aren't doing a thing. She gets an anonymous letter and not a single one of you has been able to work out who sent it.'

'We can't just—' begins Noorda, but I interrupt him.

'If you policemen paid less attention to the rules when questioning people, perhaps the truth might come out. We'd be better off considering the victim's rights for once.'

I throw my cigarette onto the ground and when Noorda doesn't react, I head for the door.

'Miss van Woerkom,' Noorda says. 'Has it ever occurred to you that Bilal Assrouti might be innocent? That someone has taken advantage of his row with your sister?'

32.

Noorda's words haunt me all evening, but each time I consider his theory, I dismiss it. I can't imagine, won't imagine, it being anyone other than Bilal.

On Saturday I go to the zoo with Raoul and Valerie. There have been so many beautiful days in a row, but we've chosen the one cold, cloudy day for an afternoon out. Valerie runs ahead, rushing to see everything, though she seems most interested in the round white stones lining the paths. We walk along behind her.

'Something strange happened recently,' I tell Raoul.

He turns to me, 'What?'

I hesitate.

'Hey!' Raoul jabs me in the arm. 'You know you can tell me anything.'

'I'm sure you won't believe me.'

Raoul looks at me and raises one eyebrow. 'I might surprise you.'

Valerie comes running up to us. 'Daddy! Daddy! Look how pretty!' She opens her hand and shows him a smooth, oval-shaped stone.

'Beautiful,' Raoul says. 'Don't you want to look at the bears, sweetie? Look! Polar bears!'

Valerie isn't listening. She turns around and runs off to look for new stones.

'Look at her with those stones.'

'That's what we paid twelve euros to come and see.'

I smile. The concentration with which my niece studies the ground reminds me of Lydia's and my chestnut hunting in the graveyard.

'What were you about to tell me?' Raoul asks. 'Something strange happened…?'

I glance at his handsome, powerful face and wonder what possessed me to want to talk to him about my feeling that Lydia was haunting me. Raoul is so sensible and practical, how could I expect him to take me seriously?

'I still get the feeling,' I begin, 'that Lydia is with me. Sometimes doors open and close inexplicably, and I keep feeling such a strange breeze around me…'

Raoul gives me the kind of look a medical practitioner uses to assess how serious their patient's condition is. Despite everything his expression makes me laugh.

'I'm not mad,' I say. 'It just sounds mad.'

'Oh…' Raoul says, only increasing my desire to convince him.

'She's here, Raoul. I feel her presence now too. She is walking with us.'

Raoul looks around and lets the observation sink in. We carry on in silence for a while, so close to each other that our hands keep touching. It must almost look like we're walking hand in hand. I wonder what Lydia thinks about that and take a step to the side.

'It's guilt,' Raoul says suddenly. 'Guilt because we're still alive and she isn't. Because we didn't do anything to prevent her death, we couldn't have done anything. Guilt because—'

He breaks off his sentence and walks on in silence, his eyes on the path.

He's right, of course we feel guilty. Because we're happy we're still alive, despite all the pain and misery, but that's not the reason that I feel Lydia around me. I don't say anything else about it.

Valerie runs past the monkey cage to the playground where ice-creams and chips are on sale.

'Daddy! Elisa! Look!' she calls out, as she climbs onto a spring-rocker. 'I can go really fast. Can I have something to eat?'

We exchange a glance.

'Shall we sit down?' Raoul proposes.

I nod and look for a free table while Raoul joins the food queue. It's cold sitting there in the wind and I'm glad when he returns, carrying three portions of chips. He takes one over to Valerie who doesn't look like she's planning on getting off the spring-rocker, and comes to the table with the other two.

There's a long silence. From time to time I look up at Raoul's expressionless face as he stares into the distance. He turns to me, and I jump at the sound of his voice.

'It wasn't going well between me and Lydia,' he says quietly. 'I think she knew I'd been in love with another woman for a long time.'

My heart races and I hardly dare look at him. I freeze, shivers running down my spine.

'Oh,' I say at last. 'I didn't know that.'

'No?' He looks at me.

I stare at the sticky table surface and try to keep my emotions under control. Restless thoughts and long-repressed feelings whirl around my head, alternating with intense joy. I didn't imagine it! I hide my happiness and lower my eyes. 'Did Lydia know?'

'I'm not sure,' Raoul says. 'I think so. Women seem to have a sixth sense about it.'

'How did she react then?'

'She didn't say much about it. I don't think she wanted to know. She threatened to divorce me if I was ever unfaithful. She said she'd take her money out of the business and I'd never see Valerie again. It sounded like she was joking, only she wasn't. She would have done it if she'd been sure I was cheating, but she wasn't sure.'

'You weren't cheating on her,' I say. 'You didn't lie, you don't need to feel guilty.'

'Thinking about someone else is also a kind of infidelity,' Raoul comments. 'It might even be more dangerous than physical infidelity.'

A fresh wave of guilt washes over me; he's right. My conscience is too strong. How can we build anything in this mess?

I look at Raoul. 'And now? What next?'

Raoul stares into the distance.

'I think it would be best to leave things be for a while,' he says quietly.

Once I'm home, I slowly recover from the shock of Raoul's veiled declaration of love. I love him, but I've got nothing to feel guilty about. Or do I? Should I have tried harder to repress my feelings? Should I have tried to invest myself more in my own relationships? Instead I kept myself available, allowing my sister's marriage to falter.

A fast-developing headache takes away any desire to cook dinner, or do any of the other chores that are waiting for me.

I throw my bag on a chair and pick up a photo from the side table. It's my sister and me, at the beach on a summer's day. We're lying on our bellies on the sand. Two identical, smiling faces with cheeks touching, looking straight at the camera.

I study my sister's face. 'I'm sorry,' I whisper. 'I'm so sorry.' Then I lay the photo back on the table, face down.

On Sunday, I visit Lydia's grave. I take white lilies and place them in tall glass bottles on the grave. I pull out a few weeds and sit down beside her for a while.

'Lydia,' I say. 'Tell me what to do. Help me! If you want me to let Raoul go, I'll do it, just tell me! I love him, but I love you more.'

I let my head drop and fight back tears. A gust of wind whistles through the treetops, brushes my cheeks and makes the lilies dance. It's short but unmistakable.

I could read something into it, tell myself that Lydia has given me a sign, but I know it's not true. This time it was just the wind.

33.

'I've got a date tomorrow.' The words dance out of Sylvie's mouth and her feet take a couple of elegant steps.

'Excellent! Who with? Do tell.'

Her smile is teasing. 'Wouldn't you like to know.'

'Is it Thomas?'

She laughs again and her feet tap out another little jig. 'He made me promise not to say anything about it, so I'm not going to.'

'Why can't you tell anyone?' I ask in surprise.

'Because it's a secret.' Sylvie laughs again and sits down on the edge of the table, crossing her arms. But less than thirty seconds later she's sauntering around the room again; she seems to crackle with static, she's got that much fresh energy.

I'm glad for her. She's my friend and I wish her the happiness she's been longing for. It's more than obvious that she's finally managed to get a date with Thomas. Yet, I still feel a painful stab. I understand why Thomas would rather I didn't know, we've been friends for so long…

'Why did you mention it then?' I ask, with light reproof in my voice.

'Because you're my friend! I'd want to know if you had a date. Men don't understand how important it is for women to talk to each other about things like this. You shouldn't feel shut out. It doesn't change anything.'

'No, it doesn't.'

'Last night, after he asked me out, I was so excited, I could barely sleep.' Sylvie is radiant.

'Did you… Did you…'

'We kissed.' She winks at me.

Kissed, they only kissed. The image of Sylvie and Thomas entwined under the sheets disappears from my mind. Why am I relieved? Still, a single kiss seems a little unlikely.

'Kissed? I hope you were careful,' I say tartly, turning back to my computer.

'You're working again!' Sylvie observes.

She looks over my shoulder at the picture I'm photoshopping. It's a still life of a bowl of fruit, on the edge of a just-visible table. Sunlight falls through an arched window, casting a golden glow onto a draped curtain and mosaic floor.

'Lovely,' Sylvie says.

'Hmm, the sunlight is too artificial.'

'It's bright.'

'That's because it isn't real – it's a laser beam.'

'A what?'

'Artificial lighting. I shone a light in through the window, but now the light is too bright. A single ray of light with specks of dust would be nice.'

'Has there been any news?' Sylvie asks, as if there's a logical connection to be made between the bowl of fruit and the police investigation. I understand what she means, but I don't answer at first.

'No,' I say. 'The investigation seems to have hit a rut. How that's possible, I don't know. It looks cut and dried to me. In a country like Holland, the criminal has more rights than the victim – that's what's probably keeping Bilal out of jail.'

'Hmmm.' Sylvie sits down again. 'You know, I've been thinking. We've been assuming that Bilal killed her. But if the police can't get anything on him then maybe he didn't do it.'

I turn to face her again. 'But who would have?'

Sylvie shrugs.

'Exactly.'

'You're convinced that Bilal did it, aren't you?' Sylvie says. 'Because he and Lydia didn't see eye to eye and because he's Moroccan you're sure that he's the murderer.'

'It's got nothing to do with racism,' I retort, 'but he had a problem with my sister and he threatened her. One plus one is still two, and I don't understand why the police can't do anything about it. And it may not have been Bilal who pulled the trigger.'

'Do you think he had accomplices?'

'He's got two older brothers who take the honour of the family name very seriously. They deny having had anything to do with Lydia's death and the police can't arrest them. But Bilal also has friends who may have wanted to do him a favour. They barely investigated that angle, they only looked to see whether he had an alibi.' I pause to catch my breath. 'You know, the last few days I've had a growing desire to talk to Bilal.'

'What?' Sylvie almost plunges from the desk. 'I hope you're not being serious!'

'I know where he lives, pretty much. I know where he goes out. I'll go and talk to him sometime. I mean it.'

Until then, it had been nothing more than a vague idea, now it turns into a firm resolution. And why not? I only have to hear him say my sister's name to know whether he's telling the truth or not.

'Please don't do that, Elisa. It seems very dangerous to me,' Sylvie says.

'I'll make out that I think he's innocent, that the police treated him badly. I can't imagine why he wouldn't talk to me then, unless he does have something to do with Lydia's death. In which case he won't be able to look me in the eye. There are all kinds of ways of betraying yourself, even if it's by saying nothing.'

'And then what?' Sylvie frowns. 'Say that his body language does betray him, what are you going to do with that knowledge?'

I hadn't thought about that, but the more sceptical Sylvie is the more I feel compelled to look for him, this very afternoon. Anything is better than acting as though life has gone back to normal.

'Well?' Sylvie insists. 'What are you going to do then?'

'We'll see.'

34.

Tussendijken has long been a problem neighbourhood, but once the City Watchdog program took control, the police closed down illegal cannabis plantations and flushed the drug addicts out, and it became a little more inhabitable. Despite this, I still feel uneasy when I walk down the street I think Bilal lives in.

The tall, dark housing blocks close ranks and seem to be watching me. A woman in a black veil holding hands with a small child passes by. Further along, a group of boys stand together, sweatshirt hoods pulled up over their heads from under their leather jackets.

I've heard that Bilal lives here, but I don't know at which house. I thought I could look at the name plates, but only a couple of the houses indicate who lives behind their closed doors. There's a tobacconist on the street corner, a small, badly lit place. A stocky middle-aged man, with a wreath of dark hair around his otherwise bald head, stands mutely behind the counter.

'Good afternoon,' I say. 'Do you sell bus passes?'

The man nods. 'A day or a month pass?'

'Day pass,' I say.

The man lays the pass down on the counter and I pay.

'You don't see many of these little corner shops anymore,' I say, to make conversation.

The man shrugs. 'I'm one of the last,' he mutters. 'Shoplifters, hold-ups…'

'I've heard it's a rough neighbourhood.'

'There are enough decent people. Last year we organised a neighbourhood barbecue and it turned into a big party. It's only a few who muck things up, but isn't that always the case?'

'Yes,' I agree. 'There are always a couple who give the rest a bad name. Bilal Assrouti lives around here, doesn't he? Do you happen to know where?'

The man looks up with a jolt and our eyes meet for a moment. 'No,' he says. 'No idea.'

Three boys of around eleven or twelve are playing among the parked cars and look at me with curiosity when I leave the shop. As I search for name plates on doors, they come after me.

'Are you looking for someone?' one of the boys asks.

'The Assrouti family. Do you know where they live?'

The boys nod.

'Bilal's not there, you know,' one of them says. 'He's gone to the mosque with his dad and his brother. His mum and his sister are the only ones home.'

'Oh,' I say. 'So Bilal's not there. Never mind. Would you tell me which house it is?'

One of the boys holds up a grubby plastic bag. 'Want a roll-up?' he asks. 'Ten cents each.'

I look at the bag of tobacco they've put together from cigarette butts picked off the street. 'No thanks.'

They turn around.

'You know what, actually I do fancy a cigarette.'

They turn back. One of the boys holds up the bag and assesses it. 'Reckon you'll get about ten out of this.'

'I'll buy them all.'

'Wicked,' the boy says, handing me the bag. I press a two-euro coin into his hand. 'That'll take care of it.'

He looks at me in silence and I return the look.

'What do you want Bilal for?' one of the other boys asks.

'Nothing special.'

His friend elbows him in the side. 'She's not from the police or nothing, you can see that.' He nods towards the other side of the street and says, 'There, number 14.'

'Thanks.'

The boys watch me cross the street.

I pause in front of the green painted door at number 14. I try to peer through the window, but the net curtains make it impossible. What now?

It's actually quite lucky that Bilal isn't home. Maybe I can talk to his mother or sister, but how should I handle it? Ring on the bell and say: Hello, I'm Elisa van Woerkom and I wanted to ask if any of you had anything to do with my sister's death? Could I come in for a moment?

I could ask for someone else, as though I had the wrong house. That would allow me a glimpse of the inhabitants. I've no idea how that might help me, but I ring the bell. I hear a door open and close inside the house. I wait, but nobody comes. I ring the bell again.

The net curtains open a chink and a woman looks out at me. She makes a helpless gesture with her hands and closes the curtain again. I stand there waiting. I don't understand.

'She's not going to open up,' a voice behind me says.

The three boys have followed me across the street.

'She's not allowed to open the door when she's on her own in the house,' one of them explains.

I give up.

35.

Once I'm on the bus, I call Sylvie on my mobile. When she answers I ask whether she feels like coming to Night City with me this evening.

'Night City? Why do you want to go there?'

I tell her that Lydia once mentioned that a lot of her students, including Bilal, go to Night City. This is met with silence. Finally Sylvie says she thinks I've gone mad.

'So you don't want to come with me?'

No, of course she's not coming with me and she doesn't think I should go either – it seems risky to her.

'Hmmm,' I say.

'Elisa, you're not going there tonight.'

'Why not? I can go where I want,' I say. 'How are you, by the way? And your new love?'

Sylvie laughs quietly, she's happy. 'Really well. Nice of you to ask. Of course I know why you're changing the subject. But now we're talking about it, I hope it doesn't bother you.'

'What?' I ask, though I know damn well what she's talking about.

'Me having a new boyfriend. It must be odd.'

'It doesn't bother me at all,' I say. 'Although I am a bit surprised.'

'Why?'

'Well, I didn't see the two of you as an obvious combination.'

Sylvie laughs again. 'Opposites attract, eh? Let's meet up soon.'

'I was trying to,' I say.

'Not in Night City,' Sylvie says. 'I'll come round to yours tonight, okay?'

'Come tomorrow instead.' With that I hang up.

Thomas isn't up for a night out either. He's not that keen on going out during the week and he really doesn't want to go to a club. I should have known that. My mobile still in my hand, I stare out of the window at the bus shelters, cyclists and pedestrians. I know that Thomas doesn't like dancing, but he could have done this for me, couldn't he? He certainly would have before. 'All right, don't come,' I say to myself. 'I'll go alone.'

Night City is a music venue and night club set up for immigrant clubbers. They have Turkish, Cape Verdian and Hindustani nights, among others, but quite a few Dutch people go too. I've never been myself. I'm not that keen on clubbing either. I've never seen the point of standing around at 3 a.m., beer glass in hand, trying to shout into someone's ear above the deafening music. I'd rather rent a couple of DVDs and spend the evening with Lydia and other friends, our feet up on the coffee table, a bottle of wine within hand's reach.

But now I want to go to Night City and I want to go tonight.

When I get there, Zuco 103 is playing and I make a few vague moves on the dance floor. The smoke machine shrouds the crowd in a red and blue cloud. The noise is ear-splitting and people are dancing with abandon. Most of the audience is foreign. I attract attention, but I'm not the only white person here.

Next to me is a Dutch girl with red-dyed cropped hair, dancing away ecstatically with a Moroccan boy. He tries to flirt with me at the same time. Despite the racket, we start chatting – we have to stand close to be able to hear each other.

'Are you here on your own?' the boy shouts in my ear.

I nod, but tell him that I'm looking for someone.

'Who?'

'Bilal,' I scream. 'Bilal Assrouti. Do you know him?'

He doesn't reply but says something to the red-haired girl. They wave goodbye to me and they're off. I watch them go in astonishment.

The same thing happens all evening. Every time I ask someone about Bilal, they disappear. I give up at last. It was a ridiculous idea to think that I would be able to find a stranger on this enormous dance floor. Instead I dance, losing myself in the music. As I move my hips, someone puts their arm around my waist. A handsome, dark face looks at me for a moment intensely and then slips away.

I spin around at once, but the boy has already disappeared into the crowd. At the same time I see someone else looking at me: a tall, dark young man who makes eye contact with another young man and gestures to him.

He pushes through the crowd towards me and out of the corner of my eye I can see that his friend is doing the same. Panic washes over me.

I wrestle towards the exit, the crowd moving aside more easily for me than for my two followers. I'm still ahead of them. I look back over my shoulder and see that the young men are being hindered from every direction.

I run to the coat check and get my jacket. My nerves calm a

little. There are two strong bouncers not far away.

The cool night air welcomes me, the silence makes my ears whistle. As I cross the street, I pull on my jacket, looking back over my shoulder from time to time, but the street is almost deserted. My pursuers are nowhere to be seen.

Lydia

36.

I'm rooted to my chair, my eyes fixed on the figure on the other side of the street. It really is Bilal standing there. He's got his hands in his pockets, a hat pulled down to his eyebrows and he's staring at me. It is him and I know right away this means bad news.

Bilal takes his hand out of his pocket and for the duration of two heartbeats I'm convinced he's pulling out a gun. But he's only making a gesture with his hand and at that moment I become aware of a couple of shapes looming in the edge of my vision.

'Elisa,' I say hoarsely.

'Yes?' Elisa is playing noughts and crosses with Valerie on the back of the bill and looks up at me.

I'm surprised by how calm and controlled I am and how quickly I come up with a plan.

'Don't look now but Bilal is standing in front of the Pathé, and a couple of guys are walking towards the terrace. Please take Valerie away at once. Do it quickly and calmly, as if nothing's happening.'

You can say a lot about Elisa, but not that she doesn't react quickly. She stands up, gathers her things, takes Valerie by the hand and immediately goes inside with her. I stand up as well, but don't go with them. At least I've got Valerie out of the way.

I leave the terrace and walk down the pavement. The two boys follow at a distance. Are they part of Bilal's gang? Was it coincidence that these guys started moving after Bilal gestured?

A group of school kids go past and I walk in their midst, ignoring their irritated glances. A bus is coming down the street so I sprint to the stop. Bilal's friends are advancing on me.

The bus stops and they quicken their pace. I help an elderly couple climb in and keep them between me and the boys. They make no attempt to get on the bus, but stand there discussing something.

'Do you see those boys there?' I ask the driver. 'Would you mind making sure they don't get on?'

A glance at them is enough to make him close the doors immediately. The boys begin to run then and bang on the doors.

The bus driver accelerates, leaving them in a cloud of diesel smoke. Weak from shock, I look out of the back window and see them glaring at the bus. They've taken their hands out of their pockets, but I don't see any weapons. Now that I know I'm safe, I begin to doubt myself. Am I imagining things? Were those boys just trying to catch a bus?

I make a call to Elisa.

'Elisa?'

'We're fine,' she says, to my great relief. 'What was the matter back there?'

'Where is Bilal?' I interrupt.

'Lydia, I didn't see him. I just wanted to get Valerie away.'

'Oh.'

'There's no one around. Perhaps you were panicking about nothing. But I do understand, you know. Of course you were terrified.' Elisa's voice is sweet and understanding.

I let my head rest against the cold windowpane. 'I'm on the bus, Elisa, I'm going straight home. Will you bring Valerie back?'

'Of course. See you in a bit.'

I spot the white envelope on the doormat right away. I take the time to close the door behind me before I slit open the envelope with my index finger and pull out a tatty sheet of paper. Pasted on it is a collection of letters cut from a newspaper in a rainbow of inks.

YOU ARE A WHORE. I WILL KILL YOU.

I stare at the lettering for a long time. My mind buzzes like an overloaded network and my body sets off all of its alarm functions. I lock the front door and pull all the blinds down. Then I ring Elisa and ask her to take Valerie to her house instead. It's dark in the house with the blinds closed. The sun shines on the windows in vain and the birdsong coming from the tree in the front garden sounds like a protest. I put the letter in a plastic bag.

Raoul's number goes straight to voicemail. It's half past three, he's probably in the gym. I try not to sound too fraught as I leave a message, but my voice cracks and breaks. I tell him what has happened and say, 'You have to come home now.' When he hears the message he'll come, no doubt about that.

37.

Raoul doesn't come home. It turns half past four, then five, and no sign of him. I try his mobile every ten minutes, but nothing. Where the hell is he?

I peer through a chink in the blinds at every person who passes the house. They might be Raoul. Or Bilal.

The ringing of the telephone breaks the silence so unexpectedly that it's like a siren going off. I jump so much that I bang my hip against one of the cabinets. A chain of curses leaves my lips. The telephone stops, but then rings again a second later. That persistence can only be my mother.

Now I have to be careful or she'll twig that something is wrong.

'Lydia Salentijn.'

My mother's voice fills my ears. 'Hi darling, how are you?'

'Fine, and you? And Dad?'

'Fantastic. Your father's working on the barbecue, but it just doesn't want to light.'

Show some interest. Remember the chitchat. If she finds out what's going on she's capable of turning up here immediately and not leaving for weeks.

'Isn't it amazing that we can have barbecues so early in the year? I can't remember beginning in April before. Have you bought a new one by the way?' I ask, as I stare out through the blinds.

'Yes, your father insisted on an old-fashioned coal one. I'm curious whether it will work tomorrow. He'd better begin lighting it early if we want to eat before 10 p.m.'

'It'll be all right,' I say.

'We'll see. How did you go with the quiche?'

Shit, the quiche.

'Oh,' I say. 'I'm going to make it later.'

'Had you forgotten?' my mother asks, her tone suggesting that nothing would surprise her.

'No, no,' I say. Through the blinds I see a shadow moving outside and I drop the receiver. Putting it back to my ear, I keep an eye on the window. The shadow disappears and I hear the sound of a key in the lock.

'What are you doing?' my mother asks.

'Nothing, I dropped the phone. Listen, Mum, Raoul is just coming in so I'm going to hang up. See you tomorrow, all right?'

'Oh.' My mother sounds put out. 'Well, if you don't have time for me…I just wanted to ask if the quiche had turned out.'

'It'll be fine,' I promise. 'See you tomorrow!'

I put the phone down, sure that my mother now knows that something's up. We usually chat for hours, whether Raoul is there or not.

I rush into the hall to Raoul, taking the letter with me. 'I've only just heard your message,' he says. He looks stressed. 'Where's the letter?'

I hand it over.

He reads it through the plastic and his expression changes to anger.

'Will you come with me to the police?' I find myself crying.

He nods, wraps one arm around me and guides me out of the front door.

The police take it seriously. When the duty officer hears what happened earlier in the week, he calls over to his colleague. The sergeant who comes to us introduces himself as David Winsemius. He leads us to a small room and offers us chairs. And then I tell my story. I tell the sergeant about the threats at school, the damage to my car and finally I show him the letter.

Winsemius takes it from me and studies the sheet of paper for a while in silence. Finally he looks up and says, 'I see that you put the letter in a plastic bag, that's very good.'

He tells us that the technical department at the station will treat the letter with a special liquid that will render any fingerprints visible. Then he picks it up again and studies it carefully.

'May I ask you why you didn't report the threats at school to the police that same day, Mrs Salentijn?'

His words seem like an accusation to me, though they might not be intended that way. 'Because I didn't want to publicise it,' I say. 'I didn't want the police to come to the school. The school's reputation, you understand…'

Winsemius nods. 'Are there witnesses to the fact that Bilal Assrouti threatened you?'

'You might say that. The whole class was there,' Raoul says.

'Could you give me a few names?' Winsemius picks up a pen.

I hesitate. 'I'm not sure if that's sensible. They're all friends of Bilal's and as I just said, I'd rather that no one at school knew that I'd gone to the police.'

'I can't take anyone in for questioning without a shred of evidence.'

true, Lydia,' Raoul says. 'Just give him the names, and ... be able to go and get the guy. A night in the cells will do him some good.'

'I'm not so sure about that,' I say. 'They won't be able to hold him for long and the second he's free again, his first stop will be my house.'

'What do you want then?' Winsemius asks.

'I want to know if there are any fingerprints on the letter,' I say. 'And if there are, I want to know if they are Bilal's.'

'Then they'll have to get him in to take his fingerprints,' Raoul points out.

'Not necessarily. I've got a pile of test papers at home, one of them is his.'

'That's indirect evidence,' Winsemius explains. 'Your husband is right, we'd have to bring the boy in to take his fingerprints.'

I look down at the anonymous letter and sigh. 'So you'll have to detain Bilal whatever happens.'

'Yes, if we want to help you.'

I close my eyes. What's the best thing to do? Let them pick up Bilal and hope he leaves me alone afterwards, or wait until he gets fed up with intimidating me?

'Madam,' the sergeant says, and I look up at him. 'The young man in question hasn't done anything to you yet, but he has committed a punishable offence. We can hold him on those grounds, but for no longer than six hours. You can also have us take down what happened and keep it on file. Then we'll be able to keep an eye on things and intervene if you need our help.'

'Next thing he'll set fire to our house,' Raoul says. 'How do you know what's going on in his head? There's a good chance you won't get the opportunity to intervene. Lydia, you have to press charges and have them pick up that bastard.'

I shake my head. 'I think he'd just be even angrier. He's just venting his anger. If I don't react he'll stop of his own accord.

But I am reassured that you know about everything now, Sergeant.'

Winsemius nods and hands me his card. 'Here's my direct line, if there are any problems.'

38.

Did I do the right thing by not pressing charges? I don't know.
Now that I've got over the initial shock of the letter, it doesn't
seem as serious.

'I think you made the wrong decision,' Raoul says in the car.
'You're letting that kid get away with it.'

'I just don't want to make things any worse.'

'No, you're letting yourself be indoctrinated by the school.
Really Lydia, I don't understand your game plan.' Raoul turns
into our street, his eyebrows knitted.

'But I did tell the police about it, didn't I? They'll keep an eye
on Bilal, and at school they'll think that I did the right thing by
keeping quiet. That's perfect, isn't it?'

'I hope so.'

Luckily, the next day proves to be a good distraction. The
weather is lovely, the barbecue lights. I'm not going to bring up
Bilal. I don't want to think about school, Bilal and all the

problems of the past week anymore.

I put on summery clothes, a pink skirt and sleeveless top, and I dress Valerie in the sweetest lime-green dress. I bring along a change of clothes just in case she gets car sick. It's rare that she doesn't cover the back seat in vomit on longer car journeys. Before we leave, I give her a travel sickness pill.

'If you feel sick, you'll say, won't you?' I tell her, once we've set off.

She nods. 'I'm already feeling a bit sick, I think, Mummy.'

Raoul opens Valerie's window a little and she leans her cheek against the lower part of the window to breathe in the fresh air. We've just got onto the motorway when there's a muffled 'Mummy' from the back seat and I look around in alarm. Valerie is resting her chalk-white face against the headrest and holding her hand in front of her mouth.

'Do you need to be sick?'

She nods with growing panic in her eyes.

'Get the salad bowl then. Where is the salad bowl?'

'On the back shelf,' Raoul says with a glance in the rear-view mirror. He pulls over to the side of the road, but it's already too late. Unsettling noises and a sour smell fill the closed space of the car. I almost throw up myself. I cast open my door then Valerie's. The damage is worse than I thought. I'll have to boil those cuddly toys and I don't think we'll get that MP3 player working again. Thank god I've got a clean skirt for Valerie, and a bottle of water to clean her off and rinse her mouth out.

I take a deep breath of fresh air, bend over Valerie and free her from her seatbelt, which is sticky with lumps.

'My throat hurts!' Valerie wails.

Raoul surveys the disgusting mess on the backseat and turns to me. 'Why did you let her eat that biscuit before we left? You know it's all going to come out again.'

'If you were so sure about it, you should have put the salad bowl on her lap,' I snap back. 'And perhaps you should drive

163

more slowly. Anyone would get sick from all that accelerating and braking. I don't feel that well either, and I never get that when I drive.'

We continue our journey in pleasant silence. Thank god my parents live close by. My old neighbourhood drowses in the sun, awash with young foliage. This area used to be heavily populated with children, but these days it's quiet and the residents are mostly elderly.

We turn into my parents' street and, as usual, emotions wash over me when I see the white house. The sight rouses precious memories. This is where I grew up, I played here, that's where I used to throw marbles, there is where I drew on the pavings with my chalks, and here's where Elisa and I used to push the doll's pram around.

I get out and survey the surroundings.

'Mummy!' Valerie knocks on her window and I help her out.

'I'm thirsty,' she complains, but then her face clears. 'Grandad! Grandad!'

I turn around and see my father. He's a tall man with a full head of grey hair. A burst of love and pride rushes through me.

'Hello!' my father calls out. He catches Valerie, who flies at him, and comes over to us, carrying her. We take the garden path together.

'Where's Mum?' I ask.

'In the garden. Isn't it lovely weather?'

'Perfect barbecuing weather,' Raoul comments.

He hates visiting people, but messing around with a barbecue and sitting in the garden with a glass of beer is something he loves.

It is wonderful to be in their enormous back garden, sitting in the shadow of the trees. I used to climb these trees with Elisa; we'd build dens and play Barbies endlessly on a rug on the lawn. In the winter, we'd ride our sleigh and in the summer we'd lie around the pool that my parents built at the bottom of the garden. It was a fantastic childhood.

I kiss my mother, and as usual my instinct is to handle her like she's made out of china. Rosalie van Woerkom is a handsome woman in her fifties. She's well groomed and elegant, always taken for younger than she is.

'How are you, darling? You look a bit peaky.'

'Oh well,' I say.

My mother carries on studying me. 'What happened?' she asks in a no-nonsense tone.

39.

Sometimes I don't feel like one of a pair of identical twins, but the third in a set of triplets. My mother has the same telepathic gift and can see right through me, in the same way as I can see through Elisa. But while Elisa always remains calm, my mother gets hysterical at the slightest hint that either of her daughters is in trouble. I'm certain that she won't be able to sleep if I tell her what the problem is.

It's better not to say anything. Luckily, pouring drinks and serving canapés is enough to keep her occupied for the moment.

A while later, we are chatting and drinking. Raoul is at his best, he can be very charming if he wants to be, but I wonder whether he'd be so relaxed if I'd decided to drink and he was driving home.

'What time is Elisa coming?' He looks around as if he's expecting my sister to jump out from behind a tree. 'I thought we were quite late.'

'She'll be here soon. She had another shoot with an actor and today was the only day he could do,' my mother says.

'An actor? Who?' Raoul asks with interest.

'Oh, I don't know. She did tell me but I never remember names,' Mum answers. 'Someone from one of those soaps.'

'Are you gossiping about me?' calls out a friendly voice from near the house.

I turn towards the direction of the sound and see my twin sister coming down the path towards us. It's perfect weather for the new outfit we bought yesterday, but my twin sister – how is it possible that we're twins! – is wearing a dark blue pair of work trousers instead, with a white jumper and chunky shoes. She looks as though she's moonlighting as a builder. It's spring for god's sake. I meet her halfway across the garden and give her a hug.

'How are you?' I ask, kissing her on the cheek.

Elisa returns my kiss. 'It's me who should be asking you. Has anything else happened?'

I shake my head as we make our way slowly over to the others. 'I haven't told Mum and Dad, so don't bring it up.'

'Why not?' Elisa smiles and waves at our parents.

'They'll only get worried, and they can't do anything about it.'

We've reached the table and chairs under the trees and Elisa hugs Mum and Dad and then Raoul before she bends down to cuddle Valerie. 'Beer please, Dad,' she replies to his question.

'How long have you been drinking beer?' Mum asks.

'For ages,' Elisa answers. 'But not constantly!'

Raoul grins and takes a sip from his bottle. 'Good choice, Elisa. Nothing nicer than a cool beer on a hot day.'

'Did you come on the train?' Mum frets.

'No, I've borrowed Thomas's car.'

Dad fetches a beer from the kitchen and puts the bottle and a glass down on the table.

'So, sweetheart, how are things? Taken any good photos recently?'

'I had to do the new actor from *Good Times*,' Elisa says. 'A young guy, lots of chitchat. Thought he'd got it made in his new role, never stopped talking.'

'That's often the best way to get good shots, better than people who sit there waiting for the flash,' Raoul says.

'True, but he was really posing. He was talking but he was very aware of how he would appear, you know?' Elisa rests her elbow on the arm of the chair, rests her chin on her index finger and stares mysteriously towards a single point, as if there were a camera there. 'Would you like to see them?'

She gets her camera out of her bag and fiddles with it. At that moment I remember something and grab for my own bag. 'That's right! I've got photos with me too. We've finally had the pictures of our skiing holiday developed.'

Mum and Dad shuffle their chairs towards me and soon they are smiling away. Almost every photo features Valerie: Valerie in her pink ski suit on the piste, Valerie in the local restaurant, Valerie on the balcony of the chalet.

'Were you and Raoul there too?' my mother jokes. 'Wow, that's a nice one! Can I have that too? Could you get me an enlargement?'

'Of course.' I turn to my sister and give her the photos that our parents have just looked at. Elisa is silent, glaring. I'm about to ask what the matter is, when she puts her camera back in her bag and takes the photos from me.

Elisa

40.

My mind at rest, I walk away from Night City towards the station. The evening air is chilly. This is a part of Rotterdam I never venture into and I don't feel entirely comfortable, but that's probably got more to do with the late hour than the area. It's half past eleven.

A taxi turns into the street. I wave it down. A dark-skinned young driver winds down the window.

'Could you take me to Kralingen?'

He nods and I climb into the back and give him my address. As we drive, I stare out of the window at the dark streets of Rotterdam, not really seeing them. We drive over Hofplein, across the Pompen Bridge and towards the Goudse Canal.

My thoughts wander as the taxi drives through the night. After a while I begin to concentrate and I realise that I don't recognise these streets. Where in god's name are we? Shouldn't we have got to Kralingen ages ago?

I frown and peer through the window trying to orientate

myself. All these dark narrow streets…Why is he taking these rather than the well-lit main roads?

'Excuse me, aren't we making a bit of a detour?'

The driver doesn't reply. He slows for a speed bump, imperturbable. He changes up to third, turns into a dark side street. I try to look at his face in the rear-view mirror, but it's too dark to make him out. My fear grows with every foot we drive.

We cross Maas Boulevard, which runs next to Kralingen. I try again, my voice trembling. 'If you turn off here, we'll be there. Why aren't you turning?'

I don't get any reaction and my panic increases. I lean back against the seat, drenched in sweat, and look out of the window. Where are we going? What does he want from me?

The tall square buildings of the Erasmus University loom up against the dark sky. We turn into Burgermeester Oud Avenue. The driver stops at Graven Road and looks left and then right.

Left, I think feverishly. Please, left.

He accelerates and goes straight, towards the Kralingse Woods. My hands are ice-cold and I can smell my own sweat. My eyes shoot from left to right, in the hope of seeing another car. Then I could jump out of the car and scream for help.

We are the only car at the black edge of the woods.

The car crawls through the woods. I could jump out now. Should I do that? If I run into the woods, I could hide. But I'd have to take my shoes off first because I won't get far in these heels.

I bend over very carefully and remove my right shoe. The driver glances at me in the rear-view mirror. I ignore him, pretend to be scratching my ankle and lean back again with the irritated expression of someone who believes she's being conned into paying more. I hold the shoe discreetly in my hand then work off my left shoe with my bare right foot.

Okay, now open the door. Carefully? Or suddenly?

I opt for the careful option and look in the opposite direction as I fumble for the door. My trembling fingers find the handle and I pull on it. There's a small click, but the door doesn't open. I try again and break out into a sweat – the door's locked. Locked! That shithead has turned on the central locking. Oh god, I'm in trouble. What can I do? Hit him on the head with one of my heels? My whole body is shaking. My legs have turned to jelly.

I fish my mobile from my bag. One text and the whole Rotterdam police force will be here. Why didn't I think of this sooner?

I cough a little to cover the sound of my fingers keying in the message. I won't have to write much: HELP! KIDNAPPED! K. WOODS!

I've finished keying in KIDNAPPED! when the taxi comes to a halt. I look up in shock.

The driver has turned around and is looking at me. Dark eyes with an evil look. I shove my mobile between my thighs.

'Give it here,' he says calmly. He holds out his hand, but instead of my phone I grab for my shoe which I'd put down the seat next to me, and stab at him. He grasps me by the wrist and turns it so sharply that I drop the shoe with a cry. His other hand grapples between my legs and I scream. He gets my mobile, opens the dashboard unit and throws it in there. Then he turns back and studies me.

'So,' he begins. 'I heard you were looking for me.'

Bilal Assrouti.

All I can do is stare, swallow.

'I take it that I don't have to introduce myself,' Bilal says. 'And you don't have to tell me who you are. I know why you're following me. This stops here.'

I nod dumbly. All kinds of things go around in my mind, what I could say, how I could explain, back out, apologise, but words don't seem enough when I look into Bilal's cruel eyes.

'I'm…I'm sorry,' I stutter.

'I'm sure you are.' Bilal looks me up and down in a detached way.

I try to think of something to say, but I can't come up with anything. It seems better to hold my tongue.

Bilal turns his back on me to light up a cigarette and inhales. 'You're her sister.'

It's impossible to deny that, so I nod.

Bilal observes me in the rear-view mirror. 'Twins then?'

'Identical.'

There's a pause. Bilal smokes and I study him in the mirror. A street lamp shines into the car and I can see enough of his face to feel a little less uneasy.

Unexpectedly our eyes meet, mine scared and his hard and accusing.

'You're going around looking for me and asking questions about me,' he says. 'I don't like that.'

I wipe my palms on my trousers and say nothing.

'Have you got any idea how pissed off I was when I heard that you were asking people about me?' He spits the words out. 'Any idea what it feels like to be ambushed by six policemen when you're walking down the street? What it feels like to see your picture in the paper and on the news and to be given the cold shoulder wherever you go after that? To fail your exams and not be able to find a job? Well, do you know what it feels like?'

I press against the back of my seat, say nothing.

'Well?' he shouts. 'You know how that feels? Not to have any chance of getting a job because you're Moroccan? To be refused service in bars and restaurants, to be discriminated against your whole life in this fucking shithole country that pretends to be so tolerant?'

'No,' I whisper.

He twists around and blows smoke through the car. I start to feel suffocated and breathe in short gasps.

'You don't know,' he says. 'You haven't got a fucking clue.'

I could argue with that, but I don't.

'I'm…I'm sorry.'

'Good.' His voice sounds friendly, threateningly friendly as he opens the glovebox and gets out a dark object. Then he turns off the central locking, nods at my door and says, 'Get out then.'

41.

I'm frozen to my seat, I can't move. Bilal walks around the taxi and opens my door. He orders me out of the car. I get out with stiff, unwilling legs. What next? What is he doing? What has he got in his hand?

I stand on the grass verge in my bare feet. Bilal is a few steps away from me. The few seconds I'd need to move forward and punch him would be enough for him to shoot me dead.

We look at each other; the silence is broken only by the whispering treetops.

'Turn around and walk into the woods.' He points towards the trees, moving gently in the wind.

'Please…I didn't mean anything by it. I only wanted to ask you something about—'

'Turn around,' he raises his voice.

I see him put his hand in his pocket. I turn on shaking legs and walk around the taxi. As I walk towards the trees, I realise that I should have jumped back into the taxi and turned on the central locking. But it's too late for that now.

I hear footsteps behind me – Bilal following me at a distance, his eyes boring into my back, forcing me to the edge of the woods. Something in his hand.

Could I sprint into the dark enclosure? Did Lydia go through the same before she was shot? This crippled, passive waiting? No, Lydia would be gone by now. Lydia would have got behind the wheel and torn off. I can run as fast as I like, but one well-aimed shot will put an end to that.

Oh, this walking, this torturous waiting for the sound, an explosion in my body. I stumble and fall forwards. Muffled footsteps approach me through the grass, and I crawl towards the bushes.

The footsteps stop and something is thrown at me. A hand grenade! All those newspaper articles about terrorist attacks, complete with bombs and hand grenades rush before my eyes.

I get up and stumble away. Into the woods. Quick!

A loud bang breaks the silence. I trip and fall flat on the ground again. But I don't feel any pain and when I try to move I can.

An engine starts up, then tyres screech. Bilal Assrouti is driving along Kralingse Road. I watch the vehicle until it's far away, no more than a yellow speck. It's the middle of the night and I'm sitting on the dark edge of the woods. I cry with relief that I'm alone again, that I'm still alive.

I sit there, one moment laughing, the next crying again and completely confused. At last I stand up and hobble towards the road. A light gleams in the grass. I walk over to it and stare in disbelief at my mobile. I put it in my pocket and walk barefoot down the road.

I can barely get the door of my house open. I've no energy left after that endless walk. I try to slide the key into the slot with trembling fingers, but I can't. Finally I give up, let my arms hang next to my body and take a few deep breaths. After a while, I try again and this time the key glides easily into the slot.

My hallway. My house. I lock the front door and turn all the catches. Once I'm sure that no one can get in, I open the door to the sitting room and turn on the light. I'm home. I'm still alive. I'm not lying dead somewhere in the woods. I'm safe.

I go into the sitting room and see the half-empty glass of wine I've left on the coffee table. Next to it are the remote control and the television guide. Did I watch TV before going to Night City? Did I drink a glass of wine? I can only vaguely remember it, as if it all took place in another life. Nothing is the same anymore.

I drink the lukewarm white wine. Drink is not really the right word, I throw it back and feel an urgent need for more. For something stronger, even. I repress the urge and peer into the empty glass. What possessed Bilal to scare the living daylights out of me? Was his plan to terrify me or did he really want to shoot me? Why did he change his mind?

With heavy, exhausted steps, I take the empty wineglass into the kitchen and check the locks on the kitchen door. I turn out the lights in the sitting room and go upstairs. Something moves behind me.

I turn around, but there's nothing on the stairs beneath me. The coats in the hall hang motionless on the rack, but my feeling of being alone has disappeared.

I drag myself up the stairs, turn on all the lights and get undressed in my bedroom. Without bothering to wash or take off my make-up, I crawl under my duvet and pull it up over my head.

42.

'He did it,' I say. 'He must have done. I don't know why he didn't shoot me, but he scared me witless.'

It's two days since my adventure with Bilal, five o'clock in the afternoon and I'm sitting around a table in a brasserie with Thomas and Sylvie. Like me, Thomas chooses his own work hours and Sylvie has left the salon an hour early to listen to my story.

They are sitting rather pointedly apart and acting normal; I sense that they've agreed on this approach. I appreciate it. I don't know if I could bear them sitting next to me like a pair of turtle doves.

They both look at me with a combination of fascination and horror.

'I still can't believe that you went to look for him.' Sylvie shakes her head. 'I did warn you, Elisa.'

'And why didn't you tell me what you had planned?' Thomas asks as he lights up a cigarette. 'You only asked me if I'd go with you, you didn't say why you wanted to go there.'

'Because you'd have tried to stop me,' I tell him.

'You're right about that,' Thomas says. 'And I'd have even made sure you didn't leave your house.'

'You'd probably have just gone with her,' Sylvie says and we all laugh. But then there's another silence.

I rotate a beer mat in my hand. 'And yet I find it strange that Bilal didn't hurt me. Everything suggests that he's the murderer, but I can't figure out why he let me go.'

'Why not?' Thomas says. 'You're no threat to him, he just wanted to scare you off.'

'He would never have got away with it if he'd shot you,' Sylvie adds. 'You asked so many people about him.'

I stare ahead. Yes, that's probably the reason that I'm still alive. To Bilal I was just an irritating fly buzzing around his head, and he wanted to swat me off.

'He must have done it though,' I muse. 'I mean, who else would have wanted to kill Lydia?'

We look at each other.

'She was good at getting people's backs up, but whether that's a reason to murder someone…' Thomas replies.

'I wasn't that fond of her either, but again that's a stretch.' Sylvie is apologetic, but I nod that I know what she means about Lydia.

'But you can't dismiss it,' Thomas says. 'What we might consider a weak motive might be reason enough for someone to commit murder. There are enough nutters around.'

'Her colleagues?' Sylvie suggests. 'There was a lot going on at that school.'

'I thought about that too, and so did the police,' I say. 'They questioned everyone but nothing came to light.'

'That doesn't mean they didn't have motives,' Thomas counters, 'just that the police couldn't find them. You'd be better off talking to her colleagues than hanging about in nightclubs and getting into cars with strange men in the middle of the night, Elisa.'

We laugh again and look around to see where our drinks have got to.

'I'll go to Rotterdam College,' I say. 'Or no, I'll go to Jasmine's house. It would be better to see her when she's got time to talk.'

Thomas goes to the bar to see where our drinks are and Sylvie's eyes track his every movement.

'Hello!' I tease.

She looks at me and lets out a guilty laugh. 'He's really nice, isn't he?'

I glance at Thomas at the bar, his broad shoulders, longish dark hair. 'Yes.'

Thomas returns with the drinks. 'Here we are, juice for the ladies and a beer for sir.'

He sets the drinks down in front of us with a flamboyant gesture.

My mobile rings.

'Elisa speaking.'

It's a fairly desperate Raoul on the line. He's horribly busy at work and the after-school club isn't going to stay open late enough for all the overtime he needs to put in. Could I help?

'Of course,' I say, glancing at my watch. 'What were you going to eat? Do you have anything in?'

'Sandwiches?'

'I thought as much. I'll go do some shopping with Val, and then I'll cook. See you whenever you get in.' I cut off his heart-felt thanks by hanging up.

'Help brigade on call again?' Thomas asks.

'He doesn't ask for that much help,' I put him straight. 'Raoul has got everything perfectly sorted.'

'I keep seeing someone else in his house more and more often when I cycle past,' Thomas says.

'What are you doing cycling past there so often?'

Thomas sips his beer and avoids my eyes. And I understand. Even though he's got something with Sylvie now, he's still not completely over me. Although I've never told him, there's no doubt that Thomas knows I've got a 'weakness' for Raoul, to put it lightly. Is he worried that I'll get into a relationship with Raoul now that the coast is clear? Is that the reason he's finally succumbed to Sylvie's advances?

As I cycle to Valerie's school, I reflect on this further and when I get to the playground I'm smiling. It's a smile I immediately feel guilty about – why shouldn't I let Sylvie have Thomas if I don't want to go out with him myself?

Valerie launches herself into my arms. 'Elisa!'

She holds me tightly, pressing her face so hard against me that I'm touched, and then concerned. Maybe I haven't been paying her enough attention recently.

'Where's Daddy? Are you staying for dinner?' Valerie asks both questions in a single breath.

'Daddy will be a bit late today. And yes, I'm staying for dinner. We'll go and do the shopping together.'

'Yes!' Valerie shouts. She says goodbye to the leader and skips out of school. 'We're not having brocklies are we?'

'No, we're not having broccoli.' I unlock my bike and put Val on the back.

'What then?' she asks.

'What would you like?'

'Chips!' Valerie shouts.

'We could also make a nice casserole.'

'Can I help?' she asks.

I nod and Valerie wraps her arms around my waist.

'Just like with Mummy,' she says. 'Mummy always let me help too.'

43.

The kitchen fills with the smell of fresh herbs: rosemary, basil and thyme. I love herbs and always use them generously. As the dish bubbles away in the oven, I lay the table and set a candelabra down in the middle.

'Can I light it?' Valerie asks.

'Soon,' I promise. 'When Daddy's home.'

'Mummy and Daddy had candles as well,' Valerie comments, giving me second thoughts about the candelabra. As I hesitate over whether to take it away or not, the doorbell rings. Valerie runs to the bay window and looks out.

'It's Jennifer's mummy!' She rushes to open the door.

Jasmine is standing on the doorstep holding a large pan, a house key dangling from her fingers. We look at each other in surprise.

'Hi,' I say.

'Hey,' she says. 'You're here? I didn't know that.'

I contemplate the pan in her hands and Jasmine notices me

looking. 'I sometimes bring Raoul something to eat. I know this is a busy week for him.'

'Oh, that's very kind, but it's really not necessary. I've cooked.'

'It smells delicious,' Jasmine gushes. 'Shall I just put this in the fridge then? Then he can have it tomorrow.'

I step aside and Jasmine comes in, carrying the pan like a carer from Meals on Wheels. A carer who feels remarkably at home here. She moves things around in the fridge to make space for the pan, then her gaze rests on the table. 'That looks cosy.'

'Yes, doesn't it?' I reply neutrally. 'Raoul called to see if I could help. He has to work late.'

'He is busy,' Jasmine says. 'I'm amazed by how he can combine his job with looking after Valerie. That's why I sometimes bring round food, or we eat together.'

I remember Thomas saying he'd seen someone in the house. 'Together?'

'Jennifer hardly eats a thing so I always cook too much,' Jasmine explains. 'And I don't know about you, but I always hate cooking for just myself.'

'But aren't you married?'

'My husband is a pilot so he's not home much. Very unsociable.'

'Aha,' is all I say.

'So…' Jasmine puts her hands together and looks around smiling. 'Everything's under control here. I'll get going.'

'Would you like a drink? My dish needs at least forty-five more minutes in the oven. I was about to have a glass of wine.'

'Oh…' Jasmine hesitates. 'I'm not sure…Well, why not. I'll just get Jennifer though – she's on her own in the house.'

'Would you like red or white?'

'Red,' Jasmine says and leaves.

I get two wine glasses out, fill one with red and the other with white and put them on the coffee table. Through the bay window

I see Jasmine returning with Jennifer. Once they've come in, the girls go off to play and Jasmine and I sit down opposite each other a little awkwardly.

I don't know Jasmine that well, though she was a good friend of Lydia's. She seems quite nice. She's also pretty, with curly red hair and warm brown eyes, but she looks pale and I notice the rings under her eyes. 'You look pretty,' I blurt out.

Jasmine has just picked up her glass and looks surprised. 'Everything's such chaos inside my head,' she says. 'I'm really looking forward to the summer holidays. I can hardly keep it together at school.'

'Why not?' I ask.

'The atmosphere has changed so much, I really miss Lydia. Everything is different. Student numbers are dropping all the time, at least five colleagues have been told that their contracts won't be renewed and it's just downright unpleasant there.'

'How terrible.'

'It had been on the cards for a while, but after Lydia's death the number of new students signing up plummeted. Hardly surprising. I wouldn't want to send my child to a school where the teachers are threatened with weapons.'

'Who exactly has been fired?'

'I'm not sure which of us you know, but perhaps you know Luke Rombouts.'

I'm shocked. 'Luke! Why?'

Jasmine shrugs. 'The excuse was that they wanted someone with more teaching experience, but that doesn't make sense. Luke is an excellent teacher. Personally I think he was fired because it got out that he was gay. He'd already been bumped out of two other schools, and he'd decided to keep quiet about it, until he had a permanent contract. He confided in Lydia. He'd have been better off not telling her because she told me, and I'm afraid she might have told other people too. In deepest confidence, of course, but if you want to be really sure a secret won't get out, you just have to keep your mouth shut. And Lydia wasn't so good at that.'

I listen with mixed feelings. On one hand I'm annoyed that Jasmine is talking about my sister in this way, on the other I sense that this was exactly what happened. I remember a group of us going out to eat at Oliva one evening and Lydia mentioning Luke's secret. I'm sure he didn't appreciate that.

'She didn't do it deliberately,' I say, feeling the need to defend my sister. 'She was just a terrible gossip.'

'I know that,' Jasmine murmurs. 'And I miss her so much. It's so strange not seeing her at school anymore. I can't get used to it.'

She's got tears in her eyes and I feel my own brimming up. I wonder if I should tell her about my adventure with Bilal, but decide not to. Instead I ask, 'The police can't get much on Bilal Assrouti. Do you think he's innocent?'

'Everything seems to point towards him but I just can't imagine that he really did it.' Jasmine sips her wine. 'I don't mean that he was an angel – I had problems with Bilal too – but I've never felt threatened by him. It was all bravado, you know, it doesn't mean anything.'

'But Bilal pulled a knife,' I remind her. 'And it wasn't long after that that Lydia was shot.'

Jasmine sighs. 'I know, that's quite a coincidence. But that doesn't mean he shot her. He was mouthy but so are a lot of them. You know, it's so easy to point the finger at a boy like that. A teacher at a school with a lot of Muslim students is shot. Conclusion – a Muslim student did it. But what if she'd been a teacher at St Lawrence's College? Would the media be so quick to condemn a difficult white student?'

We sit there for a while drinking our wine.

'Jasmine, I want to ask you something,' I say. 'It's a bit of a strange subject, but did Lydia ever discuss her marriage with you?'

'What do you mean?'

'Every marriage has its problems,' I reply. 'I wonder if she'd have confided in you if she'd had problems with Raoul. I mean you were close friends, weren't you?'

'Yes.'

'So she did confide in you?'

'She'd sometimes tell me about the arguments she had with Raoul, and I told her the things that bothered me about my husband. But what are you getting at? I presume she also talked about that kind of thing with you.'

I ignore that last comment. 'How serious do you think their arguments were? What were they about?'

'I'm not sure exactly,' Jasmine reflects. 'Just the usual, that Raoul would rather she stopped working. He can be a bit old-fashioned, don't you think?'

'Do you think Raoul was seeing anyone else?'

Jasmine peers into her glass for a long time before answering. 'Yes,' she says quietly. 'I saw him in the Euromast restaurant just before Lydia's death and he was with another woman. I told Lydia about it, not that she did much about it. Raoul was on a pretty long leash with her. She really loved him, you know.'

'Yes,' I say in a choked voice. 'I know that.'

'Are you all right? You look so pale.'

'I've got a bit of a headache.'

'Then I'll get going. We've still got to eat.' Jasmine stands up and calls her daughter.

I watch them crossing the street. Jasmine saw Raoul with another woman. That means that Lydia and I weren't the only women in his life. I recall Jasmine's expression when she came across me here unexpectedly, the house key she was holding and I wonder how much to trust her story.

44.

'Jasmine has just been round,' I mention as we're eating.

'And I played with Jennifer,' Valerie adds.

'Oh?' Raoul says with little interest.

'She brought a pan of food with her.'

'She does that quite often.' Raoul's voice doesn't sound as grateful or tender as I'd expected, giving me a sudden and shameful vision of myself as a jealous, suspicious wife. Look at me here, at my sister's dining table, in her house, with her husband. There's no doubt Lydia sat here with exactly the same feelings and had exactly the same kind of conversation with Raoul. Thank god I put the candelabra away at the last minute.

My appetite has disappeared and I push my plate away.

'Finished already?' Raoul, who is clearly enjoying his food, looks up in surprise.

'It's a little rich,' I say.

He nods, but that doesn't stop him from taking another

serving. 'It's delicious,' he says with such a sweet smile that I forget Jasmine and her pan of food in an instant. 'You're a good cook, just as good as Lydia.'

Go on Raoul, put Lydia back in between us again, help me remember the terrible reason I'm sitting here in her chair, remind me that she'll always be joining us.

I don't wait for Raoul to take a third portion. 'I have to go, I've still got a tonne of things to do this evening.'

He doesn't protest. No disappointed 'must you go?' or 'stay a little bit longer'. But his eyes do follow me as I get my bag from the window seat, put on my jacket and button it up.

'Bye-bye, Valerie darling. Do I get a kiss?'

Valerie jumps up from her chair, runs to me and gives me a cuddle. 'Will you come again soon?'

I promise I will and give Raoul a cheerful wave.

'I'll see you out.' Raoul follows me into the hall. 'You finish your dinner,' he says to Valerie, and closes the door behind me. Then he turns to me and looks at me with that special, half smile I've always found so sexy. Again I feel my belly churning.

He looks me in the eyes and whispers, 'Thank you.'

Nothing more. We're so close in the enclosed hall. For a second I think he's going to kiss me, but he turns around and goes back to Valerie without saying another word.

Am I disappointed? Would I really have let him kiss me, here in Lydia's house? What am I expecting from Raoul? I don't even know what I expect from myself.

As I cycle home, my thoughts take another direction. I think back to my conversation with Jasmine and what she said about Luke and Lydia.

I should have a chat with Luke. But how should I approach this? I barely know him. I can't ask him right out if he thinks Lydia was responsible for him losing his job, and how angry he was about it.

He was still working at the school when she was killed, so it can't have been him. But did he sense he was about to be sacked? Did he already know about it? Did Lydia just give him that last push towards the dole?

I decide not to approach Luke, but to run this information by Noorda. After my adventures with Bilal, I don't feel like playing detective anymore.

At home, there's a message on my answering machine. It's someone from a women's magazine I regularly take portrait photos for. I haven't had many commissions from them recently – if you turn anyone down a couple of times in a row, they look for someone else to use. But it seems the magazine hasn't forgotten me because another photographer is ill and now they want me to photograph a well-known writer. Can I call back on the editor's mobile?

I stare at my answering machine undecided. I haven't done anything for ages. But the thought of work gives me a buzz somewhere deep down. For the first time.

Photography has always been my great love and the realisation that I feel the same way about it despite everything else changing in my life sends a wave of relief through me.

I'll go back to work. I'll accept that job and take some good photos of the writer. I'll open my studio again and force my way back into the world of photography. Maybe I'll even travel, do a reportage piece. Edinburgh Festival is coming up. Last year I went to a festival in Lucerne and took pictures which I sold afterwards to a travel magazine.

I pick up the phone.

The writer is an attractive but serious man of around forty-five who sits up very straight and has rather pointedly stacked up some copies of his new novel on a table. He is being interviewed in his home in Utrecht and I've taken the train there to do the photos afterwards.

It's a wonderful feeling, holding my camera again, setting up my equipment and working out the best composition. Photography is fantastic. The man facing me constructs a world with words, but I write with light. A good photo can say so much, and it's often all about the details.

I've got the newest digital camera on the market, with a super-fast shutter speed. I took some wonderful shots of fireworks with it, with long trails of light. Those photos are hanging in my studio now, in the exhibition space.

As the writer straightens his pile of books and pulls down his jacket, I put up a circular silver screen to reflect the light. I move the pile of books into the frame to create depth in the photo and focus on his eyes.

'I'm just going to click away,' I announce. 'Try to look as relaxed as possible.'

For most people that's a difficult request. As soon as a camera is pointed at them they stiffen and all spontaneity is lost. I chat away casually to relax the atmosphere, to reanimate his face. When did your book come out? How many is that now? You've written a lot, haven't you? I don't know where writers get so many ideas from. What's your source of inspiration? Meanwhile I capture an unexpected smile with my camera.

Not that an unnatural pose is the only problem I have to deal with when I'm taking pictures. I've been working for fifteen minutes before I spot that the writer's fly is open. How could I have missed that? Of course I can use a close-up, but the magazine asked for a full-length shot.

For form's sake, I snap away as I try to work out the best way to solve this. I've got the impression that this man has quite a well-developed ego and that a direct approach won't increase the chances of a successful shoot.

'I think we've got a few good shots there. Lovely, but…'

'But what?' the writer asks.

'Maybe it would be nice if you put that pile of books on your lap and read one.'

Getting the book in the picture is always attractive for writers and the man immediately collects the books. I click away. Lovely, at least I've got that, despite it being an extremely traditional photograph. Not something I'd want to hand in, but there's no alternative.

I carry on for so long that the author takes a toilet break. When he returns his zips are closed and I take a few more shots of him. Shortly after that I'm leaving with a series of wonderful pictures: nonchalant, stylish and, most importantly, with all the author's zips done up. In the train back to Rotterdam, I realise that during that hour I felt fully myself again.

45.

Sometimes a fear of forgetting Lydia takes hold of me. Not really forgetting, of course, but it's as if the real Lydia keeps stepping backwards, leaving only a weak reflection behind. She's been dead for two months now and I don't want to say I've forgotten what her face looks like, or that the sound of her voice has faded in my memory, but the image of her has become blurred in my mind.

The fact that we're identical twins should give me a clear visualisation of her face, but it doesn't. I catch myself staring in the mirror for minutes on end, my nose almost pressed to the glass, looking for her. The sun has given me a rash of freckles on my nose. Did she have those too? I don't know, I never paid much attention. And that mole on her chin, was it on the right or the left?

How can I have forgotten something like that when I've known her face for thirty years? What else am I going to forget?

I put a large picture of her on my desk and throw myself into my work. I begin with two days of cleaning. I tackle all the shelves and drawers, carrying bags of old paperwork to the recycling bin. I take every commission I'm given, which means I regularly go off on jobs, and if I don't have any work, I roam around with my camera.

Summer is now in full swing in Rotterdam. They've built an artificial beach next to the River Maas again, where young and old lie sunning themselves or play ball games. I wander around, snapping away. The summer carnival is upon us too, a street party full of colours and music. My camera captures everything and forces me back into the world of the living.

The pictures in the exhibition space in my studio need changing. I take all the frames down and spend a whole morning selecting new photos. I'm re-hanging them, my neck dripping with sweat, when someone comes in.

I hang onto the frame to stop it falling from its hook, and glance over my shoulder. Behind me is a slender, well-dressed woman in her mid-forties. She smiles at me in a way that reminds me of someone.

'Good afternoon,' she says.

'Good afternoon.' I let go of the frame, keeping my hands ready to catch it, but it stays up. I turn around with a smile. 'Can I help you?'

The woman hesitates and looks around her. 'Actually I wanted to ask something, but am I disturbing you?'

'Absolutely not. What did you want to know?'

'It might sound a bit odd,' the woman begins, 'but I think you're a friend of my daughter's.'

I take a good look at the woman and see that she's nearer fifty than forty. She appeared much younger at first glance. Her hair has been highlighted in a natural way with different shades of blonde, and her make-up is lightweight but effective. She's a beautiful woman and it's not surprising she looks familiar. I don't even have to ask who her daughter is.

'Sylvie…' I say at once.

She smiles in surprise and holds out her hand. 'Yes, that's right. I'm Linda, Sylvie's mother.'

I shake her hand and introduce myself. 'Elisa van Woerkom. Would you like a cup of tea?'

'Yes, please.' She looks relieved. This reminds me that Sylvie hasn't been in touch with her mother for years, and there are reasons for that. I'd better be careful. After all, I've no idea what Sylvie's mother wants.

I go to the kitchen and put on the kettle. Linda follows me.

'We can sit here,' I say, gesturing towards the kitchen table.

Sylvie's mother sits down and waits until I've finished making the tea and then she launches into her speech.

'If you're such a good friend of Sylvie's, you'll know that we haven't been in touch for years. It hurts.' Linda drops a sugar lump into her cup and stirs it. 'Over the years I've tried everything to get back in touch with her, but she doesn't want to know.'

I remain silent.

'Do you know what happened?' Linda looks up at me with the same clear blue eyes as Sylvie.

'Sylvie has told me a few things,' I say.

Linda purses her lips. She doesn't seem to have much confidence in Sylvie, which diminishes my sympathy.

'Might I ask what she told you?' Linda says.

I begin to wonder what I'm doing here with this woman. Can't she just approach Sylvie? On the other hand, perhaps this is a good opportunity to reunite mother and daughter. Wouldn't it be wonderful if I could orchestrate that? I get a sudden vision of them arm in arm with tears in their eyes, thanking me for my help.

'Sylvie told me that her father abandoned her and she didn't get on with your new boyfriend. She told me that he abused her and you didn't want to believe her.' I keep my voice as neutral as

193

possible, but deep inside are the first stirrings of anger.

Linda looks up from her tea.

'That's not true,' she says.

I make a vague gesture with my hand.

'It's not,' Linda insists. 'He's not that kind of man, I wouldn't have married him last year if he was.'

In order to do something with my hands, I pick up my cup and take a sip.

'I don't know him,' I say as Linda continues to stare at me. 'But you do hear of women turning a blind eye to certain character traits in men. How many women were abused by their fathers while their mothers failed to notice? That doesn't mean nothing happened.'

'You're right about that, but it's really not true,' Linda says. 'You should know that Sylvie…what can I say…that she's got an active imagination. When she was a teenager, for instance, she told everyone that her father was dying. Of course there are all kinds of psychological explanations for that, but she told her teacher that her father was dying of cancer, with tears in her eyes. To prevent her from mentioning it to me, she managed to convince her that I didn't want to talk about it. She said I couldn't handle the situation, that I never got out of bed and that she was doing all the housework. This earned her a lot of goodwill at school. Hadn't done her homework? The teachers overlooked it. One mark too low to make the grade? The teachers would find her a couple of extra per cent. She wasn't a very talented student and the exams were too difficult for her, but she got through.'

I shrug. I don't see what this has to do with her stepfather.

'And just because she was a little creative with the truth at school means that she made up that story about being abused?'

'That's a nice way of putting it – creative with the truth.' Linda smiles, but it's not a happy smile. 'That's what she always was. Her father didn't abandon her in the way she's had you believe. Martin made quite reasonable efforts to stay in touch with her. He phoned, wrote letters, sent presents, came round to visit, but Sylvie just didn't want to know. He'd left the house and she felt so terribly abandoned that he could never make it up to her. Sylvie's like that – inflexible. You're either for her or against her. In her eyes, Martin was against her, so she banished him from her life. When I met my new husband she needed a bit of time to get used to him because we'd spent a long period with just the two of us. But it went well initially. They liked each other and Sylvie accepted him as her second father. Now in retrospect, I realise that he wasn't so much a father figure to her as…' Linda hesitates, and after a couple of seconds of indecision continues, 'She was in love with him. At the time I wasn't aware of it, but now I am. He was handsome, a bit younger than me. Too old for Sylvie, of course, but adolescent girls always see those things differently. I didn't think there was anything strange about the fact that she was always hanging around his neck and wanted them to do everything together. Why should I? I was just happy that things were going so well between them, despite my impression that Bert sometimes felt a bit uncomfortable. Sylvie is not good with boundaries. She follows her feelings without considering the consequences.' Again she hesitates, and her reluctance begins to make her story seem credible.

She finds her voice again. 'Sylvie was in love with Bert. He maintained that she tried to seduce him and not the other way round, that he held her away from him and that she began to take her clothes off and tried to kiss him. When he pushed her away, she fell and became furious. After that there was this story that Bert had tried to abuse her.'

I sit holding my cup, unable to drink. My head spins with all this information. What is true and what is not? That's always the problem when you hear things from both sides. The different versions are coloured with personal truths and conclusions.

'I don't know what to think,' I say to Linda.

'I can imagine,' she responds.

'Why are you telling me all of this?'

'She's my daughter. I miss her. She was fifteen when this all happened, still a child. Heavens, does she want this to come between us for the rest of our lives? I don't blame her anymore, and neither does Bert. She was confused, her own worst enemy. We want to start again, but there's no way she'll see us. This afternoon I went to her house, she wasn't in but her upstairs neighbour was just leaving. We chatted a while and I learned that Sylvie had a good friend who worked at the photography studio on Karel Doorman Street, so I decided to come and see you. I don't know why.' Linda's voice doesn't sound like she's expecting to have convinced me and she's right.

'I wouldn't mind talking to her,' I say slowly, 'but I've no reason to think that Sylvie lied. Nor do I have any reason to think you're lying, but I know Sylvie. I only met you half an hour ago and I don't know Bert at all. I'd rather not get involved, is that all right?'

Linda nods dejectedly. 'Of course I understand. But honestly, Bert is not the kind of man who would abuse a young girl. He was working for the vice squad at the time. Every day he was confronted with the effects of abuse. Sometimes he came home in pieces and spent the entire evening cursing whatever bastard had done that. Victim statements gave him nightmares. He was protective of me and Sylvie because he knows what a dangerous world we live in. And to think he'd abuse his step-daughter? No…'

I want to agree with her, but they are only words. I wasn't there, I don't know Bert.

Linda gets a card from her bag and pushes it towards me. 'If you ever change your mind…' I study the card and cold tea floods over the edge of my cup, onto my hand and my sleeve.

'Linda Ykema,' I say in astonishment.

'Yes, you can always call me.'

I look at Linda wide-eyed and my heart begins to pound. My mind has difficulty accepting this news.

'Is Bert your husband's full name?' I enquire.

Linda gives me a funny look. 'No, it's Hubert.'

46.

Linda has left and I don't stir from the kitchen table.

This truth.

Bert Ykema.

The policeman whose service weapon went missing. Why is Sylvie the link with the missing pistol? I can't think of a single reason for her to have wanted to kill Lydia. Lydia teased her sometimes, but that's no reason to kill someone.

Let's imagine that Linda's story is true, and Sylvie does reinvent reality in ways that are advantageous to her, what else might she have lied about?

I massage my temples, but no revelations come to me. The only way I can find out more is to talk to Sylvie, ask a few questions and see what comes of it.

I get up, pull on a denim jacket and get my bag and soon I'm on my way to the Essenburg Canal. It's going to be a difficult conversation, but we have to have it. What am I actually going to say? The truth is the best. I'll tell her that her mother turned up and told me her version of events. But how am I going to bring up the gun? If Sylvie did shoot Lydia, wouldn't she pull a gun on me just as easily? Perhaps I should go to the police.

Sylvie is the best friend I've ever had. This has to be a mistake. Sylvie hasn't been lying to me, it must be her mother. Lydia must have known Sylvie's stepfather somehow, I refuse to believe that Sylvie has anything to do with this.

I cycle so fast that I'm out of breath. It's a long cycle to the Essenburg Canal and I don't want to arrive panting and with a pounding heart.

Sylvie lives right at the end of the Essenburg Canal. When I arrive I stop to catch my breath. I ring the doorbell. No one comes. I look at my watch, it's half past five – too early. She's probably still at work or on her way home.

I get out my mobile and dial Sylvie's number. It rings for a while before she picks up.

'Sylvie here.'

'Hi, it's Elisa. I'm outside your door. Are you almost home?'

'Oh Elisa, I've got a dinner date,' Sylvie says. 'I'm going to Cafe Flor with a colleague.'

'Oh,' I say. 'Have a good time then. I'll talk to you later.'

'Okay! See you.'

I hang up, take a step backwards and look in through the windows of Sylvie's apartment. Might one of her neighbours have a key? These are the kind of buildings you lock yourself out of accidentally if you let the front door close after you. It's worth a try.

I ring the upstairs neighbour's bell and soon the front door opens. 'Yes?' somebody shouts down the stairs.

I climb the stairs and halfway up I meet a skinny woman with very short, bleached hair.

'Hello,' I say. 'I'm a friend of Sylvie's but she's not in. I've left my house keys in her flat. Do you happen to have her spare key, so that I could go in and pick them up?'

The neighbour studies me.

'You must be the one with the photography studio,' the woman says. 'I'm Nanda.' She offers me her hand and I shake it.

'She's never given me a key, but I do have one. From the previous occupants,' Nanda says with a guilty expression. 'I've never given it back, silly, isn't it? I'll go and fetch it.'

Nanda goes upstairs and I wait in front of Sylvie's door. As soon as she comes down, I hold out my hand and Nanda hands over the key, but not without hesitation. She remains close behind me. It would seem odd if I sent her away now, so I just accept her presence.

I go inside. Nanda waits in the doorway with her arms folded. I proceed further, uneasy now that I'm breaking and entering into Sylvie's home.

'Strange, they're not on the table. I'll check in the kitchen.'

I go into the kitchen and pull open the drawer she keeps her bits and bobs in. There are a few keys in it and I put one in my trouser pocket just in case. I hear footsteps coming into the sitting room and get my own set of keys from my bag. Just as Nanda comes in, I turn around and hold them up, smiling.

'Found them!'

'Great.' Nanda nods at me and looks at the key in my hand, the one she's had all this time. I put it into my pocket and say, 'I'll give the key back to Sylvie and explain how I got it. Thanks for your help.'

Nanda nods but doesn't dare ask for the key back. I'd hoped she wouldn't, but if that failed I still had the key from the kitchen drawer.

I follow Nanda into the hall and say goodbye. As I descend the stairs, I hear her go upstairs and, a few seconds later, she locks her front door. For form's sake, I open the outside door and let it slam shut again. Then I go back upstairs and open Sylvie's door.

Now, let's get to work. Sylvie's not coming home any time soon so I've got time. Nevertheless, I hurry, driven by an unsettling feeling.

I begin with the dresser in the sitting room and make a fleet-fingered search of its cubby holes. Bank statements, insurance paperwork, the telephone book, Yellow Pages, a pile of old magazines. Nothing special. The drawers don't contain anything interesting either.

I go to the wall cabinet in the corner, but there's nothing in it except crockery. I tiptoe into the bedroom, as if someone might hear me, and open Sylvie's wardrobe. I'm acting strangely, I realise. At least, if Sylvie doesn't have anything to hide. How would I explain this if she suddenly arrived home?

My hand gropes into the space behind her tidy piles of clothes, but discovers nothing. I carry on searching – my eye falls upon a row of photo albums on the lowest shelf. I sit down on the edge of the bed and leaf through them. Baby photos, school photos, Sylvie on her father's lap, pictures of Santa Claus, Christmas and birthdays. And then just photos of Sylvie and her mother, probably taken with the self-timer.

They go up to when Sylvie was around thirteen, after that there are a few empty pages, and you can see from the damaged cardboard that a few photographs have been torn out.

I set the albums back, get up and look around the bedroom. If I wanted to hide something in here, where would I put it?

I pull open the drawers of the dressing table. Nothing. I look around and in a final attempt I lift up the mattress.

Bingo.

There's no gun here, but there is a scrapbook on top of the bed slats.

I hold the mattress with one hand and reach for the book with the other. I drop the mattress, sit down on the bed, and open the book.

Raoul and Sylvie look back at me, their cheeks pressed

together, big smiles on their faces. On the next page they sit together on a sunny terrace with their arms around each other, there are lots of close ups of Raoul's face, taken by an infatuated Sylvie.

I leaf through the book with cold, stiff fingers. It's full of tickets and hotel and restaurant receipts. And love letters. Lots of love letters. The receipts date to a year ago and stop abruptly, but they tell a clear story. A story of a scale that doesn't quite sink in.

Each new page is like a stab in the heart, but I can't stop myself from looking. I read each love letter that Sylvie has carefully hoarded and stuck in, and I let pain take control of me. At last I drop the book on the bed, too shocked to cry.

47.

I sit very still as my brain processes what my eyes have seen. A sudden wave of nausea sends me to the bathroom, my hand over my mouth. I lean over the toilet bowl, but nothing happens and the feeling recedes. I get up, take a sip of water from the tap and peer at my pale face in the mirror. So it was Sylvie. Her motive is as clear as day.

And what's going on with Thomas then? Is she really seeing him? Perhaps she's using him as a decoy.

On an impulse, I get my mobile out of my pocket and call Thomas. To my despair, I get his voicemail and, after wondering what to do, I leave a message.

'Thomas, it's Elisa. There's something I want to ask you – are you seeing Sylvie? Has anything ever happened between you? You'll probably wonder why I want to know, but I'll explain.' I pause, intending to hang up, then add: 'I'm at Sylvie's house and I've found photos of her with Raoul. And I found out something else, you'll never believe it. You know Noorda asked if I knew someone called Hubert Ykema? He was the owner of the gun used to kill Lydia. Well, he's Sylvie's stepfather.'

I hang up and look around. There's only a small chance the gun is here. She probably got rid of it. Perhaps I should go, I need to talk to Noorda.

I hear the door downstairs opening. Fast footsteps coming up the stairs. Shit, that can't be Sylvie! No, it's not, it's only quarter past six. It must be someone who lives above her. But that's Nanda, and she's home.

A key is pushed into the lock and I freeze. My eyes search for a hiding place, but there's no time. Sylvie comes in carrying a plastic bag that stinks of cooking fat. When she sees me she stops.

'Elisa, what are you doing here?'

I look at her with a forced smile and decide to tell the same story I told Nanda. 'I've lost my house keys and thought I might have given you a spare set at some point.'

'Not that I remember.'

We stand there just staring at each other. My heart races and I feel the heat in my face. Sylvie studies me.

'How did you get in?'

'Nanda still had a key,' I explain. 'From the previous occupants.'

'Wonderful!' Sylvie walks past me into the kitchen and I realise that the scrapbook is still on her bed. The hope that she won't see it disappears as quickly as it arises. As she goes past, Sylvie glances into her bedroom, at the bed, where the book is spread open on her duvet. She turns towards me.

'Did you think your key was under my mattress?'

I don't say anything. Neither of us do.

'So, now you know,' Sylvie says. 'Raoul and I are seeing each other. Given the circumstances we've laid it to rest for a while, but in a few month's time we'll be going public. Would you like a drink? I'm having a glass of wine, you too?' I follow her into the kitchen and wait in the doorway. Sylvie puts the plastic bag down on the work surface and removes two small Turkish wraps from it.

'Want one?'

I shake my head.

'The dinner was cancelled,' Sylvie says. 'My colleague felt ill, so I just took her home.'

I can't stop staring at her. I'd rather fly at her throat, slap her around the face or sink my nails into her perfect skin, but I'm paralysed by shock. Sylvie is seeing Raoul. They're waiting a while before telling everyone. And what about me? And Lydia?

Sylvie lays the table. She puts out two place mats, two glasses of wine and fetches the plates with the wraps from the kitchen.

'Sit down.' It sounds like an order.

I sit down, but only because I want some answers from her. The door isn't locked and I'm near enough to it. I can escape if necessary.

'Go on, take your coat off. It's not that cold, is it?' Sylvie sits down and I join her at the table.

'So Nanda still had a key? Strange that she never gave it back.' Sylvie cuts a strip from her Turkish wrap and puts it into her mouth.

'It was left over from the previous occupants,' I repeat. 'She said she'd forgotten about it.'

'Where's the key now?'

I fish it from my trouser pocket and put it on the table. 'I kept it for you.'

'How nice of you,' Sylvie says as she takes the key. 'And then you thought you'd just take a look under the mattress?'

I say nothing.

Sylvie looks at me over the rim of her wineglass. 'Or did you just happen to lift up the mattress and there was my scrapbook?'

It's time for me to get down from the dock and begin my own

line of questioning. I lean back, trying to seem relaxed as possible and look at Sylvie. 'How long have you been seeing Raoul?'

On the surface it's a cosy picture, two girlfriends sitting down to a bottle of wine and a take-away, but the tension between us is like a magnetic field.

'About a year and a half. Although we've hardly seen each other the past six months.'

'Why not?'

Sylvie pauses for a while. 'Raoul thought it would be better,' she says, and I hear a tinge of bitterness in her voice. 'I thought we'd done a good job of keeping our affair secret. How did you find out?'

'I suspected it.'

'And so you decided to come and have a rummage around my house. You could have just asked me, Elisa.'

'Would you have admitted it? After you'd kept quiet about it for so long?'

Sylvie takes a mouthful of food and nods. 'Yes, I would have admitted it. What's the point of denying it when it's clear enough. I love him. I don't have to be ashamed of my feelings.'

'Don't you? He was married, and the father of a small child,' I snap.

Sylvie doesn't seem bothered by this comment. 'You know, what we've got together is so deep and so real that I've never doubted that we'd end up together.' She talks with her mouth full. 'I knew we'd end up together.'

'Really? Were you so sure?' I lean towards her. 'I'm going to ask you a single question, Sylvie, and I expect an honest answer.'

Sylvie takes a sip of wine.

I force myself to look her in the eye. My friend, my rival. Raoul's mistress. 'Sylvie,' I say, my voice shaking, 'did you kill Lydia?'

Lydia

48.

The preparations for the barbecue have us all busy. My mother and I go into the kitchen to make the salads; my father and Raoul mess around with briquettes on the barbecue next to the terrace, and Elisa lays the table, assisted by Valerie.

'Nice isn't it, all of us together?' My mother is washing the lettuce and shakes the colander to get rid of the water. 'We should do this more often.'

'Yes, it is lovely,' I admit, and I mean it. I love going home. I have a very strong bond with my parents and I miss them when I haven't spoken to them for a while. I chat to my mother on the phone a couple of times a week, or she'll come to Rotterdam on her free day and we'll go shopping together. We have lunch somewhere or drink coffee in one of the cafes, discussing all kinds of things. That's why I'm finding it hard not to talk about my current problems.

Each time I take a deep breath, ready to pour my heart out, my mouth fills with so much air that the words seem blocked in.

I'm sure my parents would be worried if they knew what had happened at school; more so, if they knew that Bilal wasn't stopping at that. Of course I can keep silent about it, but I know myself. Once I begin to tell something, the whole story comes rushing out and I can no longer stop.

'You're quiet today.' My mother looks at me. 'Is there something wrong, Lydia?'

I respond with a simple shake of my head. 'Bit tired.'

'Hmm.' She looks like she doesn't believe it. 'Everything all right with you and Raoul?'

I look at my husband out of the kitchen window, he's in the process of helping my sister move the table so it's not in the full sun. The table has already been laid which is why they are walking very carefully and when a row of plates begin to slide, their giggled warnings resound through the garden.

'They get on well, don't they?' my mother comments. 'It could have been very different, you hear those stories sometimes… Did you know that Tinny's daughter Annelise never comes home anymore because she's fallen out with Christie's husband? It's pretty serious. Tinny asked me if we have the same problem, because she knows how close you two are. But I said, 'Not at all, it's going well with us. Elisa and Raoul got on really well right from the start.'

'It wasn't always like that. There was a time when we used to slag off each other's boyfriends,' I say.

'That was because you were so attached to each other,' my mother says. 'That whole separation process needed to happen and boyfriends are a big threat.'

I cut up the tomatoes, slipping a slice into my mouth as I look out of the window again. Raoul and Lydia are drinking beer, Raoul's third and Elisa's second. They're standing a bit to one side, near the trees, and they seem caught up in an involved discussion, so involved they haven't noticed that my father is dilly-dallying with the briquettes, he can't get them to light, and

208

that Valerie is dangerously close to the edge of the swimming pool.

I put down the knife, wipe my hands on a tea towel and step outside.

'Raoul,' I shout, hearing the sharpness in my voice. 'Keep an eye on Valerie, will you? And my father might need some help.' I go back into the kitchen without waiting for a reaction. My mother gives me a look and gets the baguettes out of their packaging. For a while the only sound is the ticking of the clock, and the crack of the bread falling apart under my mother's knife. Finally my mother puts the slices into a round dish and says, 'Just tell me what the matter is.'

And I burst into tears.

Of course we talk about nothing else after that. My father comes into the kitchen, not suspecting a thing, sees that I'm crying and panics right away. I must sit down, not say anything for a while, drink water. My mother attempts to console me, my father dismisses her words impatiently, then they have a discussion about what should or shouldn't be said in this kind of situation, all the while advising me to 'stay calm'.

I take a deep breath and explain what happened at school in as few words as possible. To be honest my parents aren't as shocked as I'd expected, which annoys me a little.

'I've always been afraid something like that would happen,' my mother says. 'You hear so much about violence in schools these days…But I didn't realise it was that bad at your school.'

'It's hardly like I'm threatened with a knife every lesson,' I say, feeling an inexplicable need to put things into perspective. 'I still enjoy working there, but I'm shocked by what happened.'

'Was it a single incident? Or have other things happened?' My father studies me intensely.

I hesitate, just for a second, but they both notice.

'There were other things,' my mother notes, crossing her

arms; she's clearly not going to give up until she's heard all the details.

'Oh, it doesn't mean much. Bilal keeps hanging around near the school and giving me threatening looks. He doesn't do anything else, but it's upsetting me. It's pure intimidation.'

'You can say that again,' my father rages. 'And it's also a punishable offence. It's a form of stalking. Have you been to the police?'

'I reported it, but didn't try to press charges. They don't do much about people pulling out knives, let alone hanging around schools,' I say.

'What are you talking about?' Suddenly Elisa is in the doorway. She doesn't wait for an answer, but asks a new question. 'Did you tell them anyway?'

I nod.

'Were you going to keep it a secret from us?' my mother says.

'I didn't want to worry you,' I say. 'But it's so hard keeping things in when they're going round in your head all the time.'

'You don't have to keep things in.' The pressure of my father's hand on my shoulder is what I've been longing for all week. I've felt that pressure on my shoulder every time I've had to go through something difficult in life. It's amazing how long you need your parents for, even into your adult years.

Now that we can talk about it, I can't stop. We discuss it over the aperitif, during the meal and when we have coffee. All possible solutions to the problem are thrown on the table and my parents apply all their experience and training. It's already getting darker and a cool breeze has risen by the time we leave.

'Do you feel a bit better now?' Elisa asks as we part.

'I do,' I say. 'It does help to talk about it.'

'As I said,' she says as she bends down to give Valerie a hug.

After a long ritual of kisses and goodbyes we set off.

'So, home,' I sigh as we drive down the street. 'I'm shattered.'

'From all that talking,' Raoul says. 'You must have a sore jaw. You went on the whole afternoon.'

'But it did do me some good. I really needed that.' I turn to Valerie who is sitting in her car seat pouting.

'What's eating you, sweetie? Are you tired?'

'No,' she says. 'I wanted to tell that joke about Sam and Moose but nobody listened.'

'Sorry.' I look in the mirror at her unhappy face and realise that we haven't paid Valerie much attention. 'Do you want to tell us the joke now?'

'No, I don't have to anymore,' Valerie replies. 'I told it to Lola.' She closes her eyes, yawns and falls asleep.

Lola is Valerie's imaginary friend. She invented her when she was three and since then Lola's been an integral part of our lives. Lola sits next to Valerie at school, sleeps with her in her bed and has to be lifted up onto the bike so that she can squeeze in next to Valerie on her seat. Sometimes there will be a period when Valerie doesn't talk about her, but then she'll suddenly reappear, out of nowhere.

I think it's amusing until I want to watch the evening news and I have to spend time cleaning Lola's teeth and singing her a lullaby. Raoul's got more patience than me and takes over the Lola activities. I've always admired his patience when it comes to Valerie.

'Lola is real to Valerie,' he said once when I complained about her. 'That makes her real enough for me to pay attention to her.'

Elisa also had an imaginary friend for a while. A few of them in fact. I read somewhere that most children grow out of it, but I don't see it wearing off with Valerie and Elisa's invisible friend was also very persistent.

She always argued that it wasn't a fantasy, that she could see real people. Spirits, she meant. I'm not sure what to think about that. When we were about ten she got interested in spirituality for a while, but that passed. My parents believed that such quirks only got worse if you paid attention to them. Their attitude helped Elisa through her spiritual phase – that was good, at times she became quite strange.

Around that age we'd go to the graveyard every September to collect chestnuts. There weren't any chestnut trees in our neighbourhood, but the graveyard was full of them. Each rush of wind would send the shiny brown balls raining down, they'd fall with dull thuds onto the gravel and the gravestones.

I would always run through the wrought-iron gates to pick them up, but Elisa would follow slowly.

'You can't get anything from that grave,' she'd say, pointing at one next to the path where the prettiest and largest chestnuts lay.

'Here then?' I'd ask.

Elisa would close her eyes and shake her head, or she'd nod and smile. Usually she'd point out the places we could carry on unbothered.

'Here is all right, those people like us to be here,' she'd say then.

That was the kind of comment I was used to. When we were babies, Elisa was calmer and more serious. She would lie calmly in the playpen and could spend so much time just looking around that you almost forgot about her. She'd often stare at a fixed point, her face screwed up in surprise; other times she'd chuckle with delight and reach her hands out towards nothing in particular.

I believe she had imaginary friends even back then.

49.

I don't spot them at first. It's another sunny Monday morning, much too nice to spend trapped in the school building, and I park my car reluctantly. I still haven't decided whether to tell my colleagues about the threatening letter, and I cross the car park thinking about it. It's not until I enter the playground that I see the cameras; they flash in my face and a journalist comes up to me and shoves a microphone under my nose.

'Mrs Salentijn, could I ask you something? According to our sources, a student held a knife to your throat last week, and at the weekend you received a threatening letter. Is that right?'

I'm so flabbergasted I begin to stutter. 'H-how do you…'

Wrong! Of course I should have said, 'No comment,' and hurried inside. Instead, I'd admitted it right away, and the cameras begin to flash again. To my amazement, I think I see Thomas standing behind them. What is he doing here?

I ignore the reporter, who fires a new round of questions at me, and walk towards Thomas. He gives me a sheepish smile, gets into his car and drives off.

That prick! How could Elisa have been stupid enough to have told Thomas about it? I reach for my mobile to call her, but the reporter asks, 'Could you tell us exactly what happened on the morning concerned? And have you ever been attacked by a student before?'

'No comment,' I snarl and move on. Clusters of students divide to let me pass and strike poses for the photographer. As I hurry up the steps to the main entrance, I glance back over my shoulder and see that the students are also under fire.

With a deep sigh I go inside and prepare myself for the storm. And it hits.

The staffroom falls silent as I enter, and then everyone starts at once. How in god's name could I have been so stupid? They'd expected a bit more discretion from me. I've disappointed them. Hadn't I stopped to think that this wasn't just about me but about the entire school?

I do my very best to make it clear that I haven't blabbed, that I didn't go looking for publicity in any way, that I'm just as surprised as they are, but it's no use. Only one person seems to believe me and gives me a sympathetic look, the rest just keep on going.

Jan van Osnabrugge walks into the fray and the attention turns to him. Jan lifts up his arms, like a Roman senator trying to calm a restless crowd.

'Silence please! You've all noticed the commotion. Unfortunately we've drawn the attention of the media, but if we all ignore them, their interest will lessen. I've refused them entrance to the school building and staff are doing their best to keep the press away from the students. Go to your classes and try to avoid saying anything if the students ask questions. We need to avoid internal unrest at all costs.'

We listen and nod. Quite a few of my colleagues continue to

stare at me and I don't have the strength to stare back at them. I look at Jan and nod clearly a couple of times to show that I completely agree with him, and that I'm a victim of this too. The result is a volley of scornful looks, grimly set mouths and whispering.

The bell goes and we disperse. I go towards Jasmine and Luke, who are standing talking in a corner, but Jan stops me.

'Lydia, I'd like to have a quick word with you,' he says.

'There's not much to say, Jan,' I answer. 'We can cover it in one sentence. No, I didn't go to the press. I was just as surprised as everyone else.'

'Shocked would be a better word,' Jan comments. 'Have you any idea how I felt when I saw that photographer standing there?'

My resignation makes way for anger and I look Jan in the eye. 'Have you any idea how I felt when they all came rushing at me, Jan? Have you any idea how I felt when I found a threatening letter on my doormat on Saturday afternoon?'

'A what?' Jan queries, his eyebrows raised.

'An anonymous letter. A genuine threat, in cut-out letters,' I say.

Colleagues are standing around us eavesdropping. Jasmine and Luke join me.

'Come on, we'll discuss this in my office.' Jan grabs me by the elbow, but I pull free.

'No, let's discuss it here. Of course we don't want any internal unrest, but I'd rather that everyone knew what was happening to me. On Saturday afternoon I bumped into Bilal and his friends in town. I was able to shake them off by jumping on a bus and asking the driver to shut the doors on them. When I got home there was an anonymous letter on the mat. YOU ARE A WHORE. I WILL KILL YOU, it said. I took it to the police station because I was terrified. Jan, this can't go on. This is not an isolated incident, something has to be done about this.'

'I see.' Jan strokes his chin. 'I can't blame you for reporting it. It's gone quite far, indeed. Where is the letter now? Can I see it?'

'I'm not trying to press charges, I just reported it and the police have got the letter. It's going to be checked for finger-prints,' I answer.

'So if it goes well, they'll be arriving soon at the school to take Bilal's fingerprints. The press will love that.'

'I'm sorry,' I say.

'Hang on! You're sorry? Why in god's name? What could you have done about it?' Luke butts in. 'The school should be sorry that this has happened to you and that it can't give you better protection. Let's talk about that!'

There are a few mutters of agreement around the room, but I'm not sure from whom.

'There's something to be said for that,' Jan responds. 'And if I'd known about this anonymous letter earlier, Lydia, I would have come along to the police with you. Don't think I'm blam-ing you, because I'm not. I just don't understand why you had to get the press involved. What did you think you'd achieve by that?' He gives me a look of incomprehension and I stare back, speechless.

'I didn't get the press involved! Why would I?!'

'I'm asking myself the same question,' Jan says as he turns around and leaves the staffroom.

50.

I haven't even entered the classroom when I realise that I'm not going to be able to do much teaching. The clamour and arguing meets me in the corridor and as I stand in the doorway, I see that the class has divided itself into two camps – Funda's and Ismael's.

Funda is supported by her gang of female friends, Ismael is being egged on by a group of jeering boys. That's half of the class, the other half is made up of silent but interested spectators, standing on chairs to get a better view. The children have clearly missed the fact that there are journalists outside the school, or they're not interested because they're wrapped up in their own problems.

'I'm going to tell your dad, Ismael! And when he hears what you've been saying, he's going to break your legs!' Funda threatens shrilly.

Ismael's reply is lost in the boys' gibing. I pull my students apart and raise my voice, 'All right, what's going on here?'

'Miss, Miss! Do you know what Ismael said to Funda? You have to hear!' The girls press around me, their eyes wide with scandal. 'He really can't say that, Miss! You have to do something about it!'

'Quiet,' I say, my hand raised in the air. 'What is going on? Funda, tell me what the problem is.'

'I was just walking across the playground with Rose and Naima,' Funda cries out. 'And when we went past the boys, Ismael shouted, "Hey, look at that tasty slut!" And it's not the first time. He's been saying it to me all day and I'm sick of it!'

She goes to punch Ismael who nimbly avoids the attack and sticks up his middle finger. His friends laugh and the girls hiss back.

I sigh. A headache is on its way, complete with rolling drums and waving banners. I'm surrounded by accusing brown eyes and high voices that reverberate inside my skull.

'Anyone who doesn't shut up and go back to their seat in the next minute is going to get thirty lines,' I say, without raising my voice.

My words are lost in the tumult, so I put up a chalk and write in large capitals on the blackboard. WRITE THE FOLLOWING LINES.

They are the magic words. The threat buzzes through the room and before I know it, everyone is back in their place. I'd prefer to just get on with the lesson, but I know that it's not practical. The children are all worked up, they won't be able to concentrate. I look at them sitting at their desks giving each other dirty looks and then glancing over at me. There's nothing for it, we'll have to address this. I could talk to the two ringleaders, but it would be better to discuss this as a class. The problem isn't just between Funda and Ismael.

'Right,' I say. 'What happened exactly, Funda?'

'Ismael insults me every day. He calls me "chickie" and "slut" and other things and if he does it again…' She throws daggers at Ismael who responds with an air kiss. His friends laugh, but not as loudly as before.

I give Ismael a stern look until the smile slides from his face.

'Why did you insult Funda, Ismael? You've got a sister, haven't you? How would you like it if a group of boys called her a slut?'

Ismael looks at me for a couple of seconds and produces an apologetic grin. 'Aw, Miss, it's just street talk. I'm not insulting Funda. That's how we talk to each other. We're always hustling chicks.'

'According to the Koran, women deserve respect,' Funda calls out. 'And if Ismael calls me that one more time, I'm going to tell my brother. You know what will happen then.' She juts out her chin and looks around the class; there are nods. Clearly Funda's brother has quite a reputation.

I rest my arms on the table and lean towards the class. 'You know what, I don't understand you lot. There's so much trouble in the world, in the Netherlands, in Rotterdam. There are so many problems between white people and immigrants, between Muslims and non-Muslims. You're all Muslims. What's the world coming to when you fly at each other's throats? What does that achieve?'

There's a moment of silence in the classroom.

'Miss, you're right.' Yussef says. Yussef has stayed back a year and is older than the rest. He's been a calming influence over the other students right from the start. 'It's not right to say those kinds of things. Women deserve respect. The Koran says that, it's true. Women are the bearers of new life, they're important.'

He doesn't address Ismael, but it's clear who he's talking to. I smile at him. Thank you, Yussef, dear Yussef, my beacon in this stormy class.

Everyone is nodding now. Ismael gazes around, sees his support dwindling and backs down, giving Funda a crooked smile.

'I was just messing, Funda. It won't happen again, all right?'

Funda nods.

'Fine.' I come out from behind my desk with a smile and stand in front of the board. 'Then I propose that we look at spelling for the rest of the lesson.'

51.

'Were they at it again?' Jasmine is waiting for me in the corridor at the end of the morning and a single glance at my face tells all.

It's nice to share these things with a colleague, particularly with Jasmine. I can discuss every trifle with her because she teaches the same children and has to deal with the same problems, big and small.

We enter the staffroom discussing the many Ismaels in this school and join the queue for the coffee machine.

When it's our turn, we fill our cups with coffee and sit down at the long table in the middle. 'What a shame you'd already taken that anonymous letter to the police. I'd have liked to have seen it,' Jasmine says.

'Who knows, perhaps I'll get another one!'

'I hope not, but why didn't you bring it to school first? Of course I believe that you got one, but some people have their doubts.'

I've just taken a salami sandwich out of my lunchbox, but Jasmine's words ruin my appetite. 'What? Do they think I made it up? But that's ridiculous. Why would I do that?'

Jasmine lays a calming hand on my arm. 'Not everyone thinks that, and I certainly don't. But there are a few colleagues who doubt you received a letter.'

'Why?' I ask, hearing my voice shake. 'Why on earth would I make something like that up? To have a reason to go to the police? If I'd wanted to go nothing would have stopped me – I already had reason enough!'

'I know that,' Jasmine placates, 'and deep down the others do too. The problem is that everybody is afraid of losing their job. There are going to be redundancies, especially now the press have got wind of this. It won't do anything for the school's reputation.'

'I'm not out to drag the school's name through the mud, but if I don't get any support here, what do you expect? I can't just drop this, can I?'

'Cut the comedy, won't you,' a voice says behind me.

I turn around and see Nora, her eyes glittering, her mouth pulled into a small strip.

'Pardon?' I say with raised eyebrows.

Nora takes up position on the other side of the table and glares at me. 'As if none of us have ever had to handle something similar. If every teacher went to the police at the drop of a hat, we'd have to shut down the school. But you, you're a rich kid, you'd be all right waiting at home for another job to come along.'

'What's that got to do with anything?' I cry out. 'I don't want another job.'

'Oh, shut up,' Nora bites back. 'It's always the same with you and your big mouth. It's attention seeking! You never stop to think that there are people in this school who depend on their jobs for survival.'

I give her a scornful look. 'I don't care what you think, Nora. It's a waste of energy discussing things with people like you.'

Nora opens her mouth to reply, but I don't give her the chance. I grab my stuff and leave the staffroom before I say something indefensible. Jasmine comes after me.

'Don't take it to heart, she's crazy. Shall we go for a drink after school?'

I shake my head. I've had it up to here with this whole school.

At three o'clock when I get into a car that feels like an oven, I wouldn't be surprised if my head actually exploded. When Valerie and I arrive home, I check the doormat right away but there's nothing there. No letters, no anonymous letters. In contrast, there are twelve messages flashing on my answering machine and when I play them back, they all turn out to be from the press.

'Good afternoon, this is the *Rotterdam Daily News*. Is it correct that…?'

'Mrs Salentijn, *The Times* would like to interview you. Would you call us back?'

'This is a message from RTL 4, we'd like to check a few facts…'

It doesn't stop, and just when I've listened to all the messages with growing astonishment, the telephone goes again. I look at the display – it's my sister.

'Elisa!' I snap. 'Why did you tell Thomas what happened? I told you in confidence. There were journalists waiting for me at school this morning!'

'I didn't tell Thomas anything. Only that you had a few problems at school, but I didn't say what they were,' Elisa retorts.

'Well, he was there waiting for me with his camera! How do you explain that?'

'How should I know?' Elisa shouts in the same tone. 'I didn't tell him. Calm down, will you?'

'Who else did you tell?' I ask. It's not meant to be an accusation, but it comes across as one, I realise. Elisa takes it the wrong way.

'If I remember correctly, we talked to Mum and Dad about it yesterday,' she says coolly. 'Perhaps you should start by asking them why they called the press.'

I'm silent for a while as I look at the answering machine with all its insistent requests. I delete them with a single press of a button. I wish I could do the same with the unsettling feeling I'm getting. Someone told the press, but who?

'Please don't take it the wrong way, but did you really not tell anyone else? Could anyone have overheard one of our phone calls?' I ask.

'Sylvie knows about it,' Elisa says. 'She came by when you were at mine, remember? But she only knew about the threats in the classroom. I didn't tell her anything about a letter. I couldn't have either, I didn't even speak to her this weekend.'

'I don't understand,' I say in exhaustion.

'Perhaps it came from the police,' Elisa proposes. 'You know how those balls get set rolling. And good god, the whole school knew about it too!'

That's true, it's probably impossible to find out who blabbed. 'Sorry that I started shouting at you.'

'You're stressed, I understand that.'

Her generosity makes me feel guilty, but I'm too tired to talk about it further. 'If you don't mind, I'm going to hang up. I've got a thumping headache and all I want to do is sink into a hot bath,' I sigh.

'Enjoy it.'

52.

As soon as I've climbed into my bubbles, the telephone rings again. Not just once, but four times within a quarter of an hour. Valerie is in her room playing with her cuddly toys and her imaginary friend and comes to the bathroom.

'Mummy, the telephone keeps ringing,' she says.

'I can hear it, darling,' I say. 'Just let it ring. Mummy doesn't feel like talking.'

She disappears back into her bedroom. I smile as I hear her playing with her Barbies.

'Don't do that, meany. You're not allowed to have a knife. I'm going to tell on you.'

My smile disappears and I feel my headache returning. I float in the warm water, my eyes closed, and massage my temples.

Something is miaowing in the bathroom. I start, still not used to the new ringtone on my mobile. I think about letting it ring, but finally grab my phone from the bathroom cabinet.

'Lydia speaking.'

It's Thomas and I'm so surprised that he's calling me that I forget to speak. He says Elisa told him he should call and apologise for taking photos of me this morning.

'I had to do it,' he says, defensively.

'Who made you? You're a freelancer, aren't you?' There's no compromise in my voice.

'In a way, yes, but I do get commissions,' Thomas answers. 'When I left the house I had no idea it was about you. I'd just heard that there was trouble at one of the local schools. I only got the details later from the journalist who's writing the piece.'

I don't know what to think, but I give him the benefit of the doubt. The damage is already done.

Thomas misinterprets my silence and says, 'Well, I just wanted to say it. Maybe you don't believe a word of it but that's not my problem. Here's Elisa for you.'

I get my sister on the line who suggests we go out for dinner. I don't feel like it, but it's more appealing than staying in and brooding. I could ask Jasmine to have Valerie over to dinner at hers.

'All right,' I say. 'But I have to make some arrangements for Valerie first.'

'I can come and get you at half past five if that works.'

I call Jasmine and arrange for Valerie to eat there.

'She can stay over too, otherwise you'll have to come home early,' Jasmine says. 'Jennifer would love it, I'm sure.'

Soon I'm outside Jasmine's front door; Valerie has a small case with her. Jasmine opens up and Valerie rushes in to find Jennifer. I set Valerie's case down under the stairs.

'You go and have a nice dinner,' Jasmine says. 'I've been thinking for ages that you don't go out enough. Raoul comes and goes but you're always home alone with Valerie. Is Raoul getting back late today as well?'

'Yes, that's how it's been recently.'

'I saw him at the weekend in the Euromast restaurant.'

Jasmine leads me into the sitting room, where the girls are already getting puzzles out of a cupboard.

I nod. 'He had to meet a customer on Saturday.'

'It was Saturday. Lydia, he was with a woman, a very beautiful woman.'

I know her well enough to realise that she's not telling me this without reason. The room full of furniture and other possessions seems to heave for a few seconds, but my face remains impassive.

'He does have some female customers. Women are doing well in business. The days are gone when only men could get into top positions. Eve is waking up!'

I force a laugh, until I see that Jasmine is giving me a sympathetic look.

'Can you describe her in detail?' I ask.

'I'm not sure anymore. Now I come to think about it, she was wearing a scarf wrapped around her hair. That was something odd, I thought – who wears a scarf like that these days? But I didn't really get a good look at her.'

You've got to be kidding, I think. You almost fell over yourself trying to see who Raoul was with. Otherwise how do you know that she was so beautiful?

I don't say anything. Jasmine is a good friend, but these are the kinds of things I don't find easy to share. I bend down to say goodbye to Valerie.

'Bye-bye darling, Daddy will fetch you tomorrow morning and take you to school. All right?'

'All right, bye Mummy!'

Two small arms wrap around my neck, I get a wet kiss and then she's back with the jigsaw puzzles. Thank god for children who part from their parents easily. On one hand it feels like a small stab to a mother's heart when they let you go without looking up, but it can also be very handy.

Elisa

53.

We don't talk for a few seconds, we just stand there. Then Sylvie begins to laugh.

'I want a lawyer!' she cries. 'I'm standing trial in my own house, who'd have thought it?'

I give her a stern look and wonder how I'm managing to stay so calm.

Sylvie smiles as she picks up her glass and takes a sip. When I don't speak, her expression turns circumspect. 'You mean it, don't you? You really think I murdered Lydia. Jesus, Elisa!'

'You have a motive,' I say.

'You do too,' Sylvie counters. 'You're crazy about Raoul. Don't think I don't know it.'

'But I know that I didn't do it.'

'Oh, so I did it then. Funny logic.'

'Not that funny,' I comment, 'given that the bullet found in Lydia's head came from your stepfather's service weapon. There has to be a connection.'

Sylvie looks at me through half-lidded eyes. For a moment she looks just like a cat, then her face relaxes. 'What's that got to do with anything? What are you talking about?'

'You're not going to deny that Hubert Ykema's your step-father, are you?'

'My mother's boyfriend,' Sylvie corrects.

'No, your mother's husband. They got married, but that's irrelevant. Years ago, fifteen years ago to be precise, Hubert Ykema reported his service weapon missing. It was a Walther P5, the gun used to kill Lydia.'

I pay close attention to Sylvie's reaction. She turns pale, but recovers quickly.

'Oh, is that what you were looking for? Aha, now I see! You didn't look very well, doll.' Sylvie pulls open a drawer in the dining table. I'd never realised that there was a drawer on that side of the table, let alone what Sylvie kept in it.

One moment she's opening the drawer and the next there's a gleaming black pistol in her hand. I stare into a dark round hole. I forget to breathe. I don't blink. I stare at the barrel of the gun. It's the same barrel Lydia looked down a few seconds before she died.

My eyes search for Sylvie's and plead for her to remember our friendship, which has been long and deep.

Sylvie closes one eye, looks along the gun and says, 'Pow!'

I recoil – I can't help it – and she laughs and puts the gun down on the table beyond my reach.

'Sorry,' she says. 'That wasn't very nice.'

I take a deep breath, tighten my muscles and relax them again. Meanwhile I keep a close eye on Sylvie's face. She's acting strangely, with a kind of forced light-heartedness – she's definitely not herself. Anyone else would have been furious to find an intruder in their house and then to be falsely accused of murder.

I study Sylvie. Her blue eyes are clear and challenging; she's not going to admit anything.

I sigh and feel my fighting instinct subside.

'Why? Why did she have to die?'

Sylvie shrugs. 'How should I know? I didn't have anything to do with it.'

'Who did do it then? Raoul perhaps?' I laugh.

But Sylvie shrugs again and says, 'Who knows. They didn't have a very violent relationship though, and he was under her thumb, both financially and emotionally.'

'It wasn't that bad,' I snap. 'They may have had a few problems, but Raoul didn't have a reason to murder her. If he'd wanted to get rid of her, he could have divorced her.'

'But that would have cost him his capital,' Sylvie reminds me. 'Lydia owned almost half of the shares of Software International. Even the house was hers. It was given to them by your parents, but it was in her name.'

'You seem to know a lot about it,' I say.

'What did you expect? I also know that he was in love with you for a while. I had difficulty with that but, oh, I knew that you didn't stand a chance. Raoul finished it a few times, but he always came back. He can't live without me.'

'How did it start?' I don't really want to know, but another part of me is desperate for information.

Sylvie pushes away her plate and leans back with her glass of wine. 'How did it start?' she reflects. 'I knew Raoul from your birthday parties, but I really got to know him in the gym. We both went two evenings a week and soon we were exercising together and having a drink afterwards. I was going through a rough patch at the time, do you remember? That was when Joachem had just dumped me. I poured my heart out to Raoul and he consoled me. You know what Raoul is like, he can be so sympathetic and kind. He can make you feel like you're the only person in the room. He got me through that patch, but he did more too, he gave me self-confidence.' Sylvie takes a sip of wine and smiles at me. 'I've never suffered from a lack of male attention,' she continues, 'but it was not the kind of attention I was looking for. Nobody ever took the trouble to look further, to get to know me as a person. Raoul did and that was what made our relationship so unusual. I was sure that I'd found someone who wouldn't let me down.'

'Raoul,' I begin, choosing my words carefully, 'is the kind of man who gets to know everyone properly. He's interested in people, and particularly in women.'

Sylvie's eyes become slits. 'And particularly in me. He wanted to leave Lydia. He promised me he'd leave her.'

'But he didn't. Is that why you killed her? Were you tired of waiting?'

Sylvie looks around the room, her gaze fixed on a past I'd never known about.

'You planned to steal Raoul off her right from the start,' I say, in an attempt at provocation. 'And you were prepared to go to extremes to get him. Isn't that right? Tell me I'm wrong.'

Sylvie gives me such a fierce look that my fear returns.

'Can't I,' she begins, full of restrained anger, 'can't I have some happiness in my life? Can't I fall in love for once and get the man? Do you know what it feels like to be dumped again and again? To have everyone abandon you?'

Sylvie turns away, her lips a tight line. I lose my patience. I throw myself at my former friend, grab the pistol from the table and turn it on her.

'Admit it! You murdered Lydia!' I scream, beside myself with fury. 'How could you, Sylvie?! How could you do that to her? How could you do that to me?'

'I didn't kill her, you bitch!' Sylvie screams back. 'I keep trying to tell you that!'

'And I'm supposed to believe that? But it doesn't matter at all what I believe. The police will decide!'

'You don't have any proof,' Sylvie says.

I walk backwards to the door, getting my bag and coat on the way, the gun pointed at Sylvie the whole time. Sylvie gets up and follows me.

'Stay there!'

'As if you'd be able to shoot,' Sylvie laughs. 'Come on, Elisa, one day we'll look back on this and find it funny.'

'Do you see me laughing? I said, stay there!'

I raise the gun and point it at her chest.

'You don't even know how it works,' Sylvie says, but she doesn't move. 'Go to the police, kid. Make yourself look ridiculous. There's not a single shred of evidence, before you know it I'll be free again.'

I walk backwards into the corridor. 'Do you think so? This gun is sufficient proof, Sylvie, and I'm going to take it straight to the police.' I see a flash of panic in her face. I pull the door shut, run down the stairs and tug open the front door. I run smack bang into a man outside. He grips me by both arms and holds me tightly. I begin to scream and try to break free, until his voice reaches me at last.

'Calm down, Elisa! What's happened? Hey, it's me, Thomas! What have you got there?'

I look in confusion at Thomas's worried face. Thomas, dear Thomas, always there when you need him the most. I glance at the pistol and then at the front door to the building, as if I'm expecting to see Sylvie appear with a bazooka. But the door remains closed and there's no sound of running footsteps in the stairwell.

'What's happened?' Thomas repeats and strokes the hair away from my burning face.

'I'll explain in a minute. Did you come in the car?' I fluster.

Thomas nods and points at his old white Opal parked a little further up. I run to it, leaving Thomas no choice but to run after me.

'Now what is…'

'To the police station,' I pant. 'Quick!'

232

Thomas starts the engine and as we drive along the Essenburg Canal, I glance up at the second floor, at Sylvie's apartment. She's at the window, her arms folded, watching us.

54.

Giving my statement takes a long time. Inspector Noorda is not there, but they call him to say that the murder weapon has been found. When he finally appears, the paperwork has been completed and I have to retell everything in great detail.

I filled in Thomas in the car and learned that I was right, he'd never had a relationship with Sylvie. When we arrive at the police station, he is still in shock. I am too. But another emotion is breaking through my anger: grief. Sylvie. Why did it have to be Sylvie, the only girlfriend I've ever had?

'So if I understand correctly, Ms Roelofs stayed behind in her apartment when you fled,' Noorda says.

'Yes, but I don't know if she's still there.'

'There's every chance she's gone.' Noorda gives orders for a car to be despatched to the Essenburger Canal right away. 'With a bit of luck, Ms Roelofs will be brought in shortly. I'd like to have a little chat with her, and with Mr Salentijn too, as it happens.'

'Will Sylvie be arrested?' Thomas enquires. I register the surprise and pain in his expression and I don't blame him. I feel the same.

'Not directly. First we'll have her in for questioning, and depending on what transpires, we'll decide whether to keep her in or not,' Noorda explains.

'I don't want to be here when she arrives,' I say.

'We'll take you home and keep you informed.'

Thomas and I stand up.

'I'll take her home,' Thomas says, and glancing at me, he adds, 'And I'll stay with you. You can't be on your own.'

'I'll manage,' I say. If I need anything right now, it's to be left in peace and quiet. And I need Raoul too, but it would be insensitive to say that. Thomas's eyes have the hopeful look of a knight protector who can't wait to rescue the princess and shower her in love. That's not what I need; not from him, in any case.

'You don't need to stay with me, Thomas,' I say as we get into the car. 'I've got a terrible headache.'

'Then you go off to bed and I'll sit downstairs,' Thomas suggests as he drives away from the police station.

'It's not necessary.'

'I think it is. Next thing you know Sylvie will be outside your door.'

'I'll lock the front door. She's lost her gun, she can't do anything.'

'I wouldn't count on it. I think she's crazy, and crazy people are unpredictable.' Thomas drives along Pompenburg, towards Kralingen.

I rest my hand on his arm. 'I want to tell Raoul about this and I need to have quite a difficult conversation with him. Could you take me to Juliana van Stolberg Avenue?'

Thomas's face tightens. 'If you want me to.'

I give him my sweetest smile. 'You're a dear.'

He smiles again, happy with the smallest scrap I throw his way. I sigh, my conscience heavy.

'The thing I don't understand,' Thomas says, 'is that you really believed I was going out with Sylvie.'

'That was what she told me.'

'And you just believed it!'

I shrug my shoulders and feel Thomas's hand on mine.

'Elisa,' he says. 'You know there's only one person for me, don't you?'

I look down at my hand, embarrassed; it's almost completely covered by his. Oh my god, he's going to declare his intentions. Dear Thomas, please don't. Please just stay my most faithful and best friend. A few more words and our friendship will be destroyed. I don't know if I could bear that.

Thomas must be telepathic because he doesn't pronounce the words that could ruin everything. He does keep holding my hand until we turn into Juliana van Stolberg Avenue. He stops right outside Raoul's door.

'Thanks,' I say. 'I'll call you, all right?'

Thomas just nods.

I get out and go down the garden path. I turn around to wave to Thomas from the doorway, but he's already gone.

'What are you doing here?' Raoul opens the door and kisses me on both cheeks.

'I need to talk to you.'

Raoul leads me into the sitting room. It's quiet, the volume on the television is turned down and Valerie is already in bed.

I stand in front of Lydia and Raoul's wedding photo, which is in a silver frame on the dresser, and look at it for a long time. Next to it is a picture of Valerie as a newborn in her mother's arms.

The pain of one particular memory shoots through me. I remember Valerie's birth, how difficult it was and what Lydia went through to bring her daughter into the world. But afterwards she was happy, so happy. She lay in bed, weak from the blood loss, but I'll never forget her expression when she looked at her baby. 'A daughter. Just what I wanted. We'll share so much.' I look at the photo with a heavy heart.

'What's this all about?'

The pictures from Sylvie's scrapbook flash through my mind, replacing the image of Lydia's wedding photo. Bitterness courses through me. I take a step towards Raoul, and slap his face. 'I know everything, Raoul.'

'Everything?' He rubs his cheek. 'Everything about what?'

'About your relationship with Sylvie.'

I see the shock in his eyes. He's taken aback for an instant, but then he recovers. 'I'm not having a relationship with Sylvie,' he says.

The wave of anger washes colour into my face. 'Don't lie,' I shout. 'Sylvie told me everything.'

Raoul represses a sigh. 'I'm not seeing Sylvie,' he repeats, as he goes towards the bar. 'Not anymore.'

I follow him with my eyes as he gets out a bottle of whisky.

'You too?' he offers.

I shake my head and continue to stare at him with furious eyes.

'We did have a relationship,' Raoul says, 'but it's been over for a long time. How did you find out about it?'

'I've seen photos.' I think about the intimate pictures, the love letters, the restaurant visiting cards, and the grief I felt when I first saw them rises up in me again.

'Photos?'

'Sylvie kept a scrapbook,' I say. 'Full of pictures of the two of you. And every note you ever scribbled to her. Restaurant and hotel receipts and cards.' Some of my pain must be visible because when our eyes meet I see it reflected in Raoul's.

'Oh, Elisa…' he says. 'I so hoped you'd never find out.'

55.

I look at the familiar face opposite me, the face of a man I've loved so much – who I still love, in spite of everything. 'Yes, I can imagine,' I say.

Raoul takes a large sip of whisky. 'I don't mean that I would have preferred to keep the lie going, but sometimes you do stupid things you can't undo afterwards,' he admits. 'Sylvie was such idiocy. A mistake, a slip up. I wanted to leave it at the one blunder, but she carried on playing up to me. She didn't care that I was married and had a child. She said that she didn't expect anything and continued to offer herself to me. I should have kept my distance, but I'll admit it, I was weak. She's so pretty. I've never seen such an attractive woman.' Raoul shrugs. 'I know it's a cliché, I don't think that you will be able to understand it, but I couldn't resist her.'

'For how long?'

'A few months,' Raoul says. 'In the beginning I couldn't get enough of her, but after a while something changed. It became obvious that we didn't have anything to talk about. I'd take her out for dinner, a long way from Rotterdam, and she'd show me how long her fingernails were, or she'd tell me every little thing she'd read about celebrities in her magazines. We didn't have much in common.' Raoul looks at me. We can talk, that glance says, we're on the same wavelength, what we have is much deeper.

'Was that what you were looking for in Sylvie? A good conversation?'

Raoul gives me an embarrassed smile and takes another sip of whisky. 'Not at first, of course, but I did find it important later. Please believe me, I really regretted it. Particularly when Lydia sensed that something was up, that I was having an affair.'

Raoul swirls the contents of his glass around and gives me a look that makes words unnecessary. I feel a shiver run through my body, but I can't say which emotion has brought it on. I stand in front of the dresser and Raoul comes towards me. I look into his dark handsome face, feel his warm fingers on my cold skin, experience the consoling caress of his thumbs. I take a deep breath, this is just his thumbs.

Nevertheless, I take a step back. 'You should have worked at your marriage, Lydia deserved that.'

Raoul's eyes travel over to his silver-framed wedding photo. 'I know I've disappointed you, but my affair with Sylvie doesn't mean anything. My feelings for Lydia and for you have always been sincere. I didn't want to take advantage of you, I didn't want to cause you any pain, I didn't want to tell you how crazy I was about you, because I didn't have anything to offer. I would never have done that to Lydia. It would have destroyed your bond.'

'How noble of you,' I say. 'You know what, Raoul, I feel like I'm only getting to know you properly now. And do you know what I'm seeing? A bastard.'

The words hit home. Raoul blanches, but I'm not sorry for what I've said.

'I was always straight with Sylvie. I told her many times that I was never going to leave Lydia.'

'That's far from how she saw it. She's convinced that you're going to carry things on with her.'

Raoul sighs and empties his glass. 'Are you sure you don't want anything?' he asks.

'Coffee,' I snap. 'And you'd better have one yourself too.'

Raoul nods and I follow him to the kitchen.

'Sylvie believed what she wanted to believe,' Raoul says as he prepares it. 'I never promised her anything, certainly not once I got to know her better.'

The coffee machine buzzes to life and the cups fill up. Raoul passes one to me and we sit down at the kitchen table.

'When I ended it, Sylvie flipped out,' Raoul tells me. 'She threatened me, stalked me. She called late at night, sent desperate emails, waited for me all over the place. It got worse after Lydia's death. She was convinced that I'd want to be with her then. Finally I talked to her a couple of times to try to get it into her head that my feelings had changed, but she wasn't having any of it. She kept on saying that she understood that I needed time and that she'd wait for me. The worst thing was that I could hardly avoid her because she's your friend. She still doesn't understand that there isn't a hope in hell we'll get back together.'

'Have you talked to Sylvie recently?'

Raoul nods. 'She kept on bothering me. I decided to have another talk with her and make it clear that this must stop.'

'So she murdered Lydia pointlessly,' I say.

Raoul looks at me with astonishment. 'I don't believe Sylvie would go that far.'

'I do. Do you remember when Noorda asked if we knew someone called Hubert Ykema?'

'Yeah, that policeman whose gun was stolen. What's that got to do with Sylvie?'

'Hubert Ykema is her mother's husband. He came into Sylvie's life when she was thirteen.'

Raoul runs his hand through his hair in amazement. 'Are you sure? But…but that doesn't mean that Sylvie shot Lydia, does it?'

'I'm afraid it does. I've already been to the police and handed in the gun. They drove straight to her house to take her in for questioning.'

Raoul looks worse by the minute. My heart burns with sympathy, but I can't express it. I'm struggling enough with my feelings for him. How can you ever recover from the realisation that you're responsible for your wife's death?

'That bitch,' he hisses. 'I'll kill her!'

Then he covers his eyes with his hands and makes a strangled noise. I look at him, but I can't bring myself to comfort him.

Sylvie's gone, Noorda tells us when he calls. But his team are trying to track her down.

After he's hung up, Raoul and I look at each other.

'She's on the run,' Raoul says.

I nod. 'Is there any better proof of guilt? She knows she hasn't got a leg to stand on.'

'Noorda wants to talk to me tomorrow morning. He didn't sound too friendly.'

We are standing very close to each other, but there's no tension. We're both too overwhelmed by what's been revealed for that.

'It's late,' Raoul says. 'Will you stay over?'

I nod. 'In the guest room.'

'Naturally.'

My anger about Raoul's infidelity has lessened a little. I'm not furious anymore, but I'm still shocked and disappointed. I'm angry with myself for having idealised Raoul all these years. I've compared so many men to him, there were so many relationships I didn't give a chance…And why? Because deep in my heart I hoped that one day my sister and brother-in-law's marriage would come to an end? Did I put my love-life on hold all this time for that?

As I get into bed, I hear Valerie crying in the next room. Raoul is taking a shower, so I go to her.

'Elisa,' she says in a tiny voice.

I sit down on the edge of her bed. Her Barbie duvet is pulled up to her chin and her blonde hair fans out over the pillow.

'What is it, sweetheart?' I ask.

'Is Mummy really never coming back?' she whispers.

'Oh, darling…Are you still waiting for Mummy?'

Valerie nods without taking her brown eyes off me. 'But Mummy is dead, right?'

I nod. 'Yes, sweetie, but Mummy hasn't gone completely. She's still with you. You can't touch her or talk to her, but she's here.'

'I know,' Valerie says. 'She's here now too, isn't she? There, next to my doll's house.'

I glance at the doll's house, then study my niece.

'Mummy talks to me all the time,' Valerie says. 'I tell her everything I've done and she listens. She talks back, too.'

'What does she say?'

Valerie hugs her teddy bear to her chest. 'She says that you are going to look after me and Daddy.'

56.

'Will you come with me to the police station? I'd rather not leave you alone,' Raoul says when he appears at breakfast the following morning. He straightens his tie and sits down at the table.

I spread butter on a rusk, put a couple of cheese slices on top and look at him. 'Because of Sylvie?'

'I'm not comfortable knowing she's somewhere around.' Raoul nods at the street. 'I can't imagine that she's very far away.'

'You don't think so? I think she's long gone from Rotterdam.'

'I disagree,' Raoul says. He pours himself a cup of coffee and takes a slice of brown bread.

I shrug. 'You don't have to babysit me, you know. Do you really think Sylvie would come after me?'

'Yes,' Raoul says.

That frightens me. Raoul notices and lays his hand on mine. 'If she's still hanging around the place, she'll have seen that you stayed the night. Perhaps she can see us now, at this very minute, having breakfast together and she's drawn her own conclusions. Believe me, Elisa, she's been stalking me for weeks. Anywhere I went, she'd turn up. I'm afraid she won't accept that there's nothing going on between us.'

'There isn't anything going on between us,' I point out.

'But she doesn't know that.'

'I don't want to come, Raoul. I'm going to my studio, I'm really busy.'

'Then lock your door. And don't let anyone in, not even customers.'

I don't want to keep the studio closed now that it's starting to go well again, but I nod in agreement.

We have a leisurely breakfast, Raoul reading his newspaper, me chatting with Valerie. We're just like any normal Dutch family with two working parents getting ready for the day ahead. After we've finished and tidied up, we get our coats. Raoul puts a box of apple juice and a slice of gingerbread into Valerie's rucksack.

We leave the house and drive Valerie to school. I catch myself looking for Sylvie on the way, but I don't see her anywhere. Once Valerie is in her classroom, we drive to the Essenburg Canal to pick up my bike, which is still outside Sylvie's front door. Raoul drops me and my bike off at the studio.

'Don't get out just yet,' he says, as I go to open the door.

He gets out, lifts my bike from the boot and sets it down. He looks around and then nods at me. His suspicion is contagious. I also look around when I get out and take my bike from him.

'Thanks,' I say.

'When I've finished with Noorda, I'll come straight to you.'

A warm feeling spreads through my belly and I suppress the temptation to kiss him. Instead I think about Sylvie's scrapbook and wheel my bike to the door.

'Elisa?'

I look around to see what he wants, wary of the gentle tone in his voice. He comes towards me with fast steps, bends down and his lips brush my own. Then he's gone.

I let the tension drain out of my body in a deep sigh, lock the studio door behind me. I have so much work to do.

The telephone rings at eleven o'clock. I pick up and answer absentmindedly. 'Elisa van Woerkom.' Only then does it occur to me that it could be Sylvie. I go to hang up in panic, but at the same instant I realise that it's too late for that. But it's not Sylvie.

'Elisa.' It's Raoul. 'Valerie has gone missing.'

'What? What do you mean?'

'I've just had a call from the school to say that Valerie isn't in the playground anymore. The infants had a break at quarter past ten, Valerie played with a go-cart for a bit, but when the children went back in she wasn't with them.'

The panic in Raoul's voice transfers to me. I hold the phone with one hand and start putting on my jacket with the other.

'Where are you now?'

'On my way to the school.'

'I'm coming.' I hang up, work my other arm into the jacket, grab my bag and dash to my bike out back. I run with it through the kitchen, through the studio, outside. Precious seconds are wasted shutting the door, doing up my jacket, but then I'm on the saddle and pedalling as fast as I can to Valerie's school. It's not far, but the streets seem to stretch out in front of me.

I arrive panting at the playground where Raoul is waiting for me in the doorway of the school building.

'Where are the police?' I ask, as I get off my bike and lock it.

'They went straight to Sylvie's house,' Raoul says. He grabs my arm and pulls me to the car.

'What are you going to do?' I ask, as he drags me along like a small child.

'Look for her, of course.'

Raoul tugs open the door and gets behind the wheel. I run to the passenger door and soon we're speeding out of the street.

'Sylvie definitely hasn't gone home. She knows that the police are watching her house,' I say. 'The best thing we can do is drive around. With a bit of luck we'll see them somewhere.' I'm not convinced that we'll have that much luck, but Raoul nods.

'Do you really think that Sylvie is behind this?' I ask.

'I don't just think it, I know it. The teachers on playground duty saw a young, blonde woman standing by the fence, just next to the shrubbery. If Valerie crawled under the fence there, the shrubs would have immediately hidden her from sight.

'Would she have just gone off with Sylvie like that? Did she know her that well?'

'Well enough, it seems,' Raoul snaps. 'You know yourself how trusting Valerie is.'

I glance over at him and see that his face is contorted with self-reproach.

'Sylvie won't do anything to Valerie,' I say with more conviction than I actually feel.

'Why has she taken her then? Give me one good reason for her to have done this!'

'Perhaps she wants to send a message to us,' I suggest.

'And what would that be?'

'That we're vulnerable.'

Raoul takes a left turn. He is still driving too fast, too pent-up. I can't do anything but anxiously ride along and check side streets to warn him of potential danger.

Of course there's no trace of Sylvie and Valerie, that would be too easy, but suddenly I get a brainwave, the kind when you can't believe you didn't think of it instantly.

'We'll call her,' I say. 'Who knows, she might pick up. She might be waiting for that.'

Raoul pulls over right away and turns off the engine.

I pass my phone to Raoul. 'You speak.'

Raoul takes the phone from me and puts it to his ear. I hear the ringing tone going on and on, but no one answers.

We look at each other in defeat.

'What now?' I say. Deep inside the panic is stirring.

I have to think, act, find Valerie. Panic leaves you paralysed. I take a deep breath.

'Where would you take a little girl you'd just snatched from the playground?' he asks.

I think long and hard. 'Somewhere little girls like, otherwise they whine and cry and want to go home. Sylvie can't drag a screaming child around, she'd be noticed. She's taken Valerie to a place where there are lots of children so that they can blend into the crowd.'

'Now you're assuming that she's not planning to do anything to Valerie,' Raoul says.

I don't reply, the fact I'm assuming that doesn't mean I'm sure of it.

Raoul starts the engine and moves away from the curb.

'Where are we going?' I ask.

'To the place Valerie likes best,' Raoul says.

'The zoo,' we say in unison.

The paths and terraces in the zoo are deserted. It's a cloudy, chilly day and there are only a few people about. Even the animals sit apathetically in their cages and stare at the visitors as if they're wondering why we don't have anything better to do.

'What did she like the last time we were here?' Raoul wonders as we come to a fork in the path.

'The stones,' I recall. 'And the monkeys. But what she really loved was that playground, do you remember?'

Raoul nods and turns left. A long footpath stretches out in front of us, passing the animals' cages. We rush to the play-ground. We can already see from a way off that there's nobody around. The terrace is empty, the seesaw rests on the grass and the swings hangs in the air.

Raoul stops. 'Shit,' he says.

At that moment my mobile goes and I'm in such a hurry to get it out of my bag that I almost drop it. Sylvie's name appears on the display. I show it to Raoul and press the green button with a shaking finger.

'Elisa here.'

'Hi Elisa, it's Sylvie,' Sylvie says in a clear and cheerful voice. 'I saw that you'd called.'

57.

At first I'm lost for words.

'Yes, that's right.' I'm wracking my brains, wondering how to approach this. Raoul tries to take the phone from me, but I turn away from him. 'We're looking for Valerie,' I say. 'She didn't return to the classroom after the break.'

'No, she didn't, she's with me,' Sylvie says, her voice warm. 'I picked her up so we could do something nice together. It's a good idea for a daughter and her new mother to do some bonding, you don't have to worry yourselves.'

I struggle to breathe and look at Raoul. 'She's with Sylvie.'

Raoul grabs the phone from my hand. 'Sylvie!' he snarls. 'What the fuck are you doing? Where are you?'

He listens to what Sylvie has to say. I stand closer to him and he stoops so that I can hear too.

'It's so lovely here. Have you ever been up the top of the Euromast? Valerie thinks it's fantastic too. What a view. No, Valerie, don't climb on anything. Come here will you!' We hear footsteps, the howl of a strong wind and Valerie's small, excited voice. Then Sylvie's back. 'Children,' she laughs. 'Climbing up everything, absolutely no sense of danger.'

Raoul gestures for me to follow him and begins running for the exit.

'Sylvie.' He's outwardly calm. 'I want you to take Valerie down to the bottom now and wait for me by the entrance.'

'Sure, that's fine,' Sylvie says. 'Valerie! Are you coming? Daddy's coming to pick us up. What? You want to have another go at looking down? Well, all right then. I'll hold onto you.'

'Sylvie!' Raoul roars.

'Just a minute, Raoul. Valerie wants to look over the top again. You've got a tough daughter, you know, no fear of heights at all! Listen, I'm going to hang up, I've got to hold onto her.'

'Take her downstairs now! What the hell do you think you're doing? I…' Raoul looks as if he wants to smash the phone.

I hurry after him. 'She's not really letting Valerie hang over the edge, is she?'

'God knows,' Raoul pants. 'That woman is totally disturbed, but if she does anything to my daughter, I'll kill her.'

The exit to the zoo looms and we're soon in the car. Raoul's tearing along the street before I've even got my door closed.

Fear shrouds us all the way to the Euromast. We race along the Gravendijkwal and I stare out of the window, waiting to see the 185-metre-high tower. In the meantime, I apprise Noorda of the situation. The Euromast comes into view. I look up at the viewing platform, tense with fear, but it's too far away for me to be able to make anything out.

'It's all my fault,' Raoul drives through a red light. 'If I'd never got involved with that woman, Lydia would still be alive and Valerie wouldn't be in danger. How could I have been such a fool!'

I don't say anything.

We drive on in silence and the Euromast gets closer. I can't see any commotion in the vicinity of the tower to suggest something dreadful has happened.

'She wouldn't do anything to a small child, surely. Valerie isn't outside anywhere.'

Raoul doesn't respond and I know what he's thinking. Anyone who shoots another woman in cold blood in order to steal her husband probably wouldn't have many scruples about a child.

Raoul parks illegally and jumps out of the car. He slams the door without taking the keys from the ignition.

I run after Raoul, risking my life across the busy road, and see him disappear through the entrance. Sylvie is nowhere to be seen and neither is Valerie.

I run inside.

There's Raoul, on his knees in the middle of the lobby, his arms around his daughter. He can't stop kissing her on both cheeks. There's no sign of Sylvie.

We head straight back to Raoul's, calling the school and the police to say we've got Valerie on the way. Afterwards Valerie's small voice breaks the silence. 'I was high up, wasn't I, Daddy? I spat down.'

'Was Sylvie holding onto you tight, darling?'

'Yes, very. She had her arms hard around me. It hurt,' Valerie says, before quickly adding, 'But she wasn't doing it deliberately. Sylvie is nice, isn't she?'

Raoul doesn't answer.

I can't speak. I lean against the passenger door, my face against the window, and weep soundlessly. Raoul glances over and rests his hand on top of mine. Although I usually prefer the person driving to keep their hands on the wheel, I don't protest. The warmth of Raoul's hand seems to spread through the rest of my body and chases away my fear.

'Where are we going? Do I have to go back to school?' Valerie asks.

'No,' Raoul says. 'You can stay at home and I don't have to go to the office. We'll take a day off, what do you think about that?'

'Good,' Valerie says and gazes out of the window. 'Are you having a day off too, Elisa?'

I open my eyes and massage my forehead. 'Yes,' I answer. 'I was due one.'

'Yay!' Valerie cheers. 'Can I watch a DVD then? With a bowl of crisps?'

'Sure,' Raoul says.

In the house, Valerie's rapid steps and happy voice fill the sitting room. She pulls open drawers, looking for her felt tips, while Raoul rummages around in the kitchen.

'Hungry?' he asks me. 'I could fry some eggs.'

'Lovely.' I lean on the bench and look through the open kitchen doors into the dining room where Valerie has settled at the table with a colouring pad. 'I hope I never have to go through anything like that again.'

'So you were worried she'd do something to Valerie,' Raoul remarks as he lights the gas.

'I couldn't imagine it, but if she's capable of murdering someone in cold blood…'

Raoul nods and puts a frying pan on the stove. He squirts a dash of liquid margarine from a bottle into it, breaks three eggs into the pan and begins to grate some cheese.

'What will they do when they find Sylvie?' I ask as I watch.

'Hang her from the highest tree,' Raoul says grimly. 'Or they'll let her off because of lack of evidence, everything will depend on that, knowing our legal system. And I'll spend the rest of my life worrying about Valerie, and about you.'

He goes to carry his plate into the dining room but I grab his arm. 'What do you mean? You don't think it's going to stop at this?'

'No, I'm rather afraid it won't.'

Lydia

58.

Elisa's at my door right on time. To my surprise she's come in a car, but before I can ask her where she got it from, I see Thomas sitting at the wheel. And if that's not enough, Sylvie's in the back seat.

'Are they coming too?' I ask, disappointed.

Elisa nods. I wish she would stop trying to force her friends on me. I nearly back out and go inside again, but then I get a better look at Sylvie.

I greet Thomas and climb in next to Sylvie. She's wearing a short red, retro-style dress and a scarf knotted around her bleached hair. Her face is carefully made up and she looks breathtakingly beautiful.

'Hi Sylvie, how lovely you're coming with us,' I say. 'Where are we going?'

'Oliva,' she says. 'Do you know it?'

I've never heard of it, but I nod. Elisa sits next to Thomas, relieved. He drives off.

I glance at Sylvie and smile. 'You look nice, Sylvie. Is that in now, a scarf around your hair?'

Sylvie looks as if she's checking for veiled sarcasm in my question, but I give her such a friendly smile that she relaxes.

'Oh, I'm not that into fashion,' she confides in me. 'I just think it looks nice, so I wear it.'

'A friend of mine spotted someone wearing a scarf around their head on Saturday. Where was it again? Oh yes, in the Euromast restaurant. That's why I thought it might be a new trend.'

Sylvie looks a bit shifty, but doesn't say anything.

'Nice dress too,' I continue. 'Bit tight though. Wasn't it difficult to get into the car?'

Elisa gives me a warning look over her shoulder.

'It's not that bad,' Sylvie says curtly. 'I often wear tight skirts and dresses, so I know how to move in them.'

'I can believe that,' I say, getting a mental image of Sylvie shimmying in front of Raoul.

Why am I going with them? These are Elisa's friends, not mine. If I'd known they'd be coming, I would have happily stayed at home. I get out my mobile and begin to type a text message. Hey Luke! Going to eat at Oliva. Want to join?

His reply comes back straight away. Was about to get takeaway. See you there!

After that I put my phone away and announce that Luke is coming too.

'Great,' Elisa says. 'Does he know where it is?'

'I think so. Luke knows all the restaurants in Rotterdam.'

'Who's Luke?' Sylvie asks.

'One of my colleagues,' I say. 'And a good friend.'

'A very good friend,' Elisa adds. 'You're always talking about him. Luke said this, Luke did that.'

'Really?' Sylvie's expression suggests she thinks I'm having an affair. Of course I could explain that Luke's gay, but what's the point. It's the same as telling Luke that Sylvie is straight.

'So Raoul will be getting home late tonight?' Elisa glances at me.

I nod. 'As usual.'

'He must be busy, being the director of such a big company,' Thomas comments.

'It's not that big,' I say. 'But he's busy, it's true. I don't think Software International is doing too well. They need a few new customers.'

'Perhaps they should annihilate it,' Sylvie suggests.

'What?'

'Annihilate,' Sylvie repeats. 'That happened to the nail studio where I worked a while back. It wasn't going well so the whole company had to be annihilated.'

'You're kidding?' I ask, but Sylvie nods with conviction.

'Really,' she says.

'The whole company?' I ask, appalled.

Sylvie nods, a little less sure of herself.

'My god,' I quaver.

I look in the wing mirror and see a smile on Thomas's lips. I don't believe I've ever seen him laugh before.

Elisa quickly changes the subject and Sylvie ignores me for the rest of the ride.

Oliva turns out to be a nice place. It's a breath of fresh air to eat Italian without having plastic bunches of grapes hanging above your head, or being ringed in by basketed chiantis. This restaurant has a young, modern atmosphere, an extensive drinks list, mellow lighting and tables made out of wood and dark-green metal. The wall paintings and large blackboards displaying the menu make the space particularly attractive.

When our aperitifs are on the table, together with dishes of olives and baskets of bread with basil oil, Luke arrives.

'Hi everyone!' he says. 'I'm Luke, a colleague of Lydia's.'

255

He shakes hands and is told several times how nice it is he's here. He squeezes in next to me and winks. 'All right?'

I smile. 'Glad you could join us.'

Sylvie is on Luke's other side and studies him with great interest. 'So you work with Lydia,' she says with her most attractive smile. 'That must mean you're a teacher as well.'

Of course Luke can't do anything but confirm this and I listen to the conversation that ensues. I had no idea that Sylvie admired teachers so much, and particularly teachers in multi-denominational state schools.

'It seems like such rewarding work,' she says, with a slight shake of the head, as if she can't imagine how altruistic you have to be to become a teacher. 'It must be lovely to be able to give so much to people.'

'It would be nice, if only they wanted to listen,' Luke confesses.

'But they do, don't they? I can't imagine that you wouldn't have authority in the classroom,' Sylvie fawns, with an admiring glance at Luke's muscular arms.

Luke throws me a pleading look, but I have no time to help him before my mobile rings. It's Raoul. I tell him where I am and that Valerie is staying over at Jasmine's.

I put my mobile back in my bag, 'Raoul's coming too.'

'Oh, lovely,' Elisa says.

Thomas gives her a sideways look. As usual he's withdrawn to the point of rudeness, but Elisa doesn't seem to notice. She chats to Luke and Sylvie. I've got Thomas on my other side, and I study him disapprovingly. Look at him slouching there, his elbows on the table. How can he think he's ever going to attract my sister if he sits there like a sack of hay, with most of his face hidden behind his long hair.

'Why are you staring at me?' Thomas asks.

'No reason.' I pick up my wine glass. I can hardly admit that he reminds me of my neighbour's dog – an animal with long wispy hair. What are they called again? Afghan hounds, or something like that.

Sylvie is getting up and going to the bathroom.

'I'll come with you.' I push my chair back and follow her into the ladies toilets. Sylvie stands in front of the mirror to fix her headscarf. I disappear into a cubicle.

When I've finished, Sylvie is still there, holding an eyeliner. I wash my hands and see she's looking at me.

'Nice guy, that colleague of yours,' she says.

'Luke? Yes, he's definitely a nice guy.' I rinse the soap from my hands.

Sylvie skilfully applies eyeliner. 'Is he married?' she asks casually.

'No.'

'So he's got a girlfriend?'

I dry my hands and lean against the sink. This is interesting. There's just one man in our group who Sylvie hasn't yet tested her skills of seduction on and, of course, she's pouncing on him.

'He hasn't got a girlfriend. I've never heard him mention any women.'

Sylvie's eyes light up and I have difficulty restraining a laugh.

'I've never seen Luke pay so much attention to a woman before.'

Sylvie smiles. 'I thought we had some chemistry.'

'I thought you liked Thomas,' I say lightly.

Sylvie pulls a face. 'Thomas has only got eyes for Elisa.'

'Maybe you should make him a bit jealous,' I suggest. 'That can work wonders.'

Sylvie studies her appearance in the mirror. Her beautiful appearance. I don't know why Thomas didn't fall head over heels long ago.

We join the others back at the table.

59.

We're well into dinner when Raoul hurries into the restaurant. His eyes glide over our group, then he bends down and kisses me. 'Hi darling.'

'Hi.' I return his kiss. 'You're actually quite early tonight!'

'The system went down and there wasn't anything else to do.' Raoul sits in the one remaining chair, to Elisa's right. He smiles at her for a moment before his eyes move on to the others. I watch him closely out of the corner of my eye. I see Sylvie's smile, Raoul's tense jaw. I register that his gaze rests a little longer on Sylvie's bare shoulders and the curve of her breasts under the tight red dress.

'Bon appétit! I'll order quickly and see if I can catch up with you. It won't be that difficult – I could eat a horse!' Raoul beckons to the waitress. She comes at once and stands over him with the expression of delight I've seen on so many women.

'Would you care to look at the menu, sir?' she asks with the sweetest smile.

'I'll just have the same as her,' Raoul says, nodding at Elisa's plate.

'Grilled tuna with roasted onions and balsamic vinegar,' Elisa says. 'Do you like that?'

'If you like it, I'm sure I will too.'

I sit at the furthest corner away, opposite them, and study them for a while before Luke kicks me under the table. To my astonishment, Sylvie has taken his hand and is admiring his fingers.

'I've never seen a man with such beautiful hands and such manicured nails,' she says. 'You look like a pianist! Do you play the piano?'

'Erm, no actually, I don't.' Luke smiles and tries to withdraw his hand, without success.

'I always pay attention to hands. I'm a nail technician, you see,' Sylvie explains. 'I recently read a book about telling people's personalities from their fingernails. Did you know, you can tell an awful lot about a person from how they look after their nails?'

'Really?' I say in interest. 'What kind of things?'

'Just things about their character,' Sylvie says.

'So if you have fake fingernails' – I glance at Sylvie's gel nails – 'what would that say about your personality?'

'I don't know,' Sylvie says. 'You tell me.'

I shake my head and open my mouth to say something, but Elisa is too quick for me.

'I wish I had such nice nails,' she says. 'You should see mine, I can't stop biting them. When are you going to give me a manicure again, Sylvie?'

'Soon,' Sylvie says stiffly.

'They look very realistic,' Luke says admiringly. 'It's really not possible to tell fake ones from real ones these days.'

'I agree,' I join in. 'I find it exhausting sometimes, don't you? I mean, what's left that's genuine these days? Pumped-up lips, hair extensions, silicone tits, plastic confidence, all of it. Some women have more paint on their faces than I've got on my front door!' I laugh but Raoul's the only one who laughs along.

'You should try going out with one of those women!' he says. 'Imagine the fright when they take it all off before bed!'

My suspicions vanish. I take a nasty pleasure in looking at Sylvie, sitting there quietly with all her wonderful make-up. Touchdown, girl.

Luke apparently feels sorry for Sylvie and begins a new conversation with her. He's such an attentive, sweet dining companion that the smile returns to her face.

Dear Luke, I think affectionately. What a shame you're gay. I'd fall for you completely if you weren't.

We sit there chatting and eating. I talk and drink too much and become aware of it, but no one seems bothered. There's a lot of laughter, and even Sylvie smiles at my stream of anecdotes. I'm probably a little drunk, this will have to be my last glass. The conversation turns to Bilal and my problems at school, but I shut it down. 'Come on, I'm having a night out!'

Luke nods. 'That's it, don't let the boy ruin your evening, Lydia.' He shifts his position to get away from Sylvie, who's leaning against him, and looks at me with despair. Once more he's been too accommodating towards her. Sylvie's left hand is on the table, but her right one has disappeared. I try to picture where it is now and have trouble keeping a straight face.

'Hey, Luke, have you left your boyfriend at home on his own? He could have come too.' I realise what I'm saying as it leaves my mouth. It's a careless slip, really it is. I didn't stop to think that no one knows that Luke is gay. But what difference does it make? It's only a secret at school, it won't matter to anyone here. Except to Sylvie. I see the confusion on her face as she looks from me to Luke. There might be a way out of this, I could say that Sven's a friend he was supposed to be meeting tonight, but the disbelief and anger that washes over Luke's face makes that impossible. And Sylvie, of course, makes it even worse.

'Your boyfriend? You're not a bit queer or something are you?'

There's a silence around the table. I fidget and don't say anything. Luke stares at his plate.

'Not a bit,' he says in a clipped voice. 'One hundred per cent.'

Another painful silence.

'Well,' Elisa says finally. 'Do we really have to be reduced to silence by this?'

'Of course not, there's nothing wrong with it,' Sylvie says. 'I've got nothing against queers. I mean, well, what a nasty word it is. It sounds so insulting. Like a swear word. Of course it's not, but...' she stops, tangled up in her own words. 'I only mean that I've got nothing against gays.'

Luke lays his hand on hers and says, 'Don't worry about it. Just eat your pudding.'

Sylvie stares at his hand on hers and turns bright red. I take another sip of wine and look away. The prank has been a complete success, but the fun's gone out of it somehow.

The conversation is resumed and when I go to the toilet a second time, Luke comes after me.

'Sorry,' I say at once as we go up the stairs. 'It just slipped out.'

'You're suffering from that quite a lot at the moment, aren't you?' Luke says. 'What did you say to Sylvie in the toilets earlier on in the evening?'

I have to hold on tightly to stop myself falling down the stairs. 'Nothing, what do you mean?'

'You didn't warn her a little so that she could have spared herself the trouble?' Luke says.

'Should I have?'

'That's what I would have expected you to do, yes. Then you would have saved us both from a painful situation.'

'Sorry,' I say, full of remorse. I giggle a little, trying to break the tension. 'But it was quite funny, don't you think?'

Luke gives me a look that I'm not used to from him. 'No,' he says. 'I don't think it was at all.'

60.

Luke doesn't look at me once after that. I play with my napkin. He's not really angry, is he? He must be able to understand that it was a joke? Irritated in turn, I ignore Luke and look at my husband, who seems to be finding it all terribly amusing. He winks at me.

That's why I love Raoul. He might not always be faithful, but he'll never leave me. We are soul mates, friends and lovers too. He'll never find this combination with another woman.

The atmosphere around the table is a little subdued. Elisa does her best to raise our spirits with a funny story, but it doesn't work. After the pudding, we stand up quickly, one by one.

'Do you want to leave now?' Raoul asks.

I shake my head. 'I quite fancy a Sambuca.'

We get up, say our farewells to everyone and sit back down again. We face each other in silence and order two Sambucas. Raoul begins to say how funny it was to see Sylvie's attitude change after Luke was forced out of the closet. He sniggers as he does an impression of her hanging onto Luke and afterwards sitting up straight like a prudish Victorian lady.

'Luke wasn't too happy,' I say.

'He'll get over it,' Raoul reassures me.

We look at each other and burst out laughing. We discuss the evening and how nice it is to sit here like this; it's been ages. The Sambucas arrive and we clink glasses. And then I remember what Jasmine told me earlier in the evening.

'Was that appointment on Saturday worthwhile?' I ask.

'Appointment?' Raoul takes a sip of Sambuca and puts his glass back down.

'With that German.'

'Oh that. Yes, that went fine.'

'You went to the Euromast, didn't you?'

'Yes, how did you know that?'

I keep my eyes fixed on his. 'Because Jasmine saw you there, with a woman.'

Raoul looks at me with a broad grin. 'That was Helga, Ernst's wife. She always goes on business trips with him.'

'Oh,' I smile back. Jasmine didn't say that he was there with two people. Logic and emotions compete to get a hold on the situation.

'Raoul…'

'Hmm?' He continues to look at me in the same sphinx-like manner, as if he's finding my questions immensely amusing.

'If you were in love with another woman, and I don't mean just a bit but properly in love, you'd tell me, wouldn't you?'

'God, no,' Raoul reacts at once. 'That would mean that you'd leave me and I wouldn't want to run that risk.'

'I wouldn't be so quick to walk, you know. We're all attracted to other people at some time or other. You just have to get over those feelings, you can't do anything about it. The point is more what you do with those feelings, how far you let it go. What would be the boundary for you if I fell in love with someone else?'

264

Raoul reflects on it. 'I don't know,' he says. 'I've never thought about it. I think this is more about where your boundaries lie.'

'Are you interested?'

'I'd like to know, yes.' He sits on the edge of his stool, wearing the same smug smile on his face and I become certain that he's taking me for a ride. Don't ask me how, but I see it on him. Usually he would have reacted with more irritation. This light-hearted, amused pose is disguising something else.

I take a deep breath and say, 'What I expect from a marriage is total fidelity, companionship and respect. Cheating doesn't go with any of those things. If I found out that you were building the same kind of relationship with another woman as you have with me—' I pause for a second so that the next words will fully sink in. I have his full attention now.

'What would you do?'

'I'd ruin you,' I say. 'I'd take out every share I have in Software International, I'd throw you out of the house my parents bought for us and I'd insist on getting full custody of Valerie. I don't really believe in co-parenting, do you?'

Raoul looks at me in disbelief.

I smile at him and smack his thigh. 'It's just as well you're not cheating, isn't it?' I laugh to break the tension.

Raoul doesn't laugh along.

It's late when we leave Oliva and walk along Witte de With Street. Raoul has left the car in the closest multi-storey car park, but it's still quite a trek.

I don't like multi-storey car parks. I refuse to park in them if I'm on my own, especially late at night, but even with Raoul close by, I feel uneasy. What would Raoul be able to do if five men suddenly confronted us? Not that that's ever happened, but still. I'm always relieved when we're safely in the car.

We go to the ticket machine and the display tells us we owe ten euros.

'Ten euros! For that short time!' Raoul says. 'You don't have a ten, do you?'

I get out my purse and take out a ten-euro note. The machine swallows it up and gives us our ticket back.

'Where's the car?' I ask.

'On the third floor. Do you want to take the lift or the stairs?' Raoul stands in front of the lift waiting for my reply.

'The stairs.' I don't like lifts. They make me claustrophobic and a lift in a car park is something I find totally unpleasant.

We walk upstairs and discuss the evening. The sound of our footsteps echoes behind us in the empty stairwell – our steps sound too loud, too present. During a moment of silence, I think I can hear the sound of footsteps somewhere below us. But we're already at the top so I carry on chatting until we get to the car.

'Shit.' Raoul feels around in his pockets and frowns.

'What is it?' I look at him over the roof of the car. 'Can't you find the keys?'

'No.' Raoul pulls the lining out of his jacket pockets and pats his trousers. 'I'm sure I put them in my jacket.'

'Trouser pockets?' I suggest.

'I just felt them, they're empty.' Just to make sure, Raoul turns his trouser pocket linings inside out. Next he checks the inside pocket of his leather jacket, but it only contains his mobile.

'Perhaps I dropped them by the ticket machine.'

'Or in the restaurant,' I say. 'We'll have to go back.' But then I rummage around in my bag and like a magician producing something from a hat, I get out my key. 'Tadaaa! I had a key in my bag.'

Raoul looks relieved, but he's still annoyed about losing his own. 'You get into the car and I'll just check that I didn't drop it next to the machine,' he says, and before I can dissuade him he's gone.

He's left me here alone. It's eleven at night in a multi-storey car park, he knows how scary I find that.

'Bastard,' I mutter as I quickly get into the car.

And then I hear them again. Footsteps.

I glance in the side mirror, but I can't see anyone. I look back over my shoulder and can't see anyone, but I can hear them. Calm, emphatic footsteps that are advancing nevertheless.

I squirm in my seat. Bloody Raoul, why did you leave me on my own! I sink down and listen hard, but all I can hear is my own heart pounding.

The footsteps have stopped, but the familiar sound of a door being opened doesn't follow. There's no engine being started up, nothing to suggest that the person has come to get their car.

The door is locked, I reassure myself. They can't do anything.

All of a sudden a dark shape surfaces right next to my door and I scream.

61.

The shape bends down and Raoul's laughing face appears through the window. He dangles the car keys between his fingers. I unlock the doors and Raoul gets in the driver's side.

'Where the hell did you get to?!' I shout, verging on hysterical. 'And what possessed you to leave me here alone, you idiot!'

Raoul looks at me with astonishment. 'You were safe in the car, though. What happened?'

'I heard footsteps!'

Raoul bursts out laughing and starts up the engine.

'Go on, laugh. If you ever leave me alone in a garage again, you'll pay for it.'

'Sorry,' Raoul apologises. 'I was only away for a couple of minutes.'

'It seemed much longer. And? Were the keys next to the machine?'

'No, there's a hole in my jacket lining and they'd fallen through.'

'And you say I'm scatterbrained!'

We leave the garage and drive into the black night. A dark blue car drives through the boomgate behind us. My attacker from in there, I think with a smile. A bit strange it took them so long to get into their car and drive off, but as we enter Hillegersberg, I forget about it.

'I'm just popping round to Jasmine's to see whether everything went all right tonight,' I say when we arrive home.

Raoul opens the front door and looks at his watch. 'This late?'

'There's still a light on, so...You never know, they might be struggling with a crying Valerie,' I say. 'Then I could bring her back with me. I'll only be a minute.'

'All right.' Raoul goes inside, throws me the bunch of keys and closes the front door behind him.

I quickly cross the road and ring on Jasmine's bell. Her husband Lex opens up.

'Hey!' he says. 'Did you have a good evening?'

'I was about to ask you that,' I say with a smile. 'Are the girls asleep?'

'They're sleeping like babies. They had a bath together and played with the Barbies in bed. Once they'd fallen asleep we had to dig out all the shoes, skirts and other stuff from around them,' Lex chuckles.

'Great. I just thought I'd come and make sure,' I say. 'Raoul will pick her up tomorrow morning.'

'Fine. Good night!' Lex raises his hand and closes the door.

I hurry over the street. The whole neighbourhood is still. The car park has made me nervous. As usual, the street seems quiet and safe. And then I hear footsteps behind me. I look back over my shoulder, but don't see anyone.

The hair on my arms and the back of my neck rises and my heart beats faster as I walk. I study the trees, someone could easily hide there, but no one jumps out. Of course not, why would they? Yes, Bilal, but I'm not scared of him anymore. Deep down, I've never believed that he would really do anything to me. I mean, then he would have done it long ago, right? He's had opportunity enough.

But there's still that fear. My mouth becomes dry as I hurry along the pavement. There's my house, my safe house. Just a few more steps and I'll be inside. There, in the hall, I'll hang up my jacket and laugh away my fears.

Again the sound of soft but fast footsteps behind me, as if someone wants to cross over without being seen or heard. I glance back but still don't see anyone. The dark silhouettes of the trees along the kerb are the only witnesses to my terror.

I walk down the garden path. There's a cracking sound behind me and I run to the door. The key, quick, quick! Bloody hell, why did Raoul lock the door behind him! He could have left it on the latch.

There's a noise behind me. The unmistakeable sound of one, two, three footsteps.

I don't look back, but panic builds up inside me. I scrape the key over the lock with jerky movements, not able to find the slot, and then finally it slides in and I can turn it. But I don't get that far.

I hear the crunch of the gravel and I know. I turn around. Someone is on our garden path, a few metres away, but I can't make them out. The moon is shining, but the trees cast shadow over the path.

'Yes?' My voice sounds high-pitched with fear. I see something glittering. I take a step backwards, so that I'm standing with my back to the door.

'What…' I stammer and try to make out the object that's pointing at me. It's a gun.

'Hello, Lydia,' a familiar voice says.

My astonishment is complete. It's as if my blood has stopped circulating. I can't believe this is happening, that the person facing me is really going to murder me. Impossible – we know each other too well.

I fiddle helplessly with the lock. The lock is obstinate and my trembling fingers can't get the key to budge.

Again the gravel crunches, my attacker comes closer. There's no point fleeing anymore, the best thing I can do is try to start up a conversation.

I turn back around, with legs of jelly, and lean my back against the front door.

'What is all this?' I rasp. 'You've got to be joking, right?'

We stand a few steps away from each other. Moonlight falls onto the face before me.

'Far from it,' a soft voice says.

How strange to hear my death sentence announced in such a friendly manner. I inch along the door, think about jumping into the bushes and hear the click of the trigger.

'No,' I say. 'Please!'

I raise my hands, as if they might protect me. But I see the finger pressed against the trigger, I see a squinted eye focusing and a body that prepares itself for the recoil.

I stare into the black circle in front of me and plead, 'Please, I don't understand why. What have I done? Please, don't do this! I don't want to die!'

But the shot still comes.

Elisa

62.

'So you've moved in with Raoul,' Thomas says. He's standing in my bedroom with his hands in his pockets. I'm throwing the contents of my wardrobe into my suitcases.

'For now,' I make the distinction. 'As long as Sylvie is still free, all three of us are in danger.'

'Do you really believe that?' Thomas picks up a jumper that has fallen from a pile and lays it in the suitcase. 'Sylvie might have lost it once but that doesn't mean she's a serial killer. She didn't do anything to Valerie.'

'She should never have taken her.' I put some summer shoes in. 'What kind of person does that?'

'Well…' Thomas frowns at the way I'm packing my cases. 'Why are you packing everything so messily? It'll crumple.'

I look at him in surprise. 'I'm in a hurry.'

'To get back to Raoul.'

'To get away from here. I'm scared of being at home on my own.'

This was also the reason I asked Thomas to come with me. Although I can hardly believe that Sylvie would do anything to me, I'm not taking any risks.

'Elisa,' Thomas begins.

I wipe a lock of hair away from my burning forehead and look at him.

'Is there any chance…I mean, do you think that we ever…' He breaks off his sentence, pushes his hands deeper into his pockets and stares at his shoes.

I straighten up and drop a few bras into my case. 'You're my best friend, Thomas,' I say. 'Always have been, and always will be.'

Of course, I understand that that's not what he means, but to avoid the sensitive subject, I carry one of the packed cases out of the bedroom. The doorbell goes downstairs and Thomas goes past me to open up. I return to the bedroom, add a couple of nightdresses to a suitcase and click it shut.

Thomas has opened the front door. I hear him talking for a while and then closing it again.

'Who was that?' I call down the stairs.

'Someone asking for directions,' Thomas says.

He rummages around in the kitchen while I wait for him to come back upstairs. Soon I hear his heavy footsteps mounting the stairs and through the bedroom door I see him picking up the case I've left on the landing.

'That's heavy,' he grumbles. 'Did you put bricks in it?'

'No, my shoes. Here's another one.' I take the second case from my bed and push it across the landing to the edge of the stairs. Thomas has gone outside and is putting the case in the boot of his car. I begin to drag a load down the stairs, but when I've got as far as the second step I realise I should have left this to Thomas.

'Thomas!' I call out.

No reply. He's probably still at the car. I wait a while, but he doesn't come back in. I sink down onto the top step, hold the case by its handle and wait for him to reappear. I think I hear him walking around in the kitchen and I lean forwards. 'Thomas!'

He comes into the hall, sees the problem and runs up the stairs to take the suitcase from me. 'That's much too heavy for you. You could have fallen down the stairs,' he says. 'I've made coffee. Shall we have a quick cup before I drop you off?'

I don't feel like coffee and certainly not the disgusting stuff he makes, but I can hardly say no now that he's gone to the trouble of helping me pack and is giving me a lift to Raoul's. Not something he's pleased about. I would never have asked him if Raoul hadn't been in meetings all afternoon.

'Okay,' I say, following him downstairs. Thomas sets the case down in the hall, goes into the kitchen and pours out two large mugs of coffee.

It's hot inside the house, so we go and sit in the garden under the pear tree. The sunlight plays through the foliage. Thomas sits there staring at me with sad eyes.

I avoid his gaze and sip my undrinkable coffee. It's hard to relax around him.

'Is the coffee nice?' Thomas asks.

'Lovely.' I take a sip.

'Not too strong?'

'A little,' I admit.

'I'll get some sugar.' Thomas gets up and returns with the sugar pot. He scoops a couple of spoonfuls into my mug. I smile at him and stir my coffee.

'Elisa,' Thomas says as he sits down. 'I want to talk to you.'

'You say that so seriously.'

'I am serious. I've been trying to talk to you for ages, but you keep avoiding me.'

I stare at the dark contents of my mug. 'If I'm avoiding you, it might be that I have a reason to.'

'Maybe, but it seems better to talk about it than to keep silent.'

'Let's not do this. It just makes everything more…difficult.'

'It's difficult already,' Thomas says. 'At least for me it is. I know that there can never be anything between us, that you only consider me a good friend, but I want to tell you how I feel, just once.'

I look at him helplessly, incapable of diverting the course of this conversation. I'm on the point of losing a very good friend.

'Say it then.'

Thomas is sitting on the edge of his chair. He bends forwards so that his long dark hair falls in front of his face. I allow him to take my hand and give it a kiss.

'Ever since we got to know each other when we were students, you've been my best friend,' he says. 'While everyone else ridiculed me and laughed behind my back, you offered me friendship, you gave me confidence. Without you, art college would have been hell. That's why you have the right to be happy too, even if that's not with me. But if it's not with me, I don't want to stick around.'

I look at him in alarm. 'What do you mean? Where are you going?'

'I'm going away.' Thomas lets go of my hand and stares at the ground.

'Where? Oh no, Thomas, don't go away! First I lose Lydia, then Sylvie and now you as well! You can't do this to me!' As I'm saying it, I realise how selfish it sounds.

'You've got Raoul,' Thomas reminds me. 'And as far as Sylvie is concerned, you haven't lost her. Really, you haven't lost her,' Thomas says. 'I've sent a letter to the police saying that she's innocent. They won't believe it straight away, but eventually they'll realise that I'm telling the truth.'

Goose bumps spread over my arms and legs.

'What do you mean? How do you know that?'

The expression on Thomas's face changes. A hard glint appears in his eyes.

'Your sister wasn't a nice person,' he says. 'She got in your way, she didn't let you make any decisions of your own, live your own life. She decided what was good for you, who your friends should be.'

'Why on earth do you think that? Lydia didn't do that at all. She interfered with my life a bit too much, but it wasn't as bad as that.'

'She didn't like me.' Thomas's eyes sparkle strangely. 'She thought I was a loser, not fit to be your friend.'

'Did she say that?' I cry out.

'She didn't have to. You must have felt it too – as soon as Lydia got to know me, you started being distant,' Thomas accuses. 'Maybe you didn't realise it, but Lydia had enormous influence over you. You took her into account in every decision you ever made in your life. We might have had a relationship if she hadn't stood in the way. Really, Elisa, you're so much better off without her.'

It's as if I'm sitting next to a stranger.

There's no point arguing, he's too convinced that he's right. I begin to feel scared. Thomas has always been different, but I liked that, it was artistic. But now he's frightening me. He must see that I don't quite understand.

'I did it for you,' he says. 'You understand that, don't you? You weren't getting any space to develop, to form your own opinions, to live a life like Lydia had. You were being suffocated. I had to intervene.'

He is begging for understanding, but the meaning of his words barely sinks in. I sit on the edge of my chair, straight-backed and cold, while my brain disassembles everything I thought I knew.

'I know that deep in your heart, you can't live without me,' Thomas continues, emotionlessly. 'Raoul is just a whim of yours.

Sooner or later he'll meet another Sylvie and he'll cheat on you. Why would you put yourself through that when you know that I'd never, ever hurt you? Don't look so frightened! I love you!'

'Sylvie,' I say with difficulty. 'Where's Sylvie?'

'How should I know? She's on the run, but they'll find her. And then they'll let her go again. Sylvie's a good girl. I've got nothing against her and she's always been kind to me. She has no idea that I found the gun in her drawer. I put it back again. I've sent a letter to the police so they'll have to let her go. I don't want her to pay for something she hasn't done.'

'You…' I whisper. 'You murdered my sister? And that letter? Did you send that to her?' I don't have to ask the question. I bury my face in my hands and mutter, 'Oh my god, so Noorda was right. He said that it was quite possible that someone else was taking advantage of the situation with Bilal. But you… Why? Why, Thomas?'

Thomas takes my hands away from my face. 'I did it for you, Elisa. I've explained that, haven't I? Lydia had to die so that you could live. That happens sometimes with embryos, one survives at the other's cost. It's as a kind of law of nature.'

I try to speak, but my throat produces only a few unintelligible sounds. I feel dizzy. My head has suddenly become too heavy to hold upright.

When I look up, Thomas touches my cheek tenderly.

'It doesn't take long,' he says. 'And it doesn't hurt either. It's awful that I have to do this to you, but there's no other way. We simply had to talk this through.'

I look at him, confused, and watch his eyes travel down to the mug on the ground. There's a layer of sediment in it. Oh my god, what was in the coffee? And I drank all of it, every last drop.

He sits there, with a concerned look on his face, his hands ready to catch me as I fall.

I shake my head slowly. The garden spins around me. If I

stood up now, I wouldn't get far. A leaden feeling spreads over me and stops me from thinking clearly. I rub my forehead and eyes with my fingertips. Don't fall asleep, keep your eyes open! What did he put in the coffee?

I get up to keep moving, intending to splash cold water on my face but I'm completely disorientated. I bump into the garden table, of which there are suddenly two, fall to the ground and have trouble getting up again. And then I see four legs and four black boots standing in front of me. Two Thomases peer down.

'Let me help you up,' he says. 'You'll hurt yourself.'

Strong arms pull me up and guide me into the house. What is he going to do now? No, I beg silently. Please not.

I fight to keep hold of my senses, but I feel myself losing the battle. I'm being sucked into a whirlpool, deeper and deeper. I gravitate towards passiveness. There's no way to fight this. I feel like I haven't slept for days. Lie down, I want to lie down. I don't want to be dragged upstairs to my bedroom, that's too far. Thomas picks me up and carries me upstairs, but I'm gone before we reach the landing. Halfway up the stairs I feel a long, damp kiss on my mouth before my vision fades and I surrender.

63.

It feels like I'm floating and my body tingles all over, as if I've been wired to an invisible energy source. It's blue around me and very bright. I move around, at the speed of my thoughts. My senses have never been this sharp and I'm aware of being on my way to a larger entity.

I'm dead. No, I'm not dead, I'm alive in the next stage. Death is not the end, it's just another natural process. I'm the same person as before.

It is getting colder. A voice reaches me and I look ahead at the trembling apparition. It gets closer all the time.

'Lydia,' I whisper.

A cautious happiness bubbles up inside. I'm crying. She approaches slowly, until she's standing right in front of me. She's not pale or transparent, but just like she always was.

'Elisa,' she says with a smile.

I can't get a single word out. We step forward and embrace. When I finally let my sister go, she seems to fade. I try to grab hold of her arm, but my hand goes through it.

'Don't go away!' I cry. 'Please!'

Lydia gives me a loving look and nods towards something below. 'You don't belong here, Elisa. Go back. It's better that way.'

When I open my eyes again, my eyelids are heavy and my lips parched. My eyes fill up with tears. For an instant, a short instant, I was with my sister again and now I have to go on without her.

I look around. It hurts to move my head. Everything is white. I'm lying in bed in a small room. There's a drip set up next to my bed. The tube runs into my hand and is attached with a large plaster. I look at it, stupefied. Where am I?

I'm in hospital. I'm not dead.

I slowly recall how I ended up here and fear strikes my heart. Thomas!

Where is he?

I try to sit up, but fall back onto my pillow groaning. What did he make me take, and why am I still alive? I feel around for the buzzer. It's not long before a nurse comes in. She hurries towards me with a big smile.

'You're back! Thank god! We were terribly worried about you.' She grasps my wrist and takes my pulse, her eyes focused on the window.

'That all seems to be fine.' She smiles again. 'How do you feel?'

'What happened?' I ask in a strange, croaky voice. 'Where's Thomas?'

Her smile is replaced with a frown. 'Did he give you that rubbish?'

'What rubbish?' My voice sounds strange to my ears, as if I'm under water and every noise is distorted when it reaches me.

'GHB,' the nurse says, or perhaps she's a doctor, because a stethoscope hangs around her neck.

'GHB? That's some kind of drug, isn't it?'

'Yes, but luckily it wasn't that much,' she says, 'but we did have to give you something to neutralise it. All in all, you've been unconscious for quite a while.'

'How…how did you know?' I say.

'Someone called to say that you were on your own at home and that you'd taken GHB,' the doctor says.

'Thomas,' I mutter. Why did he give me drugs only to tell the hospital afterwards? He wasn't planning on murdering me. So why did he confess about Lydia and then knock me out?

I'm suddenly very worried and I grab the doctor's arm. 'Thomas,' I repeat. 'Where is he?'

She looks down at me, full of compassion. 'He was a good friend of yours, wasn't he?'

'Was?' My voice sounds husky. Deep down inside I know they are using the past tense because our friendship is now over.

The doctor hesitates. 'Shall we talk about it later?' she suggests.

'No, I want to know. Tell me, please,' I insist.

She continues to hesitate.

'He's dead then?' I say in a strangled voice.

She realises that I won't be able to rest until I know the truth.

'Did he commit suicide?' I ask.

She nods. 'He took GHB too, but in a larger dose. He was lying next to you in the bed. We couldn't save him.'

In spite of everything, I begin to cry for Thomas, for the lonely, hung-up soul he was, who didn't know how to get any more out of life than this. I cry until the tears run dry. From my bed I can see the hospital entrance and a stream of visitors coming in through the revolving doors, their arms full of presents and flowers.

It's a lovely day. Outside the window, the heavy foliage of the trees sways in the breeze. The sky is blue and shimmers with warmth and promise.

I'm alive. Slowly a feeling of gratitude rises up in me, I'd thought that everything was over, but I'm still alive. I'll have to manage without my sister, but not forever. I'm sure of that.

I gaze at the cloudless blue sky for a long time and I can't stop a hesitant smile from spreading over my face.